Through the Eyes of a Black Butterfly

In the beginning there is life...
then the lessons... and misfortunes... and transformations...

Karen L. Williams

Dedication

This novel is dedicated to "My Girls". My daughter Dazia, who has been my motivation to strive for greatness since the day she was born. My granddaughters, Raven and Kennedi. My mother Nadine, who has always shown me in her own special way how to be a strong independent woman. My grandmother in heaven, Miss Lorris Helen Williams-King, thank you for always giving me unconditional love and guidance. And to the "prettiest girl in the world" my aunt Stephanie King, thank you for always being my cheerleader and making sure I believed in myself and intellectual abilities! Thank you all for being **A Beautiful Black Butterfly.**

Lastly, thank you Pop for being the strong man that you are! Always loving, always encouraging, always there for me. Together forever in love!

Chapter 1

"You stupid punk!!" I yelled as I fell and got scratched and scraped up. I was simply doing what I was told to do, go to the mailbox and get the mail. But just as I was about to open the old metal box, he ran right into me with his bike. He was about 9 years old and I had just turned 8. I ran in the house lugging my physical pain and hurt feelings. I told my mama!

"That boy run me over with his bike!" I exclaimed, crying to my mom. She came out, cursed him out and went down the street and told his parents, Lester and Monique Wallace what happened. Of course, they did nothing about it except tell my mother she shouldn't be talking to their son in that manner. They had just moved to Desoto Place on Rolland Street, which is a small community in Acres Homes, about a month ago and was not expecting the unannounced intrusion from their new neighbors.

"Well you keep his bad ass down here at his own house and you won't have to worry about me saying a damn thing to him anymore!" And that would be their first encounter with my momma, but definitely not the last.

Their only child, Jason Alexander Wallace, was an annoyingly spoiled and impolite brat that had very little regards for the adults and girls he came in contact with. However, as the years went by, I often found it ironic that his encounters with guys were totally different. He was always centered around a number of boys playing organized sports, riding their bikes or simply just hanging out. He was the cool guy in the group, a team player, everybody's friend. He always had the latest toys, the coolest bike to ride up and down the street, the newest football to play with in the open field at the back of the neighborhood. The best basketball and basketball goal to play with in his backyard when no one felt like going to the park to shoot hoops. And when it was time to play America's favorite pastime, he provided the baseball, bat and gloves! All the guys in our small community wanted to be his friend and keep him as a close ally. But my momma was fierce and didn't take no shit from anyone, especially from an uppity couple and their privileged, mischievous son! She didn't always treat us that great, but she was definitely not going to let someone treat us bad, after all, she was a single parent raising four kids on her own.

My mother, Ms. Deborah Rochelle Jones, 36-years-young, with four kids, two baby daddies, and a mouth so bad she could put pirates to shame. She wanted a partner in life and love, but would definitely trade it all for a man with some money.

"Never fuck for free," is her favorite motherly advice given while dangling a cigarette from her mouth. "Not that your ass should be fucking in the first place, but when you grown and start having your little relationships.... never have sex with a man without him giving you something good in return. Never fuck dirty dicks and never ever go where you not wanted. You hear me girl! Life is a bitch! It's hard on everybody, it don't discriminate...and believe me the wrong man in your life will take you for everything you got! Just always stay two steps ahead of them." These were clearly words my mom lived by, but not I!

My oldest brother Raymond or Ray Ray, is 19 and always in trouble; I can still remember when he was just 13-years-old and was accused of stealing a bicycle right out of the owner's garage. When he brought it home that evening, he told my mom it belonged to his friend, "He let me ride it home because it was getting dark. He said I can keep it because he had another bike to ride!" Raymond said happily while admiring the 10 speed Huffy. The light green dirt bike appeared to be in brand new condition, but Raymond insisted that it was old and his friend no longer had use for it.

"I ain't ever known anyone to give away something so nice...," said Deborah while glaring deep at the bike with suspicion in her eyes. "No, you take it back tomorrow to whoever it belongs to. You have a perfectly good bike in your room you never ride...hell if you want something better, then go get a job and earn the money to buy yourself one...but you take that shit back to wherever it came from!"

Well the next morning before I could get out the crust that was collected throughout the night centered across my eye, there was a loud-bang! bang! bang! on the door. The pounding was intensified to a louder pitch because the person on the other side was beating on the screen door that was attached. "Police, open up!" yelled the outsider. The cops, what did they want? Did they have the correct house? "Police, open up!" I could hear my mother rushing frantically to the door yelling.

"What the hell is going on?" As she looked through the peep hole to make sure it was the men in blue violating her door. "What do you want?" yelling at the front entrance before opening.

"We are looking for a Raymond Jones ma'am...please open the door; it is in regards to theft," one of the cops stated firmly. My mother reluctantly opened the door and a tall, medium build white man with dark brown hair, wearing a blue suit and glasses said, "I am looking for a Raymond Jones, we have reason to believe he stole a bike from the residence at 1893 Sue Marie Ln, in Shepard Park Terrace." The officer was reading from a pad with a straight face and firm tone, "Witnesses say he entered the opened garage at this residence at approximately 2:32pm yesterday and ran off with a mint green Huffy, 10 speed bike." Oh no, this was the bike he brought home yesterday! Shepard Park Terrace was a very nice subdivision outside of Acres Homes, where the upper middle class lived. It wasn't too far from our home, but it was definitely a good distance when traveling on foot. My next question was how did he get way over there and why was he there in the first place? I ran to a window to look outside and noticed a man with a young boy standing by the cop car.

"Raymond, come here!" yelled my mom. "Now I know my son may be a lot of things but he ain't no thief! He said one of his friends gave him that bike." Raymond slowly walked into the living room as if he were contemplating a getaway. "Is this true?" My mother yelled out the question in anger. "Did you steal a bike?" The look of guilt in his eyes said it all. "Boy...have you lost yo mind boy... go get that damn bike!"

The boy identified my brother as the assailant, and he was arrested at once. A week later my mom paid a lawyer for him; he was able to walk away with the judge sentencing him to only six months of probation and 30 hours of community service. This of course would not be his last time breaking the law. He was constantly getting kicked out of school for fighting his classmates, harassing teachers and cursing out school administrators. When teachers would find out he was my older sibling, they would always have the same response, "you guys are like night and day! You two are nothing alike!" And they were correct in their assumptions, I didn't have the nerves to break any rules at school or at home!

One time at school, he ran right outside the principal's office and threatened to kill everyone there! All staff members were ordered to go into lock down mode until the Aldine ISD Police arrived to apprehend him and take him into custody. He was arrested and later sent to an alternative school for six weeks as a punishment, but immediately after serving his time he was allowed to return to school and his behavior got worse. Raymond began skipping class to hang out with other young male thugs in Acres Homes. They were often caught drinking alcohol, getting high off marijuana, and committing various petty crimes in the area. Then finally at the tender age 17, just two months shy of his 18th birthday, he was caught driving while drunk in a stolen car. The judge found him guilty of all charges and declared him a menace to society and sentenced him to two years in a state jail about an hour away from home. That was about nine months ago, he still has a little over a year to finish out his sentence.

The two youngest members of the family were my sisters Reba, age 6 and Renee, age 7. They were 10 months apart in age. I still remember my mom breast feeding Renee as an infant while pregnant with Reba. She had always said she didn't want me to be the only girl, and I guess the Lord heard her prayers above all others because she was definitely twice blessed. Then there was me, Regina Denise Jones, 16 years old, the second oldest child and the oldest girl. My mother told me I was named after a woman that lost her baby the same day I was born. She would tell me stories of how the hospital rooms back then housed at least four ladies to a room after their child was delivered. Well, when the nurse brought my mother to her room, the patient sharing the space next to her was crying. My mother's first thought was to go off on the nurse and demand that she take her to another room. She would always say giving birth to me was the hardest thing she had ever done; it was 18 hours of pure agonizing pain! Therefore, she was not in the mood to hear some woman crying because her "baby daddy" didn't show up! But she said it was something about the way the woman was crying, a sort of a sad soft whimper from the heart. When she asked the nurse why the lady was so upset, the nurse explained to her that her baby did not make it during labor and delivery. But what really made my mother's heart drop was the child's father had died in a car wreck just six months ago and this was to be their first child. She was to be named Regina Denise Porter. My mother decided she was only going to send her condolences to the fragile young female, but instead my mom ended up spending the rest of that night talking to her and feeding me. My mom would always say, "that Jackie girl ...she was good people." She would never go into details about what she meant, but I know the lady had to be something special for my mother to not only like her, but also name me-- her first daughter after the lady's unborn child.

Now, even though I was the only girl, the baby of the house for approximately eight years and specially named after a baby that passed away, there was nothing special about my life! First of all, even though I was the second born, I always felt like the eldest since my brother Ray-Ray was always in trouble and never around. My mother depended on me for so much at times, as if I were an adult. I babysat my sisters daily, kept their hair combed and bodies bathed; I even cooked dinner when she worked late or hung out at local neighborhood cafes with her friend Ms. Carolyn- which was most of the time. Therefore, I was often left at home with my young siblings to watch over, with an abundance of chores to complete and many responsibilities to keep track of. These tasks included washing the dishes, cleaning the bathroom, vacuuming the carpet in the entire house and washing clothes. My mom would always get one of her guy friend's cars to transport us to our bi-weekly trips to the local laundry mat, which basically meant I had to help her wash, fold and fluff large bundles of clothes, even though everybody's weekly attire went for a spin in the large commercial machines. This wasn't too bad though, mainly because once the clothes went in the machines, my mom would leave to run errands, or do what she called "take care of business" which was cool because it was my alone time, something I never get any of when I'm at home. Therefore, I always bring a book to read to temporarily escape the harsh realities of adolescent life. However, when the machines stop spinning, reality continues and the fantasy ends or its at least placed on hold until my opportunity to indulge in my current favorite genre presents itself again.

Oh yeah, I'm a voracious reader, I will read and analyze any and every literary work I can get my hands on. My love of books started at an early age, I guess I was around six years old when my grandmother bought me the Walt Disney Classic book collection. The collection included *Snow White and the Seven Dwarfs, Dumbo, Aladdin, Bambi, Sleeping Beauty* and my favorite, *Cinderella.* I guess it's no real mystery as to why I can relate to the main character Cinderella and the story's plot; a young girl that's treated like a slave by her stepmother and sisters after her real father dies. Then, the story takes an interesting turn when she is visited by a fairy godmother who grants her a wish that allows her to attend the ball in a beautiful gown that attracts the prince. She runs off, but he eventually finds her and marries her, because he fell in love with her! Love, deep passionate affection, passion and desire for another individual. And this is what I wanted for my life, to be loved by someone. I wanted that special someone to find me, marry me, because he fell in love with me and wisped me away to live happily ever after.

I went on to read more book collections by various authors like Beverly Cleary's *Ramona Quimby* collections, Judy Blume's *Super Fudge*, C.S. Lewis *The Chronicles of Narnia*, I even read poetry by Roald Dahl. And even though these authors and the characters were Caucasian, I still enjoyed them and had no problem with relating to the various storylines. These kid friendly tales were loaded with action and adventures, which kept my immature mind occupied at a very early age. However, after the tender age of nine I realized these books lacked the drama and love I longed for. I wanted to read about drama that was often portrayed in the different movies I would watch. I guess that's what led me to the novel *The Pigman* by Paul Zindel when I was in 5th grade. It was different from what I was used to reading and was probably my favorite realistic fiction piece. I got caught up in the complexity of the two main characters, John and Lorraine. I remember picking the book off the shelf in the school library and thinking it was a love story since main characters were a male and female, John and Lorraine, I soon discovered it wasn't. And even though it wasn't exactly what I expected, the storyline was quite intriguing. They were high school sophomores who develop a relationship with an elderly man they originally intended to deceive. These two teenagers' quest for fun results in the death of a man they grew to love and forces them to do some much-needed maturing.

This reminds me of the life altering events that forced me to develop at an early age. I wasn't exactly in search of mischievous fun, but instead an escape from the harsh realities of my everyday life. It all began the summer I turned 16, I remember like it was yesterday, just days after my birthday, he was standing near my house in the street with a group of guys, staring at me. At first, I thought he was looking past me at the other females on the street, but his intense stares seemed to burn right through me. I was a chubby girl, at least

20 pounds larger than most girls my age, or at least I think I still was. I did notice that I was taller than my friends on the street this summer, not to mention my clothes seemed a little looser than before. But that didn't mean anything, I was just this super thick, dark skinned girl that all the boys teased. They annoyed me so much that I stayed in the house most of the time to avoid the constant name calling that usually drove me to tears. So why would he be staring at me, so intensely? Did I do something to him; is something wrong with what I am wearing? Well, whatever the reason, I needed to make myself unavailable for him or anyone else to talk about.

Three days later I was walking home and noticed him standing there in the street in front of my house. My mother had sent me to the corner store for cigarettes and a loaf of bread and I was a hot mess, a straight target for insults. I had on an old t-shirt with the sleeves cut off because my arms had gotten so fat, with a pair of cutoff jeans that probably belonged to my older brother. At first, I was reluctant to pass by him, but I had to get into my house.

"Hey Regina," said Jason. Not sure why he is talking to me; he never talks to me...ever...well...at least not on purpose.

"Oh...hey Jason," I muttered looking down the entire time at the ground as if I would turn into stone if I dared give him any eye contact. Jason was about 6'1, with a golden honey almond colored skin tone and light brown eyes. He was very handsome to me, tall, muscular and very athletic. So why was he talking to me? I hurried myself into the house and closed the door as quickly as I had opened it, hoping he didn't notice the dried-up food stains on my shirt from the chili dog I ate earlier.

Later that day I noticed him standing in front of my house again, but this time he was surrounded by a few guys that lived on the street: Larry, Isaiah and Trent. Although he was talking, I noticed him turning around and staring directly at my house—as if he was waiting for something to happen. Oh, hell no! He was not going to do something to embarrass me if I came outside. Like once while I was with my friends Vanessa and Rachel, Jason passed by me putting his butt on my back and passed gas...fucking childish! Well, I wasn't going to give him the satisfaction this time. But I couldn't help but notice the sincerity in his voice when he spoke to me yesterday, not to mention all the stares he has been giving me lately. I began to chuckle at the thought of him having feelings for me, Regina Denise Jones...now that's funny. The chubby, chocolate girl with big eyes, big legs and a big ass butte! Lately however, I have been going out of my way to look decent when I come outside to hang out. School was going to start in a couple of weeks and I made sure I had nice clothes to wear from the money I earned working a summer job program in June and July. Momma let me wear make-up when I turned 15, so I always have on my lipstick, eyeliner and mascara. I placed a lot of emphasis on my eye wear to help tone down these big ass head lights. And my hair was always done, even though it was done by me-it was perfectly curled and styled with each ringlet intact, and I thought it was cute for a kitchen do. But of course, even with all the prissy prepping I had done before coming outside, he just went on to play basketball with the guys on the street.

That night after the sun finally hid itself and the darkness was a blanket covering the sky, I laid in bed looking out the window at the diamond studded twinkling of the stars and I couldn't help but think about Jason. Wow, what if he did have just an ounce of attraction to me, would he want me to be his girlfriend: hold my hand when we walked together, carry my books at school, walk me to class, talk to me on the phone? Yeah right, come on Gina girl, that stuff only happens in the movies! Yeah sure, I was the typical hopeless romantic, but Aphrodite did not release her son Cupid from Mt Olympus to come down to the hood, draw back his bow and let his arrow go straight into Jason's heart just as I was walking by so we could fall madly in love with each other! Get out of la la land Gina!

Chapter 2

My Sweet 16, my passage into early adulthood, my introduction to society--it was a new stage in my life. I was coming out and transitioning from a girl to a woman, or at least that's how it was supposed to be, right? Well, I turned 16 years old Sunday, July 19th, and this meant nothing to no one. It was simply just another day in the Jones' household, with no celebration on my behalf at all. Traditionally, young girls would participate in a father daughter dance that I'm sure symbolizes the bond a daddy shares with his little girl and then he proudly presents his pride and joy to society. Since I have no dad in my life to share a bond or shake a tail feather with, there could not be a father-daughter dance!

Also, parents typically pass down a valuable keepsake to their sweet 16, but the only family valuable that came close to being considered a heirloom to pass down, was a necklace given to my mom when she was a young girl from her parents.

"My husband worked a many hour at HISD School District as a janitor...jus so he could earn a-nuff money to buy that necklace for my baby girl. He wanted to show her his love fo her!" My nana would tell me.

Of course, my mom couldn't wear it at the time so he held on to it and planned to present the lovely 18 carat gold chain with an attached gold locket to her when she became a teenager. Since he died before he could give the necklace to my mother, my grandmother presented to her just before the funeral proceedings and told her to wear it to represent his love for her. My mom wore it that day and that day only. I found out a few years ago from my nana that mom pawned the necklace when I was a baby to buy me some diapers! Well--there goes the family heirloom!

So, as you can see nothing great ever happens in my life, I've dealt with more let downs then come ups. Therefore, that summer of my 16th was truly a turning point in my life. First, I woke up one morning and my breast had grown to at least a C cup, but I was forced to wear a B cup bra because my mom had no intentions on buying me a new one that fit. My grandmother eventually purchased me two white laced Playtex bras with the pointed cup from the Sears on N. Shepard Dr. I still remember them being brand new, one was still in the box, the other I had taken out to try on to ensure a semi-perfect fit after the saleslady measured me. "No brasserie is going to ever fit you perfect baby," my nana would always say. I just shrugged my shoulders in compliance; heck I was just grateful I no longer had to squeeze two oranges into-two irregular small pouches...when I wasn't trying to make orange juice!

My taste in books also began to evolve. I still remember reading *To Kill a Mockingbird* by Harper Lee in school the previous year. I was amused at the way the other students in my class responded to the fictitious narrative. Many of my classmates, Black and White students became angry at how the all-White jury wrongfully convicted a Black man accused of raping a White woman in the 1930's rural south, during the Great Depression. But in actuality, it was a coming of age story centered around a girl who had to learn many important lessons in life at a very young age. Lessons like, keeping the fight going, even when you know you might not win. How the world we live in can be scary and simply unfair, but how there sometimes can be value in the unfairness we witness. Now, before reading this book I had never seen a mockingbird, but I felt an instant connection. You should never kill a mockingbird, since it doesn't harm anything or anyone. I know none of my classmates understood that metaphorically that meant you should never take advantage of someone that is weaker than you. I am a mockingbird; I'm weak and lack power and everyone I come in contact with sees this lack of strength in my personality and feels the need to overpower me. To Kill Regina Jones.

I guess it's the reason for my also choosing to read *The Color Purple* by Alice Walker. I can still hear my best friend Diane looking at me cross when I picked the book up at the school library and checked it out. "Where you going with that textbook?" she would ask laughing at her own question while poking fun at me. "Girl, you and those books! I wish I read like that!" But books were my means of escaping reality. It was my only opportunity to reside in a world before my time. I had often wondered how and if I were able to adapt to a time period where racism and segregation was so prevalent. But in both books, *To Kill A Mockingbird* and *The Color Purple*, the stories of racial injustices that are embedded in the storyline are just small subplots of the actual dramas.

Well, maybe I am the weaker species or the mockingbird that flies around and hums all day without bothering anyone or anything. Because Jason just didn't understand the importance of showing kindness to a feeble being. Like one day he is speaking to me all nice and polite, the next day he decides to cut through a layer of my skin so he could get under it, in an effort to hurt my fragile demeanor and humiliate me in front of our peers. And this really kills the anticipation I develop for wanting to mix and mingle with the other kids in our small neighborhood. I never come outside like the rest of the kids on the street because I am always busy doing other things in the house like cleaning, cooking or babysitting, you would think he would give me a break! I'm fortunate to have the rare opportunities to socialize with my peers, since my mother is so strict about my whereabouts, always thinking I'm going to get pregnant from merely holding an innocent conversation with a boy!

Well days after Jason's polite greeting to me, Rachel and Vanessa, a couple of teenage girls I hung out with at home that lived on the street, came over to my house and asked me to come outside and hang out. It was a little after six o'clock in the evening, which was good timing because the sun finally decided to head to the west, set, and give us Houstonians a little relief from the summer heat. And since my mom was at home in a very mellow mood from inhaling one can of malt liquor after the next, while glued to the couch watching re-runs of the show "Good Times," she didn't mind me going outside, as long as I kept an eye on my sisters. But to my surprise, Reba and Renee were actually in their room playing with their toys and reading books. They were not at all concerned with any outdoor activities, so I, of course, took advantage of this rare occurrence!

Well, ever since Jason spoke to me the other day and I knew he would be outside with his buddies, I wanted to wear something that would definitely capture his attention. Afterall, let's face it, good or bad, I liked the attention he had been giving me lately. So, I changed into my cute brown, thigh-high shorts with the matching halter top and when my mother got up to use the bathroom, I quickly headed outside with the other neighborhood girls. I simply did not need my mother, Ms. Deborah Jones to interfere with my wardrobe selection!

The girls and I walked over to the basketball court where all the guys on our street played ball; we found a seat on the bench and sat down to watch them finish their game. And before my butte cheeks could meet the lumbar framework, there it was: that intense stare from Jason that sent my body into a shivery state. But this time he said nothing to me the entire time we were there. After about two hours of watching the fellows dribble the ball back and forth down the court, talk a ton of smack to one another about their capabilities, they finally called it quits. As night time quickly began to close in on our outing, the girls and I got up to leave the basketball court and head home with the rest of the kids, including Jason. While walking home Isaiah, my 17-year-old next door neighbor, said, "What's up with them shorts you got on covering all that booty. Gina, you know your butte is too big for those shorts...while you walking...and jiggling like jelly!" and of course, everyone started to laugh.

"I don't know why in the fuck she got them little bitty ass shorts on anyway!" yelled Jason out of nowhere. Okay what the hell was that? "You need to take yo ass in the house and change...matter of fact you just need to take yo ass in the house!"

The words hit me like the release of a belt to backside of an unruly child. "Ooooo!" said everyone. "Dang, dang man...damn dog!" was all you heard. I turned his way and saw the distinct look of anger taking over his face, while staring straight at me, through me! Rage had completely taken over his mind, body, and spirit.

"You don't need to be worried about what I have on, this is my body...I can wear what the fuck I want to wear... don't none of you niggas buy my clothes!" I yelled in retaliation.

"Look," said Isaiah, "I was just trying to help you out. Hell, the way they are wedged up your ass they probably stank!" Of course, everybody laughed again, including Jason.

"Fuck all of yall!" I yelled then ran home. The tears from my eyes began to run out in puddles. How stupid can I be, to think that bastard actually liked me! And my so-called friends Vanessa and Rachel stood by and said nothing, I'm almost certain I seen at least one of them chuckle. I walked to the side of the house and entered through the back door because I didn't want anyone to see me crying. I was not sure why I was allowing this situation to affect me in this manner but it did, and I didn't want to be bothered by anyone. Yeah right, here comes Reba and Rene playing in the hallway, in my way as I struggled to get to my bedroom without them noticing the flow of tears from my eyes.

My mom was getting ready to go out with her new friend. She had already drunk an entire six pack of beers while listening to the blues playing on the radio and watching a muted television periodically screaming at my sisters, "Yall better sit yall asses down somewhere before I get the belt!" I was thinking, yeah right, they might have got it on a sober day, but not on a going out night—and ruin her buzz. I began cleaning up the kitchen, wondering when she would finish getting dressed so she could hurry up and leave. "Look my friend will be here in a minute and I don't want to hear nothing about anybody being in my house, you hear me girl!" said momma.

"Yes ma'am," I replied to my mother, Ms. Deborah Rochelle Jones, 36-years-young, with four kids, two baby daddies, and a mouth so bad she would put pirates to shame.

An hour later she left with some unknown random guy that didn't even feel the need to come to our home's entrance and knock for her...he simply blew his horn and out the front door she went. "Momma be back...yall be good" looking at Reba and Rene. "And Gina don't have nobody in my house!"

"Yes ma'am."

I looked out the window and watched as they backed the old 1974 Buick into the street from the driveway to begin their journey to the local juke joint. I could hear the loud knocking from the engine as the vehicle took off down the road. I guess this guy could be her life partner, maybe. It could be love, possibly, but a man with money...I doubt it!!

After I put the girls to bed, I went to sit on the couch in the living room. I sat in front of the floor model television set, gazing past the dark blank screen deep in thought about what happened earlier with Jason; okay I guess I never really stopped thinking about it. What got into him? Why was he so upset? Also, what about the constant stares and him speaking to me all the time lately? I was so confused. I got up to turn on the floor model television set and settled on watching the end of an episode of the show "Dallas" while Reba and Rene, who should have been sleeping, played together in their room.

About an hour had gone by when I heard a knock on the kitchen door, which was odd because no one ever comes through the back yard and knock on the back door—ever. Slowly and timidly I walked to the kitchen towards the door in fear of the unknown. Criminals and drug-addicts didn't usually hang out in our area, but you never know—villains can be lurking around at any given moment waiting for the perfect opportunity to appear unannounced and take an unexpecting family for everything they got.

"Who is it?" I yelled once I approached the door. There was no response. "Who is it?" I repeated. "What do you want?"

"It's Jay..." the familiar baritone voice responded back in a low tone. Could it be? I pulled back the curtains on the window next to the door just enough to sneak a peek, and I instantly recognized the reflection peering back at me. The cut off sleeves of his t-shirt revealing his muscular biceps; his baggy, white, basketball shorts covering the bottom half of his slender athletic body; it was Jason. I open the door.

"Yes." I said trying to appear annoyed, yet still confused at his knocking on the back door. "Why you in my backyard, knocking on my back door?" I asked with my left hand gripping my left hip. Although, it was probably best he did come to the back since our neighbors were nosey and had no problem informing my mother, Ms. Deborah Rochelle Jones, about the goings on at her house when she wasn't present. Not because they liked her, because they didn't; it was mostly because of the traditional values established in the neighborhood that a child should stay in a child's place and should not be participating in any activity that would result in any type of sexual activity.

Actually, the vast majority of the adults living on the street considered my mother to be beneath them because they didn't agree with her party girl lifestyle or the fact that she had a house full of bastard kids with no husband, no car, no money. Most of the neighbors merely tolerated her because they knew she was here to stay and wasn't going anywhere since the house we lived in was paid for, courtesy of my grandfather, her father, and his insurance policy when he died. It was actually the house she and my uncle grew up in. They were a two parent, two kid household in the 1950's with both parents gainfully employed; they lived the ideal middle-class life. While Grandpa worked full-time for HISD, Grandma was also employed working ten hours a day for a rich family in the Galleria area. They were living the African American dream in Acres Homes as a thriving middle-class family. They were actually the second family to purchase a brick home on this street in this small community, Desoto Place; the Smiths, who lived on the corner were the first. Back then almost all the homes in Acres Homes were old wooden shot-gun houses; brick homes were almost unheard of!

After grandpa died the burden of raising two rebellious teenagers on her own became so overwhelming that my grandmother, Mrs. Laura Jones, decided to begin making plans to leave the city and return to her roots in the country. My Uncle Lonnie eventually got his life together, landing a job at St. Joseph's Hospital in downtown Houston then marrying his first wife. But my mother, Ms. Deborah Rochelle Jones could never get it together. She was pregnant by the age of 16, which resulted in a miscarriage. The very next year she gave birth to Raymond, and three years later I was born.

By the time my mother met Reba and Rene's dad, my grandmother had decided to move out and away to Dobbin, Texas, where she was originally from. My grandfather was from Acres Homes and relocated her here after they married in 1949, which was the year my uncle Lonnie was born. A year later Grandpa was drafted into the army and served in the Korean War. While on medical leave from a bullet piercing his right thigh during combat in 1951, my mother was conceived. He returned to Korea for an additional year and returned home for good in 1953 when the war ended.

I was seven years old when my grandmother left my mother her house and used her retirement money to move into a manufactured home in Dobbin. I cried every day for a month when she left!

"Oh...my bad! Shid, I just didn't want these nosey ass neighbors to see me! But damn...it's like that, I can't come in?" Jason said with a slick grin to the side. Damn he looked good! Even after working out on the basketball court all afternoon, the sweat on his forehead seem to rolled down like golden chunks against his honey golden complexion. And those pretty ass straight pearl white teeth that seem to stand at attention and salute every female in sight.

"What do you want?" I asked, still trying to sound irritated.

"I just wanted to borrow some sugar... I wanted to make some kool-aid. You got some."

"Sugar? You came all the way down here...to my back door to borrow sugar" I asked. "Yeah right! What you want Jason?"

"Some sugar! Why I got to be lying?"

"Okay...let me see if we have any...stay right here" I sighed and walked off leaving the door open behind me. I was glad the girls were asleep, or they would definitely have plenty of information to report to my mom.

"I see you still have on them shorts," but this time he sounded interested instead of upset. As I searched the cabinets for the sugar, I heard the door close. I turned away from the pantry and Jason was inside.

"I don't know why my clothes are such a hot topic for you today, but I really wish you would leave me alone about them. Last time I checked—I buy my clothes...not you or your silly ass friends!"

"Alright, my bad," holding his hands up to surrender to the lost battle. I turned my back to him again to look for the sugar in the cabinet and didn't see any. As I turned in his direction to check the pantry, there it was his Johnson waiting to greet me in a solid state. Jason had pulled down his pants to reveal his prized possession in hopes that it would receive yet another award. I couldn't move, all I could do was stare...and I did, for what seemed like forever, but actually it only calculated to about 15 seconds. Once I fell out of the trance I ran into the bathroom, with him following me with the live snake fully erected. He pushed his way into the bathroom before I could close the door behind him and he managed to quietly connect it to its hinges without using force.

"What are you doing, my momma is going to get you!" I said in a quiet but stern tone.

"I saw Ms. Deborah leave earlier; ain't nobody here but you and your sisters, and they must be sleep because I haven't heard them since I got here," said Jason while coming closer. "What's wrong baby, did I scare you? I don't want you to be scared, I want you to be willing," he said while gently grabbing my hand and standing so close to me I could feel the warmth of his breath on my forehead. The sexy scent of cologne mixed with sweat filled my nostrils as he released my hand and put both of his arms around my waistline pulling me so close to him that I could feel his penis jabbing me in the stomach. I looked down the entire time, not knowing what to do. I was a virgin and no one has ever seduced me in this manner; hell no one has ever come on to me at all!

"Why are you doing this?" I said still looking down. "I thought you didn't like me, the way you talk about me and make fun of me, it hurts my feelings," I said in a sad sincere tone I usually use with my grandmother when I want something or want to have my way.

He then took his right hand and softly lifted my head so our eyes could meet, then he gently kissed me on the lips. "I'm sorry for hurting your feelings," he whispered. I felt his penis getting soft. "Do you accept my apology..." he kissed me again just as gentle as the first. "I don't want you to be mad at me...." he kissed me again. "Do you forgive me?" I felt like butter melting at the instant touch of a heated surface. I nodded my head slowly up and down and this time when his lips began to touch mine, I returned the favor. Oh my-- was all I could think as our tongues touched and intertwined in the moistened, hollow spaces. He began to caress my back and from out of nowhere his hand was on my thigh. He carefully pushed me back up against the wall and lifted my leg. He pretended to duel with the buckle of my pants, I guess to see how I would respond. I didn't decline his gesture; so, he began to unbuttoned my shorts giving himself permission to enter. I could tell my innocence was driving him to seek a place in me that no man has ever gone before. He slid my bottoms down and ran his fingers over the upper layers of my vagina until he found what he was in search of. He rubbed the area with his index finger with the perfect amount of aggression and gentleness until I exploded with pure delight into his hands. "You forgive me now baby...?" And with that last statement he released me from his grasp, pulled his pants up and left me in a delighted state of confusion. "What the hell just happened?"

Chapter 3

This is too confusing one minute a man has his hands all up in your business and the next minute he doesn't know you exist. After our encounter in the bathroom two nights ago, Jason has not said a single word to me. Fuck him! But I like him. The way he made me feel while he had me in his arms, I remembered enjoying his every touch. The way he kissed me—I wanted to keep kissing him all night. He held me in such a protected manner that all I could think about was being in his arms and when will I have the pleasure of being in them again? He still stares but that's all he does is stare—watching my every move. Does he like me or not? Or does he like me and doesn't want anyone to know. Fuck him! But I like him. The way he made me feel, it was indescribable! It's all that I could think of since it happened. But, fuck him! That's just too much time and energy on something that will never be!

Later that night while watching television Rene was working my last nerve, all the playing, whining and throwing tantrums to get attention when she couldn't have her way. "Sit down somewhere Renee; you're getting on my nerves!" I yelled.

"Stop hollering at my baby; your ass ain't grown!" yelled my mother. I find it amazing that they are her babies when she is mad at her man and want to put them off on me.

"Momma, she keeps playing in front of the t.v. and I can't see."

"I don't care, you stop talking to her like that, I'm the only momma in this house damn it!" I was not in the mood to hear this; so, I dropped the remote control on the table and proceeded to get up; the loud thud from the remote's impact made Renee and Reba jump. I headed to my room and closed the door and within minutes of my arrival an unwelcomed guest barged in with the ends of a leather strap tightly wrapped around her hand. "Who the fuck you think you are slamming shit in my house?!" Wap, right across my right arm. WAP, WAP, WAP, to my backside, my chest, my legs! They were coming with intense speed and aggression sending surges of intense pain throughout my body. "I'm the only grown-up in this house..do you understand? I said do you understand me?" WAP WAP WAP.

"Yes ma'am." That night I cried myself to sleep. Why does everyone hate me? I am a mockingbird, I'm weak and lack power and everyone I come in contact with sees this lack of strength in my personality and feels the need to overpower me. To Kill Regina Jones.

🦋 🦋 🦋

Well school started and Jason finally talked to me, I guess if that's what you want to call it. He whispered, "Hey sexy." In my ear as he passed me in the hallway at school while I was putting my books in the locker. He thinks I'm sexy? Well, I did stay up late doing my hair and the outfit I had on was new and very cute, but this big ass butte of mine; that's all I need is for him to make a comment and start unnecessary commotion about it. I mean really there was nowhere to run in this crowded hallway filled with eager, obnoxious students looking for a good laugh. But he thinks I look sexy...wow! Why hadn't he said anything to me until now...and in such a secretive manner? I must admit since that incident with my mom I hadn't really come outside. On my birthday last month, my mom borrowed her friend's car to take me to my grandmother's house in the country, since my nana, Mrs. Laura didn't drive in the city. I ended up staying there a couple of days. So, I guess there was no way Jason could communicate any form of compliment, comment or criticism to me.

Jason stopped a few yards away from me to talk to a group of athletes. DAMN! he looked good with his tight white t- shirt and fresh haircut. I finished putting away my books and checked my make-up and clothing...well everything appeared to be in place. Why is he watching me with those deep dark mysterious eyes? Could he be thinking about that night too? I know I was...hell it was all I could think of. He was as mighty as a lion but as gentle as a baby lamb. But more important, it was all about me...he left me curious and longing for more. Was this part of his scheme to seduce me; but why me— Jason was very handsome and last I heard he had a girlfriend... Lisa. Well at least she was last year and I know I saw her on our street a couple of times in the beginning of summer.

As I closed my locker door and headed down the hallway, I notice a few guys checking me out, but they too were probably thinking my butte was too big for the outfit I was wearing. I was sporting a short, acid washed, denim skirt, with a hot pink cotton tee and hot pink bobbie socks to match. Even though I wore this skirt a lot, I thought it was cute, plus it was all I had! When school started my mom of course never bought me new clothes, I guess making sure that I had what I needed to be a success in class cut too deep into her party and bill money. So, my nana would send me clothes she bought in the country and $70 from her fixed income to help supply my clothing needs. This school year, with that $70, I was able to purchase this skirt, two pairs of jeans and three tees from Weiner's Department Store, with a pair of cloth white Keds from Payless Shoe Store. My sisters had their grandparents on their father's side to accommodate their needs, so there was always an abundance of new clothes and new shoes for the girls each new school year.

I found my two best friends Diana Walters and Freddy Boyd in the cafeteria. We grabbed our food together as usual then proceeded to our table to have lunch. Diana and I go way back to elementary school, where we met in the second grade during recess. We were two little girls just having fun on the playground, taking turns reaching our arms, swinging our bodies, and dangling our feet, all while our hands maintained a tight grip on the monkey bars, we've been best friends ever since. We eventually met Freddy the beginning of our 6th grade year at Hoffman Middle School. He was and still is, very feminine, very loud and very flamboyant. Diana on the other hand was a say what she gotta say kinda girl, yet very intelligent and pretty. But more important she was thin, lucky bitch! No, my friend isn't a bitch but she is lucky. She was a true friend to me—giving it to me straight whether it hurt my feelings or not. She was the only one I told about the incident with Jason. She thinks he's full of shit and no good; a master manipulator that did whatever it took to get what he wanted. DAMN! Tell me how you really feel Diana!

"He probably just wants to have sex with you...that's all! You remember what he did to Mary last year...he flirted with her until he got what he wanted...a good fuck! And all he did was come to school and tell all the guys in the locker room while they got dressed about how she was a hoe and let him do her anyway he wanted. As a matter of fact, she continued buying him gifts and running behind him for a minute," Diana exclaimed just before taking a bite of her burger.

"Yeah but Mary is a slut and did pretty much the same thing to Devin Terry last year," I said defensively.

"Look, I'm just calling it like it is, don't get mad at me for looking out for my friend, plus girl you look good! You don't need him...but...the brotha is fine though..." she said laughing while looking in the direction of the school's athletes. They all seemed to have congregated together at the far end of the cafeteria, as if to show the student body of Eisenhower High School who was running things.

I must admit, all of what Diana said was true and she had no problem laying it on thick! You gotta love her for trying to look out for me but she didn't understand what I was feeling. I felt something special there, that night, his touch, he was so sincere. And I was too curious at this point to let it go. I decided I was going to proceed on...either becoming his next love or next victim, depending on how the cards are dealt.

Afterschool, I walked in the house to be greeted by my mom's new man. Dexter Rhodes, 62-year-old retired truck driver. He had a cocoa brown skin tone with deep tiny little beady eyes attached to a face that had been harden over time. Struggling to get off the couch, he stood up and extended his hand to mine, "How you doing baby?" he said in a sly tone. He appeared to be about 5"8 and about 250 pounds. He was short and stubby with salt and pepper hair and mustache that was in dire need of a trim. "Deborah, you didn't tell me you had such a pretty daughter." I took my hand back, smiled and went to my room. As I headed towards the hallway, I couldn't help but notice the foul scent that seemed to fill the room. The combination of cheap liquor, dirty clothes, musty underarms, tobacco and bad breath. How do you kiss this?

When I entered my room, I placed my books down on the bed and proceeded to change my clothes so I can head outside to get Reba and Renee off the bus. Just as I was unbuckling my skirt, the door swung open. "Ugh... make sure you put on some decent clothes...I don't need you prancing around my man in that little shit you call clothes," my mother said in a low tone, as to not be heard by her guest. "I don't need that nigga looking at nobody but me! You hear me girl."

"Yes ma'am," was all I could utter as I stood there a little startled at her sudden entrance into my room.

"Well...what you think?" My mom asked sitting down on my bed. She does this every time she brings home a new man, as if my opinion meant anything to her. I know he a little rough around the edges, and the mother fucker do stink—but I met him the other night and he got some cash...and that's all I needed to see! Shit girl, you better learn now that a good fuck is nothing and leads to shit you either don't want or don't need: babies, diseases, or heartache—cause nine times out of ten he is fucking someone else on the side too. Shit I need some cash! That shit lasts a lifetime, love don't pay the bills or put food on the table...only that all mighty dollar!"

Okay gross! Why in the hell would I want to entice a dirty old drunk that's old enough to be my grandfather! Two, I don't give a damn about who you talk to...that's your business and your nose to smell his ass! But the part about the good fuck, I mean I get the picture about just going around having good sex with men that can't do anything for you...but what if its love. Real love...the kind you read about, or see on television. The kind of sincere love a woman gets from a man that desires her. I want to be desire, I want to be made love too, hell I just want to be loved by someone. I want someone to take care of me instead of me always taking care of everyone.

"Yes Ma'am,"

She left me in the room to change. I guess she gets frustrated with me because I don't really respond to the stupid shit, she tells me. Why should I listen to her—she doesn't know what she's talking about. What the fuck does she know about having a "good" man. I can only remember one decent boyfriend of hers, and that was Anthony Cobb. Although I was pretty young at the time, I understood at an early age that a woman can pretty much run a man off with all her unnecessary hell raising, her unfair accusations about him being with other women, and her always having her hands out for money. Anthony was a truck driver and traveled for days at a time. When he came home to us, his hands were always filled with goodies. One bag would be full of food for the house and the other was filled with gifts. He would always get Raymond a baseball cap and me a stuffed animal. At the time it was just my mom, me and my brother Raymond; the girls hadn't been born yet. The last night he was with us, I was in my room reading my book when I heard a loud crash. I quickly ran to the door to take a peek and there was Anthony sitting on the floor in a pile of what appeared to be thousands of tiny glass chunks. My mom was standing over him with a knife yelling, "motha fucker I know yo ass been up to no good, I ain't stupid that's perfume I smell on your clothes!" She didn't seem to be afraid instead she had the distinct look of revenge on her face.

As he stood, "Bitch I'm tired of this shit! Cain't no man make yo crazy ass happy...and hell I'm tired of trying, I told you I was at my mother's house, that's her perfume you smell, you want to fight and argue- do it by your damn self!" And with that last statement he was gone like a thief in the night.

Hell, I have only seen pictures of my dad before we were told he was shot and killed by some woman's husband he was messing with at a local café and bar many adults hung out in. My father, James Nelms was ten years my mother's elder and is actually Raymond's dad also. Raymond was conceived while my mother was still in high school, and he was very married with children. This is the reason why we took our mother's last name Jones, because we were a part of his hidden secret life. James Nelms, a husband, a father, an adulter, a child sex offender and the daddy I never knew! My grandmother would tell me stories of how my mom would sneak out the window in the middle of the night to go lay up with him at a local motel.

"He always made sure he brought her back in time for school the next morning." I could hear my grandmother's voice in my ear, "Then that ass got pregnant and broke my heart...her daddy must have turned over twice in his grave...God rest his soul." My grandfather Jeremiah Jones, a handsome, proud Black man that took care of his family, died from a heart attack when my mom and uncle Lonnie were young. My mom was about 14 and my uncle was 16 years old.

"Everything took a turn for the worse", I could hear my grandma Laura saying. "Even though the house was paid for...thank God! I still had to get two jobs to make ends meat...I had two teenagers to take care of! And that wasn't easy in the late 60's, so they were left alone many times, enough for your uncle Lonnie to get caught up hanging with the wrong crowd and your mother experimenting with sex at such an early age."

Ah, and then there is Ricky Moore—Renee and Reba's dad who burned out on us when they were just toddlers. When he came to our home, he stayed weeks at a time and then he would disappear for about a month, but he would always return. My memories of him before Renee and Reba were born are pretty vague; however, I can recall my mom getting up and going to work, while Raymond and I went to school. When we left in the morning, Ricky lay in bed asleep and when we returned that afternoon, he was in the bed still napping. He only got up to go to the bathroom or kitchen wearing only a pair of shorts and no shirt. Other than the few times I would catch him in the kitchen mixing sugar in a large glass of water, I hardly ever talked to him.

Then my mom got pregnant with Renee and things began to change. Ricky would get up every day and work with his dad doing construction. In the evenings he would return completely drenched in dirt and sweat, carrying a bag full of foods my mom craved. There was always an abundance of ice cream, pickles, Coca-Cola, sour cream potato chips and a box of fried chicken from Hartz restaurant for my mom to consume.

He would sit on the couch watching television and rubbing her feet every night while she polished off a bowl of Blue Bell's Rocky Road, with a sour dill pickle on the side! When Renee was born, his mom and dad, Ricky Sr. and Betty Moore brought tons of baby clothes, diapers and wipes. Renee was Ricky's pride and joy, he packed her everywhere. He made bottles, fed her, bathe her, rocked her to sleep and let her sleep on his chest every night. "You gonna spoil that girl!" was all I ever heard my mom say. Her comments went ignored and he continued to overindulge in Renee, making her the center of his attention and his only concern. However, they somehow made time to conceive Reba.

Reba's conception must have been immediately after the doctor gave his consent to have sexual intercourse because Renee was still an infant when my mom started to show. And I guess that was too much responsibility for old Ricky to handle because he slowly brought catering to my pregnant mom and his infant baby girl to a halt. He began to gradually revert back to his old ways and by the time my mom was at the end of her third trimester he had disappeared. Reba was born towards the end of August on the first day of school. The night before, Raymond and I could barely sleep, anxiously awaiting the next morning to get up and show off the new clothes our grandmother bought us for the brand-new school year.

My grandmother Mrs. Laura Jones wanted to ensure that her neglected eldest grandchildren didn't return to John F. Kennedy Elementary School another year looking unkept and unwanted because our mother—her daughter Deborah Jones, didn't feel the need to supply us with the barest of essentials.

"Call an ambulance!" My mom shouted from her bedroom. "OOOOUUCCCHH! Call the damn ambulance now! I'm in labor damnit!" Raymond called 911 while I helped my mom get dressed. When the ambulance arrived, my mother put up a big fight, refusing to be taken out of the house in a stretcher.

"I got it! Hell...I ain't dying...I'm havin a damn baby...don't need no bed on wheels!" She headed out the door, rushing and waddling towards the ambulance when suddenly a large contraction hit her as she was about to step up on to the medical vehicle. She missed the step and fell backwards into the ditch in front of the house and lay there in the dirt filled with labor pains, unable to move. It took the paramedics almost an hour to get her out of the ditch and on the stretcher, this time not taking no for an answer.

Both Raymond and I rode to the hospital in the ambulance with my mother. She held my hand the entire time, giving it an unusually hard squeeze periodically letting me know every time she felt a contraction. Needless to say, she refused to release my hand, completely ignoring the nursing staff about the liabilities of having a minor in the room. I ended up holding her hand throughout the entire birth process in the labor and delivery. I was barely ten years old; yet my mother felt I possessed the necessary strength needed to carry her during this defining moment. Her sweat, screams and cries were simply a mask to hide the hurt, fears and disappointments that she was forced to revisit when Ricky didn't show up for the birth of her baby girl. As I wiped the sweat from her drenched, feeble body, I knew I had to be strong.

Reba was born at Jefferson Davis Hospital less than an hour later at 5:31 pm on the first day of school. But instead of the nurses taking the precious infant to the nursery, she was immediately rushed to Pediatric ICU.

"Where my baby...where yall take my baby?" my mother's questions remained unanswered as the medical staff exited the room. My mother raised her weakened, fragile body up from the labor and delivery bed, trying to build up enough energy to remove her legs from the attached stirrups.

"Mama...what you doing?" I asked, still at her side assisting her.

"Where the hell they take my baby? Where my baby at?" she began to scream with tears rushing down her face.

"I don't know mama...but you can't get up...you too weak...she alright..."

"I ain't too weak to get my baby!" Ms. Deborah Jones said while continuing to get out of bed, but failed at her attempts; she eventually collapsed in my arms in tears. As I consoled her an older Caucasian, female nurse dressed in all white came in to talk with her.

"Everything is going to be fine Ms. Jones; your baby girl's kidneys were damaged and she had to be rushed to PICU to be put in an incubator to assist with the development of her little organs," said nurse Nancy in a patient sincere tone. "The patient escorts will be here soon to transport you to your room and later on tonight...and whenever you feel up to it, you can go see your little baby girl." Nurse Nancy left the room leaving me with the responsibility of consoling a woman that carried the weight of guilt on her shoulders knowing she was possibley the reason for her baby's unexpected fate. Raymond and I never did make it to John F. Kennedy Elementary that day!

Ricky eventually showed up at the house with pampers, wipes, clothes and toys for both Reba and Renee about a month later, shortly after Reba was released from the hospital. He stayed around consistently for almost a year, mainly just to spoil the girls, argue with my mother and ignore Raymond and I. Then one morning as we headed out the front door to go to school, there was a large trash bag filled with clothes sitting next to the front door. When we returned from school that afternoon, both the bag of clothes and Ricky were gone. That was six years ago and we haven't seen him since.

Chapter 4

Was what the letter read that Jason tossed in my locker as he slowly walked passed me at the end of the school day. Just as I closed my locker door, he whispered in my ear, "I will be waiting," and he lightly tapped my ass. Damn, a splurge of moister instantly hit the inner lining of my panties as I headed to the bus ramp. My first question was how was this plan supposed to be executed? At 7:00 my mom was usually at home watching her favorite shows on the television. Then there was Reba and Renee's bad asses that instantly became my shadows the minute I collected them from the school bus. Think Regina…think…okay, I could tell my mom I was walking to Rachel's house to get my sweater that I left on the bus. Hopefully this will fly since she doesn't like our belongings scattered all over the place.

This was too easy, my mom called just as I walked in the front door saying her friend took her to pick up Reba and Renee from school early because Renee was sick and she just went ahead and took Reba too. She was at the county emergency room since we didn't have insurance, and they said it will be a while before they are seen since Renee only had a fever that had gone down after the nurse gave her children's Tylenol. "I didn't cook, but I left some meat out, you can cook that…Reba sit your ass down somewhere!" I could hear her screaming in the background at her baby girl. "Oh Lord, these two little girls gonna drive me crazy! Anyway, cook that meat so we have something to eat when we come home…my lil friend left me a lil change last night…so I bought some thangs for us from the store! That damn Dexter might stank a bit…but he is very generous. That bastard said he wanted to take care of me and my kids…well I'm gonna let him do just that! My mom chuckled a bit. " Reba!!" she yelled out of nowhere. "Gina, let me go get this damn girl before I hurt her! Oh, and don't have nobody in my house! You hear me girl?"

"Yes, ma'am," and I hung up the phone.

It was already 3:16 pm, one hour and 44 minutes till show time. I immediately went to the kitchen and saw a large package of pork chops on the black and white tiled countertop. The checkered patterned counter with matching black and white checkered floors were redone just before my grandmother moved out. However, pure neglect and lack of appreciation over the past few years caused the pretty tile to chip and dull too soon. Even though she was repeatedly told not to, my mother threw straight bleach on the tile to keep it clean. The girls were always playing in the kitchen with their toys and there was a cracked stain on the corner surface where Raymond dropped his friend's carburetor on two years ago while working on his car. I took out a pan and decided to bake the chops; that way while they are cooking, I could get cleaned up and dressed to meet Jason, my love.

I showered to cleanse myself of all the bad debris that made contact with my body that day. The water and soap drenched my body from head to toe returning my anatomy to its natural state of softness. I dried off, then took my time and touched up my makeup, brushed my hair and curled my bangs. I wanted to be perfect for him. Now, what do I wear? Jeans? Shorts? No, a dress would be perfect, nice sexy not to mention easy access for whatever he has in mind. My mind was racing a mile a minute. Will he embrace me in his arms and gaze into my eyes telling me how much he loved me? Or will he feed me strawberries and whip cream with two glasses of wine while we sit in front of the fireplace and talk? Oh my, his hands will get to wondering after he tells me he loves me and has loved me for a long time now, and then he kisses me...the way he kissed me that night...and touches me...the way he touched me that night. "Okay Regina snap out of it!" Five o'clock was quickly approaching leaving no time for day dreaming.

I decided on a knee length black and white polka dot halter dress that flared out at the bottom. It hugged my mid-section and lifted my breast-making me feel sexy and empowered. I just wish my butte and legs were a little smaller so my dress wouldn't hike up in the back. It would just be nice to not have to pull it down after every five seconds. Oh well, I love this dress, it makes me look and feel like the diamond in the showcase that everybody wanted but couldn't afford to get.

Six o'clock on the dot;, it was show time! I turned off the oven, slipped on my shoes and out the door I went. Oh shit! Let me leave a note for my mom just in case she makes it home before me. I will just tell her I walked to the store to get something to drink or something...whatever, I was ready to go! So, I left and hurried down the street to my destination. As I approached Jason's yard my heart began to race in mini sprints within the walls of my chest. Nervousness had taken over as the perspiration exploded like a time bomb on my hands and face. Great, now I was perspiring! So, I slowed down and took deep breaths to calm myself down, and by the time I made it to the door I was relaxed.

His parent's car was gone so I could only assume they were gone like he told me they would be. I lightly tapped the door and no response. I knocked a little harder and waited patiently for a response, but still no answer. I put my head to the door and could hear the television playing in the background, so I knocked a little louder and a tad bit longer. I heard the television mute and a loud, "Who is it?"

"Aww...its, um.." I muttered.

"Who?" the deep baritone voice appeared again.

I got scared and turned to walk away when the door popped open. Jason. He stood in the door way stretching long and hard apparently just awakening from a nap. Just like a man—they come as is. I could almost guarantee that he wasn't bathing, fixing his face and attire, while anxiously awaiting my arrival. Nope, he simply came home and took a nap.

"Where you going girl?" he said with that slick grin to the side. "You leaving, I thought you came to see me, I see you got all jazzed up...come here." He extended his hand out for me to grab, I took hold and followed him into the house.

"When you asked who it was, I guess I got scared...it didn't sound like you." I responded in a low tone. I heard the door close and lock behind me. No turning back now Ms. Regina Jones.

"Damn you look good, girl!" he said while grabbing me around my waist with his strong arms. I didn't respond by hugging him back instead I played hard to get, just to let him know I was not the type of girl that was going to just let him have his way with me. So, I pulled back gently. He released me and I sat down on the oversized peanut butter brown sectional that took up over half of the living space in the room. There was a cherry wood colored floor model RCA television on the opposite end of the room, with a large JVC stereo system next to it. In the corner were pictures of Jason and the rest of his family, but mostly Jason. There were baby pictures and team pictures of just him...Jason Alexander Wallace.

"I'm dressed this way because I'm going to the movies with my friends. I stopped by here because of that letter you dropped in my lap on the bus." I lied.

"To the movies?" Jason asked as he sat down next to me, "Girl you ain't going to no movies- unless the star is me and it's set at my house! Shit...you staying here with me, looking all sexy...I don't need some other niggas looking at you!" he said with a smirking grin on his face moving closer to me.

"Boy please, I'm leaving in a few minutes," I said, looking down at my watch, "I have a date! I'm going out... to be around people that's ain't ashamed of being seen around me! You know...people like you that only talk to me on the cool when ain't nobody paying attention."

"Okay... now you trippin, I don't talk to you because your mean ass always talking crazy to me...shit, you don't think I want to talk to you, as fine as your ass is...why you think I am always starting arguments with you...especially when you wear them lil ass clothes. I hate to see guys looking at you, talking about they wanna fuck you and shit! I want to talk to you...I want to be your man," he said, calming down in a sweet seductive tone, he moved in closer, "don't you want to be my gal?" Jason asked kissing me on the neck. "Don't you?" kissing me on the cheek.

My mouth was speechless but my vagina seemed to have no problem responding to his seduction, with every touch it seemed to release floods of bodily fluids. He kissed my cheek again—but this time closer to my lips with his hand on my thigh. He took his other hand and turned my face to his and kissed me on the lips softly. He kissed me again and with his lips he parted mine for the full effect. Our tongues touched and danced a sweet tune together in the hollow spaces. He pulled me into his arms in a protective manner as if the fate of my life was determined by me being placed securely in his arm. I must admit it felt good to be loved. I could stay this way forever, in his arms in love!

"Come here," he stood up and reached for my hand.

"Where we going?" I asked.

"My room, I want you to see something."

I slowly stood and followed him up the hallway to his bedroom. The house was dimly lit with the smell of incense and cigarette smoke in the air. The cigarette smoke I assumed came from his parents' tobacco habit. The scent seemed to be embedded in every piece of furniture we passed. We made it to a room at the end of the hall and Jason flipped on the light. As we entered, I could feel the stench of tobacco leave my nostrils and replaced by the light smell of feet and musty under arms. "Sit down," he gestured towards the bed. I walked over to a twin bed that sat up against the wall and took a seat. The bed wasn't made up so I moved the blankets to the side and sat on the bottom fitted sheet. I couldn't believe he still slept on Superman sheets. I scanned the room and saw little league basketball trophies and certificates on a tall cherry oak bookcase with two drawers at the bottom filled with clothes, there were several pieces hanging out. A nightstand, with multiple sport designs tabletop lamp stood next to his bed. A 13-inch, black and white, RCA television set sat on top of a chest that matched the bed and nightstand. The chest sat near the foot of the bed next to a door that I can only assume lead to his closet. There were posters of Majic Johnson, LL Cool J, Janet Jackson and Salt n' Peppa on the wall. A desk and chair sat in the far corner of the room with a few pieces of clothing tossed here and there.

"So...what's up," said Jason while closing the bedroom door. He turned off the lights and walked over to me as the room instantly became dark.

"Wait, why did you turn off....," before I could finish, the lights to a small lamp on his desk came on. "Damn, you sure like dim light," I said.

"What you fussing about girl," he said with that sly school boy grin. Damn! Once again, the vagina lost its fluids.

As he walked towards me, he began to undress, his shirt went over his head while dropping his shorts to the ground. Lastly, there went his underwear that enclosed that signature prize possession I had the pleasure of viewing just a few nights ago. He walked over and lay directly behind me. All I could think of was, "What the hell have I gotten myself into! He wants sex fool—not love—SEX! So, what are you going to do now Gina? Say "no thanks" and walk on home? Oh, there must have been some sort of misunderstanding Jason; I was looking to be fed strawberries and champagne in front of candle light while listening to Marvin Gaye on the radio. What happened to whispering sweet nothings in my ear? Okay Gina, you watch way too much television.

"Lay down and relax...you can take your shoes off. He pulled me down on him just as I took off my last shoe. With one arm under my neck and the other under my dress he wasted no time aggressively kissing me and undressing me. His hands moved swiftly throughout my body unbuttoning, untying, unraveling and unfastening any and everything that got in his way. Before I knew it, I was naked.

"Wait Jason," I finally managed to say. "You're moving too fast; I have never done this before!" I said as fast as I could before he made another move. He paused and stared at me for a minute, then lay down and stared straight at the ceiling. I paused momentarily from his reaction then proceeded to get up.

"Wait," he said grabbing my arm. "Where you think you going, I'm not finished with you yet," pulling me back down under him. This time he got on top with his body completely covering mine. His Johnson, jabbing through my thighs, was already wearing its hard hat in search of its new found damp and dark place to go to work in. "You don't want to make love to me Gina?" kissing me on my lips, while his eyes refused to make eye contact with me.

"I don't know...I mean, you don't love me...how you gonna make love to me when you don't love me!" I began to plead my case. "Dang, I've only been here 20 minutes and look at this, you led me to your room, took off all my clothes before I could say yes to anything." My legs remained closed. "Let me up, I want to go home." I attempted to rise up from under him, but he tightened his grip and wouldn't let me budge. I tried squirming and wiggling, but his massive body wouldn't give way.

"Girl how you gonna tell me how I feel about you!" He said this time staring straight through me. "Why you think I keep picking arguments with you when you wear them little ass clothes, why you think I wanted you to come to my house tonight...I might not be in love, but I know what I like and I like you...a lot. I want you Gina...right now and I don't want you with nobody else." He kissed me, "you hear me Gina, I want you and I don't want you with anybody else—you belong to me." He kissed me, again and again and again. My thighs slowly parted and his penis slowly found its way to its domain. "Hold my neck baby."

The pain from having sex for the first time was almost unbearable. I wanted to scream out loud from the unpleasant sensation I felt as he pierced my vaginal wall. The pressure forced me to pull forward in an attempt to reduce the pain and agony of making love for the first time. "Where you going?" said Jason, realizing I was slipping away and gently pulled me back under his control. I held his neck tighter, biting down on my lip to keep from crying out. How could a world of pleasure be accompanied by so much pain? "Hold my neck tight when it hurts baby," he whispered again as he continued to grind and grind his massive head into my lower extremities. I held his neck even tighter.

We had sex! The wild thing! Sexual intercourse! A BOOTY CALL! And my virginity no longer existed, it was gone...history...bye bye! A lifetime of purity lost for 22 minutes of what was supposed to be pleasure. I mean I guess it was pleasure; Jason sure seemed happy especially at the end when he began to stroke at an increased pace making my encounter almost unbearable, and just when I thought I couldn't take anymore he immediately came to a stop, let out a loud shriek, and his entire body began to make multiple contractions all at once. "Did you cum?" was what he asked as he lifted himself off me. Come where? What was that? He didn't wait for a response; instead his body fell limp next to mine and he fell fast asleep like an infant after receiving a warm bath and bottle at bedtime.

It was 6:28 when I finally slid myself from under Jason's tall frame. I slipped onto the floor, right foot first careful not to wake the sleeping giant. I could still feel the cool breeze from the fan hit my naked body sending chills throughout. I gathered up my clothes, and as I got dressed, Jason awoke. He groggily sat up on the end of the bed saying nothing with his Johnson hanging limp still losing fluids. He silently put back on his shorts as I got dressed; then, he walked me to the door. Not a single word was spoken—not one single word. I didn't bother waiting for the door to close; as soon as I stepped outside, I began to run.

I was at home in the shower all within an eleven-minute time frame. I was in the bed when my mother and sisters made it home from the hospital. I pretended to be asleep when my mom walked in and turned on the light to check on me. I didn't want to talk to anyone, I didn't want to hear what anyone had to say. I just wanted to be left alone and think about what happened between Jason and I. Where do we go from here? The last thing I remember hearing was my mom screaming at Reba to take a bath and go to bed.

Chapter 5

Watching the sun slowly creep up from the east side of the sky, I stared out of the school bus window while in route to school. As dusk became dawn, I began reminiscing about what happened last night with Jason. It all seems so surreal at the moment as if it were all a mere figment of my imagination. But the soreness of my lower extremities proves that the night of passion definitely happened.

Jason usually drove his parents' blue four door Caprice Classic to school, but before I boarded the big yellow school bus this morning, I noticed the vehicle was still parked in the driveway. I didn't see him leave this morning, nor did I recall seeing him at school at all that day. I just went about my daily ritual and met up with Diana and Freddy in the cafeteria that morning to have our usual breakfast date. I of course didn't dare tell them about what happened the night before. I wasn't ready, I mean I don't know, I don't think I want anyone to know yet--or at all! I wasn't sure if it were too soon to profess my feelings for Jason; after all, he didn't talk to me at all after our encounter last night. I just kept pondering on his statements about how he felt, "I might not be in love, but I know what I like and I like you...a lot." These were his words spoken to me, to let me know how he really feels, then we made love...? "What a fool I've been," I instantly thought as the light bulb popped on in my brain. I was Jason's fool! The weaker species. To Kill Regina Jones.

Time just seemed to move at a glacier pace the entire day. I moved from class to class completing tasks, solving for "x", conjugating verbs, recalling facts and making educated guesses while conducting experiments. My body and brain seemed to participate in my learning, but my heart didn't; it simply wanted to go home and sulk in its own foolishness. Each crucial minute that passed seemed to be torture to my heart's dying spirit. Why did I allow him in; what was I thinking? Having sex with my arch enemy! Damn Gina, that was not the plan! You allowed a guy to enter into your temple, play in your garden and sample your forbidden fruit with no strawberries, no champagne, and Marvin Gaye definitely not singing in the background. The only noise heard were the occasional grunts and groans made by Jason during our sexual encounter. But he said he loved me...or liked me...I think...I mean...hell I don't even know!!

Finally, the school day came to an end and time to return home. After the

38-minute commute to Acres Homes, the bus stopped in front of Rolland Street and released a handful of us anxious teenagers. It's funny how we walk around like zombies all day in the graveyard of educational learning. but seem to quickly recover from the lack of energy that school seemed to have sucked out of us at the mere sound of the signal that indicates it's time to stop learning and time to go home! The mere sound of the 3:00 release bell sends a bolt of energy throughout our bodies that seems to make us come alive. Even I felt the electronic waves filter throughout my nervous system as I exited the yellow bus and began a conversation with Vanessa and Rachel.

"Where are you guys headed?" I asked.

"Home, I have homework and hell I need a nap before I crack open a damn Biology book!" Vanessa laughed.

"Girl you and me both! Ms. Andrews gets on my nerves with all this work we have to do at home, I ain't tryin to be no Scientist!" exclaimed Rachel.

Rachel, Vanessa and I were 16-year old juniors and we took most of our classes together at Eisenhower High School. We weren't the smartest girls, but we did get our work done. Rachel Murdock, the bad girl of the bunch was a "goody two shoes" that thought she was better than both Vanessa and I because she lived with both her parents and we didn't. I blame this superior attitude on her parents, James and Virginia Murdock who owned two dry cleaners in the community and actively participated in community events. They were far from broke, but they were definitely not as rich as they thought they were, or wanted people to believe.

Rachel was not the only child in her family, she had two older siblings, her sister Stacy was a 29 -year-old registered nurse at St. Joseph Hospital downtown. Rachel's parents are always bragging about how she graduated top of her class at Eisenhower and was accepted to The University of Texas in Austin. Then there was Rachel's unstable older brother Adam, a 31-year-old with four kids and at least three baby mamas! He occasionally worked at the cleaners his parent's owned, that is if he weren't partying or laid up with different women. He was even more spoiled than Rachel and definitely did not fit into the well-to-do middle class African

American family lifestyle his parents have worked so hard to create for them.

Rachel was the only child living at home and it showed! She always seemed to let it be known that she only shopped at Dillard's or Foley's, while the rest of us bought our clothing at the discount retailers up the street Weiner's or Kmart. She wasn't the prettiest girl but according to the guys she had a killer body! Rumor has it, she and Jeremiah had sex the entire summer last year and she got pregnant. Her mom supposedly took her to the clinic to get rid of it. The Murdock's couldn't let their reputation—or--I mean, their child's future be interrupted over a simple mistake like teenage-pregnancy.

Vanessa on the other hand lived with her dad, grandmother and two brothers, Bud 12, and Tim nine. Her mother, Mrs. Janet Wright, died in a car wreck when she was about 6 years old, which was shortly after Tim was born. She was the only one of the siblings that has any recollection of their mom since she was the oldest. She didn't talk much about Mrs. Janet, but she kept a picture of her on the mirror in her bedroom. She would always say her mother was her guardian angel and was always watching over her. This kept her out of a lot of trouble because she never wanted to disappoint her mom. Her dad, John Wright worked long hours at a nearby steel company called Forge Vessel, Monday –Friday and hung out with his friends drinking and gambling on Friday and Saturday nights. On Sunday her grandmother, Grandma Pearl made sure everyone went to church. Grandma Pearl was truly the glue that held down their family. She cooked, cleaned and made sure everyone in the family was taken care of. She often took care of the neighborhood kids to supplement her meager income of $500.00 a month.

Vanessa was cool but a bit of a flunky for Rachel at times. If Rachel liked something, Vanessa liked it too. If Rachel wanted to go skating, Vanessa wanted to go too. Last year for Vanessa's birthday she put together a girl's outing since her dad was unable to pay for her a sweet 16 party. Her plans were to go to the mall early in the day, have lunch at her favorite restaurant, Red Lobster and go to the movies that night to see the movie *Ghost Busters*, because she had a thing for Dan Aykroyd ever since she saw him in the movie "Trading Places" with her favorite comedian Eddie Murphy. Well, at the last minute, Rachel decided she wanted to go to the skating rink since Larry, Isiah, Trent and Jason were going to be there along with some other jocks from school. Rachel spoke and Vanessa changed her plans.

"Well I have to go home and watch Reba and Renee while my mama goes to work."

"Your bad ass little sisters can watch themselves, shit...I would prop them up in front of the t.v. and dare them to say anything!" murmured Rachel. "That's why I'm glad I don't have any siblings; kids get on my nerves!"

"Whatever...I gotta go...bye!"I said annoyed.

"See ya later Gina" said Vanessa.

"Bye girl" said Rachel.

Damn Rachel gets on my nerves sometimes, silly BITCH!! Whatever, I have bigger fish to fry like where was Jason and why didn't he come to school today. I glared down at his house and saw the cars parked in the driveway. This was a bit strange since his parent's car is usually gone. Then suddenly the tail end of his parent's powder blue Caprice Classic began to slowly back out of the driveway. I squinted my eyes to its lowest form in order to make out the image of the individual operating the motorized vehicle, hoping to project Jason's image behind the wheel. I slowly etched my way down the street towards my house, keeping one eye glued to the clear glass shadowing the individual driving. It was Jason! I could feel my heart sink to the deepest corners of my abdomen as the car backed out into the street heading in my direction. I swallowed long and hard, trying to keep from appearing too nervous as the vehicle crept up the dusty gravel road towards me. The rays of the sun slammed down onto the car's glossy chrome trim sending a variety of ultraviolet rays in my direction. Jason stopped the car once he reached my side. I could feel the blaring heat from the running engine as it purred melancholy songs of a well-engineered machine at work.

As my heart continued to make its way to the southern part of my anatomy, I saw a familiar face but with an unfamiliar look. This Jason was not the Jason I was used to seeing. His smile, his sly school boy grin, was replaced by a look of sadness and sorrow, screaming for solace from a terrible incident.

"What sup girl," he murmured as if it were hard to speak.

"What's up...missed you at school today," I said as I stared at the ground, too shy to make eye contact.

"Yeah...my grandma past away this morning and I went to her house with my moms and pops."

"Oh wow...I'm so sorry Jason!" I said staring into his distant eyes. "You gonna be okay?"

"Yeah, but I'm gonna miss ol' grams! She was my best girl. DAMN man!!" he screamed while hitting the steering wheel simultaneously. He hung his head low fighting off tears. "I mean I knew she was sick but I just thought she was gonna get better. Hell, I was supposed to go see her in the hospital last weekend, but I let my homeboy Rick talk me into going to the mall to hang out and now...shit...she's gone."

His grief-stricken demeanor made me want to embrace him in my arms and hold him until the sadness exited his mind and spirit. I wanted him to seek comfort in me like a crying baby needing his mother's love.

"Hey, what you about to do? Come ride with me to the store," murmured Jason in a sad solemn tone.

I began thinking to myself, I had two choices; decision A or decision B. Decision A was safe, I politely tell Jason "no, I can't ride with you because I need to get home to babysit my sisters so my mother can go out or entertain her guy friend Dexter." With decision A, I go home like a good girl and clean up, get my sisters off the bus and cook. However, with choice B, I am with the man I love and can't seem to get off my mind since our previous night of passion. Decision A has a positive outcome. Choice B, a risk that a woman in love, like myself, was willing to take and deal with the consequences later.

My once settled curly bang stood up and attempted to make its way to the back of my head as the gusty winds circled the interior of the car. We traveled down the dark winding road

towards the corner food store right outside of the neighborhood. He didn't say much but his silence spoke volumes. After making a steep turn onto Carver Road, he slowly released his right hand from the steering wheel and casually placed it on my knee.

"You close to yo grandma?" Jason asked in a sullen voice.

"She is my favorite adult in the world..." I murmured, choosing my words carefully. "It hurt my heart when she moved away...I don't know what I would do if something happened to her."

Nana, Big Mama, Grandma Laura Jones...my mother's mom and the one person I could always count on, no matter what the situation maybe. She has always made me feel so special, so extra-ordinary from everyone else, even my siblings. When she lived with us, we would sit and watch movies for hours at a time together. Raymond was always outside playing, in trouble or just simply couldn't sit still long enough to watch a 30-minute sitcom, let alone a two-hour movie. Whenever I visit her at her house, she always prepares my favorite meals and at Christmas I always get the most gifts out of all the grandchildren. But the best thing about my granny is that she gives my mother back some of what she dishes out, and my mother never argues back. She just gets mad, leaves and orders me to follow.

We didn't say much while in route, but I could tell his heart was troubled. He just kept sighing and saying he was going to miss her. We made it to the corner store at the corner of Carver Rd and West Little York in about 13 minutes. As usual the outside parking lot was crawling with drunken alcoholics and drug addicts looking for their next fix. A Black female weighing no more than 100 pounds, wearing a skin tight off white halter dress that was in need of a wash approached the driver's side of the car. She reeked of booze, musk and cigarettes.

"You got some blow baby?" she asked Jason as he got out of the car.

"Bitch, hell no! Get the fuck out of my face," he screamed. These damn crack heads be trippin! I be right back."

He slowly walked towards the store scanning the scenery and paying close attention to his surroundings. It was a well-known fact that drug addicts will jack you and run; and everyone knows you can't catch a crack head on the run! As he opened the door to walk in the store, I noticed Steven, a guy from school walk out. They gave each other dab and a half hug, the typical hood-boy greeting. They exchanged a few words then proceeded in their opposite directions. Steven, an 18-year-old, that dropped out of school last year to get a job, if you call selling drugs a career. Steven was somewhat tall and handsome...in a thug like...gansta way! He had gold teeth, gold chains and a gleaming gold watch that seem to reflect the sun's rays from every direction. As Steven headed for his car, he glanced my way.

"What's up girl?" he shouted.

"Hey Steven," I replied. He began to head my way dressed in a solid white t-shirt and white jeans that were so white, they looked as if he had fallen in a bottle of bleach. He wore a huge gold belt buckle and white and gold Nike tennis shoes.

"Say what you doin ridin with ole boy...yall talking?" Steven asked as he approached the window.

"Aw well...," I didn't know how to respond... what exactly were we? What were we doing? Who was I to Jason in his life?

"So, what's up? I saw you the other day getting off the bus in them damn shorts!" he exclaimed. "Hell, I had to look again...when you get so damn sexy?"

What? Me...sexy? Wow. Steven had bank and was known for hustling in the street. There were several girls-or shall I say "gold diggers" that wanted to talk to him, and he was *well* respected by the fellas who wanted to be like him, and he thinks I'm sexy? "Oh, Jason asked me to ride to the store with him," I replied bashfully.

"So, what sup, when you goin home?"

I began to look down at my hands popping my knuckles wondering where this conversation was going. "I don't know," shrugging my shoulders. Before I could utter another word, the door to the store swung open and out walked Jason cradling a small paper bag in his left arm. He stared intensely at Steven, then at me, back at Steven then settled his beaming gaze directly on my face. I immediately looked down like a child with his hands caught in the cookie jar that he was told not to touch.

"Alright Steven...I'll catch up to you later man," uttered Jason still glaring my way opening the driver side door.

"Yeah...alright Jay, holla at me sometimes bruh" Steven said not realizing Jason had walked up. "I see you later Miss Lady!" Steven uttered looking back at me as he began to walk off.

The slam from the door aggravated the windows in the car as they shook profusely in theirs hinges while sitting half way out of their hiding place. The engine let out a loud roar after the ignition signaled for it to wake up. The gear shifted and was followed by an immediate jerk backwards. Jason backed the car up, changed gears again and headed towards our home. Angry. We were two blocks from our house when he pulled the car into an empty lot.

He put the car in park and immediately grabbed my arm, yanking me under his right wing and shoving his tongue down my throat. The unforeseen force from him took my breath away. I couldn't breathe; I couldn't break loose from his firm grip. His right arm slithered quickly around my shoulders to the back of my neck, while his left hand made its way up my right thigh heading straight to my glutes finally settling on gripping my right butt cheek pulling me in so close that we were one. I began to tug and jerk away from his firm grip, but the more I fought the tighter his grip became. I surrendered to his will, becoming a weak, helpless kitten captured by an angry hound!

But why was he so angry? What did I do? How can I make this right? I kissed him. He loosened his grip. I kissed him again and again. Then suddenly his lips were pressed against mine; he parted my lips and pushed his tongue into my mouth with so much force it took my breath away.

"Get in the back seat! Jason demanded while releasing my lips.

I hopped in back, with Jason quickly on my tail following me. And before I could hit the seat, he grabbed my hips and pulled me into a doggy style position. He grabbed my ass, pushed up my skirt, pulled my panties to the side and rammed his dick inside me from behind. He fucked me...hard. I began to cry. I screamed out so loud my head began to explode from the intensity. The explosions continued to go off in my mind like fireworks on the 4th of July. That's when I realized I hadn't made a single sound. The screams, the explosions, the intensity never left my head. After about 2 minutes I managed to let out a weak, "Stop please...stop!" I collapsed with Jason's body instantly caving in and landing on my lower back and butte, breathing like he had just completed a 100-meter dash.

All I could think was, "What the hell was that!" Jason tucked his penis back inside his underwear, zipped his pants and returned to the front seat not saying a single word. We rode home in silence; no words were uttered not a single question was asked.

I am a mockingbird, I'm weak and lack power and everyone I come in contact with sees this lack of strength in my personality and feels the need to overpower me. To Kill Regina Jones.

Chapter 6

The house was mysteriously dark and quiet for reasons unknown. I know Jason and I rode around for several hours, but it was still only little after seven o'clock, still too early for anyone's bedtime. I slowly turned the knob and stuck my head through the small gap between the door and entryway to get a sneak peek of the surroundings before entering. There was only darkness, not a single soul in sight. Hmmm I wondered, "Where was everyone?" Reba and Rene typically play in their room around this time, but my mother's routine never changes. When she came home from work, she did a quick change of clothes, grabbed a beer and flopped on the couch. I quietly crept through the front door of my house careful not to let a single hinge rotate too abruptly, while attempting to prevent any creaking. I didn't want to ignite a single sound while entering my family's dwelling, knowing full well that the slightest disturbance would create a huge commotion between me and my mother. After turning the bolt to lock the door, I proceeded down the long corridor in my stocking feet and headed towards my bedroom. Just as I was about to reach my safe haven, I felt the sting of the rawhide leather slice the middle segment of my back multiple times.

"Where in the hell have you been!" my mother screamed angrily. "I saw you getting out of the car with that no-good ass boy down the street, what the hell y'all been doing...fucking!"

The force from the blows caused me to lose my balance and fall, but before I could hit the floor several additional zingers sliced my right arm while bright red fluid began to drip from my mouth. This made my mother stop swinging. The torture I felt from the licks seemed to over shadow the pain I was experiencing from the busted lip I got falling face first unto the floor. The sight of my blood covering my hands and spilling all over the floor sent me into a hysterical outrage. I quickly jumped up and flew right pass my mother, nearly knocking her down and headed towards the front door. I could hear screams from both my mother and my sisters, but I didn't stop, I couldn't stop; my feet wouldn't allow it. I continued out the door into the dark lonely street without looking back once while streams of hot tears ran down my face. It wasn't until I reached my friend Candace's house three blocks over that I decided to stop and catch my breath.

Since we lived so close to one another I sometimes hung out with Candace Robinson, a 17-year-old school acquaintance outside of school. I knocked on her door and her mother, Mrs. Robinson, a short plus size woman with a pretty face greeted me with a smile. "Hi Gina baby, Candace is in the kitchen feeding her face as usual...are you okay?" Mrs. Robinson asked as her greeting turned into concern.

"Yes Ma'am," I said barely able to keep from crying.

"Come in." she said while stepping back to allow me to enter. She rushed out of the room calling Candace's name.

Eating a piece of homemade fried chicken, Candace came out from the kitchen dressed in a green tank top and denim shorts. She was the splitting image of her mother, short with peanut butter brown skin and a pretty face. Only she was 20 years younger and wore thick black framed glasses.

"Hey Gina, what you doing here?" murmured Candace. "Damn girl...you alright?" Candace asked with the same look of concern her mother had. A few minutes later her mother returned with a soapy wet towel and handed it to me.

"You bleeding baby," said Mrs. Robinson. "Did someone hit you? Where is your mother? Did you have a fight?"

"No ma'am...I fell on the way over here," I lied not wanting to go into details about what happened; I just asked if I could use the phone so I could call my grandmother.

My trembling fingers seemed to miss the buttons as I dialed the familiar number on the mustard yellow, plastic, wall phone. It was mounted up next to the beige, top freezer refrigerator that seemed to house every piece of artwork Candace's 6-year-old baby sister has ever drawn.

No answer. I called again and still no words were returned on my end of the line. I hung up the receiver and slowly sat down at the kitchen table still feeling the pinch and soreness from my earlier sexual encounter. I was exhausted. My head was throbbing from the injury to my mouth and a bright red bruise seemed to have formed on my arm from the belt lashes. I knew I was wrong for leaving with Jason but why does my mother have to be so damn mean!!

I glanced over at Candace as she devoured another chicken leg and thought how lucky she was to have a mother who loves her. I bet she didn't have to worry about not being allowed to talk to boys and constant beatings to maintain control over the weaker being. Candace was so fortunate to not be a mockingbird, the weak that lacked power. And her mother, Mrs. Robinson was strong, nurturing, and didn't treat her like the weaker species and feel the need to overpower her.

"Hey, I have to take some stuff to my auntie's house. You feel like riding with me?" Candace asked while washing the chicken grease from her hands. "She stay in Studewood by Booker T. Washington High School...shouldn't take long."

"Okay..." I responded back. Studewood wasn't too far away by car, I'd just try calling my nana when we returned.

We headed down towards West Little York Road in her mother's black Baby Cadillac. The ride was so smooth as we glided down the dark street. The digital time glowing in bright green from the dash board read 9:06p.m. I let out a deep sigh as I sunk down into the velvety soft burgundy seats thinking, "What have I done? What am I going to do? Should I go home? Then there was Jason; should I call him and see if he was still upset?

While shaking me, Candice shouted, "Gina...Gina... girl wake up!". I must have dozed off to sleep in the extra plush seat. "I be right back; I just need to go inside and get something from my baby Eric."

Rising up to check out my surroundings, I asked drowsily, "Where are we?" Since we were still in Acres Homes, parked in front of an old classic white, one story narrow, rectangular shaped, shotgun house raised on brick piers. It had a set of wooden porch steps on the side of the house that lead to a narrow porch covered by a roof apron, which was supported by two white columns posted on either side. It sat on about one fourth acre of land with one tree in the front yard and a long dirt driveway on the side that dead ended to a small white wooden detached garage. The property was completely enclosed by a silver steal chain linked fence with the gate door in the front entrance to the yard. The gate had a tarnished gold pad lock dangling from the gate latch which I assumed was to keep intruders out, but not only was it not locked; the door wasn't even closed. As a matter of fact from its appearance it hadn't been fastened for a while and seemed to be neglected by the residents inside.

Eric was a 22-year-old drug hustler that Candace met at Big Tex Lanes Bowling Alley or at least that's what she told me. The bowling alley was near our neighborhood and was typically crowded on Friday, Saturday and Sunday nights. Most of the people that hung out there were drug dealers, drop outs and boppers. Boppers, which were girls looking to hook up with someone to get their hair and nails done and buy their babies' a pair of Air Jordan tennis shoes. At any given time during a visit at Big Tex, you would hear the constant bang of firearms exploding in the air surrounding the parking lot. The discharge of the bullets from the guns would send everyone there in a state of panic, forcing them to scatter like ants, and seek refuge and shelter among the parked vehicles. This hang-out spot was always getting raided by the cops, and someone was always going to jail. Just last year the place was on the 10:00 p.m. news because a random drug dealer and known gang member was shot and killed there. The lanes closed temporarily but managed to re-open after being out of service for about a month. I heard the owner promised to beef up security by adding additional security guards to monitor the outside premises; however, I still heard the girls complaining in the locker room at school about how they scraped up their knees on the ground dodging bullets while trying to locate the car and person they had ridden there with.

I've only been to Big Tex Lanes once with Diana and Freddy. Freddy borrowed his mother's car one-night Dianna had a sleep over at her house. Diana and I crept out of her bedroom window when her parents fell asleep, hopped in the car with Freddy and didn't make it back home until after 2a.m. Luckily her parents' room was in the back of the house, and they slept very soundly because they didn't notice we were gone. I, of course, was scared half out of my mind, but Dianna reassured me that we would be fine.

"Girl, ain't nothing gonna happen to us...DAMN stop being so scary! Ms. Deborah ain't gonna find out!" Diana said while in route. I simply let out a deep sigh and said a quick prayer thinking, peer pressure is real and powerful to the weaker species. To Kill Regina Jones.

Candance disappeared into the house while I sat in the parked car on the street. I sank deep down in the plush seat allowing my mind to play a recap of the events of that day, while my eyes were fixated on the bright green light from the time displayed on the dash board. It was now 9:13, and if I were at home, I would be in my room reading a romance novel thinking about Jason and I making love. I just can't understand what got into him today, why was he so mean, so forceful...why was he trying to hurt me?

I also wondered what my mom was doing? My mother, Ms. Deborah Rochelle Jones, 36-years-young, with four kids, two baby daddies, and a mouth so bad she could put pirates to shame. She was probably glad I was gone so she could finally have the house to herself and her man with money. She's going to miss me not being there to babysit Reba and Renee.

Suddenly, a super bright head light jumping up and down in the rear-view mirror brought me out of my daydream. The light grew larger and stronger as it got closer. The beam finally sat still, creating a glare in the mirror making it difficult for me to see any reflections. And just like that the light vanished into the night, leaving behind a trace of illumination that eventually disappeared too. Moments later I could see the image of someone heading towards the car. Where was Candace? I instantly felt afraid; I just realized I was alone in a car in front of an old house in the hood. Technically it was my hood, but I lived on the other side of the tracks...the safer side. What if the person was trying to jack me for a car that didn't even belong to me! A knock on the window made me jump, but when I looked at the familiar face, I was relieved. Steven, with his gleaming gold teeth was smiling at me through the window.

"Let the window down," he yelled. I hurriedly push the button that controlled the locks accidently, then hit the button for the window and watched it slowly depart from the top and head downward until disappearing completely. "What you doing over here girl?" murmured Steven. The smell of Busch beer and marijuana began to flow inside the car hitting my nostrils from every angle; this dude was drunk and high!

"I rode over with Candace... she's in the house talking to Eric," I said nervously. Why was he here? "You came to see Eric too?"

"Eric my cousin... we stay here with our grandma," he said with a drunken smile plastered on his face. "Why Candace got you sitting out here, come in girl... anybody could walk up and do somethin to you." Steven pulled the door latch attempting to open the door to the car for me but came up short. I looked at him, then at the manual door lock, then back at him and decided to unlock the small, silver, chrome knob. Steven pulled the door latch again, this time the door opened. He stepped back stumbling a little on the gravel as I got out of the car and pulled down my short skirt. I really didn't want to go inside; I was fine sitting in the car thinking about Jason and wondering what he was doing and if he was still upset with me.

"I see ya girl; you ain't got to pull it down! Damn you sexy!" stated Steven sluggishly. He was eying me up and down like I was a piece of meat waiting to be devoured at the dinner table by a hungry family. I bashfully lowered my head looking at the ground as I passed through the silver gate door heading towards the house with Steven in close proximity. He was unable to walk a straight line but had no problem grabbing my ass.

"Stop!" I said in a low tone while pushing his hands away.

"When you get so damn sexy?" Steven asked drunkenly as we approached the steps of the house. I just shrugged my shoulders and continued up the rickety steps that led to the porch. Just as I approached one of the white column posts, he grabbed my right arm, pulled me towards him and wrapped his arms around me in an intense bear hug, locking me into his control. I could feel his heavy breathing on my forehead as I continued to look down still in shock from the sudden gesture.

"Can you let me go!" I said tugging and pulling. His grip was so tight I could barely move.

"I can't hug you?" he said with the smell of malt liquor and marijuana simmering from his breath. "Damn baby, what happen to your mouth?"

"Nothing," I said breaking free from his drunken hold. I headed towards the old wooden door covered with scratches from years of abuse and neglect and proceeded to knock when Steven jolted ahead of me and turned the knob, pushing his way through the entrance. I followed closely behind.

Once inside the house I instantly noticed the framed picture of Jesus on the far wall to the right. A tan couch with a multicolored crocheted throw placed neatly on top of the back, rested against the right wall. A wooden floor model television was centered on the other wall with an elderly woman with short curly salt and pepper colored hair rocking back and forth in a matching tan arm chair watching the nightly news. She wore a pale pink house coat that fastened in the front and white socks with pink slippers on her feet. Steven instantly straightened up and walked over to her and gave her a kiss on the left cheek. The surprised kiss must have startled her, she jumped.

"Oh baby, when you come in, you scared me.

"My bad--Granny," Steven murmured while rising up from the small peck. "This my friend Gina." Before she could respond..." where Eric at?"

"He in the room with his friend...how you doing baby?" said Mrs. Barbara Thomas.

"I'm fine," I said innocently.

"Have a seat baby, you Steven friend?" asked Granny.

"We about to go to the back with Eric Granny," Steven said while pulling my right arm, leading me out the living room.

"It was nice meeting you," I managed to say before leaving her presence.

Steven lead me down a dark hallway with only one single dim light coming from the bottom of the third door to the right. As we approached the door, I could hear the faint sound of music; however, it was being drowned out by the sounds of a headboard hitting the wall, the bed squeaking and loud moaning. "I guess your girl and Eric is gettin they freak on!" said Steven as he quietly cracked the door open to peek in.

"Close the fucking door!" yelled Eric while throwing a shoe aiming for Steven.

"My bad bruh...my bad!" Steven said closing the door. He turned to face me. "Let's go in my room..."

"Nah, I think Ima go back to the living room with your granny and wait for Candace." How do I manage to get in these situations was all I could think at the moment? I wanted to go home, I wanted to talk to Jason and see why he was so upset, but I couldn't, my ride was in the room getting her groove on.

"Look, I don't know you like that and I'm not trying to go there with you." I turned to walk away when he grabbed my arm and pulled me towards him.

"So... wassup, Jason your man?" Steven asked spraying the scent of malt liquor drenched in saliva on my face. He only stood about 5'11 and even though it was dark the gold on his tooth seem to set off a soft glow between us.

"I just want to go back and watch t.v. and wait for Candace...that's all." I said slowly pulling away from his grasp. I stepped back slowly but he stepped forward trying to keep the proximity between us as close as possible. He tried to kiss my neck, I pulled back...he came closer and aimed for the other side of my neck, I again stepped back and again he moved forward. Before I knew it, I was pinned against the wall with him kissing my neck trying to put his arm around my waist and the other hand on my behind. When I resisted him, he put both his hands flat on the wall on either side of me, I was trapped and he knew it. The scent from his intoxication made me noxious, yuck! His touch started to make my skin crawl, it wasn't Jason's touch and that's the touch I had grown accustomed too. I instantly began to think about Jason and what happened earlier in the car. Thoughts of his sudden anger, the painful intercourse and the silent ride home was beginning to make my head spin.

"Come on girl, come go in the room with me, I ain't gonna do nothin...I just wanna talk," Steven said interrupting my flashback.

"No! I'm just gonna go back in the living room and wait." I said ducking down under his arm away from his control. Just as I turned to head towards the living area, Steven grabbed my arm so tight, I could feel his nails deeply embedded into the surface of my skin. He aggressively pulled me back towards him and our eyes locked.

"Say lil lady, why you trippin? Nigga just want to spend a little time with you that's all, damn! You ackin like I'm gonna do somethin to you!" Steven said, still piercing the skin of my upper arm with his nails.

"Let me go!!" I screamed, jerking away from his control. The force from my reaction in conjunction with his intoxication made him stumble a little. I slowly backed up not giving him a chance to rebound and make another play. We made eye contact, and judging from the rage in his eyes I was not going to hang around to see what was going to happen next. I quickly turned around and raced to the front door screaming out Candace's name. As I turned the knob, I could hear his grandmother voice faintly asking, "What the matter?" But I didn't stop to answer, I turned the knob swung open the door and ran as fast as I could. I slipped on the last step of the porch causing me to scrape and injure my left knee. I got up and continued running in full force all the way through the fence and down the dimly lit, sleeping street. I didn't stop until I saw a heavily lit convenient store at the corner of W. Montgomery Rd. and W. Little York, which was about two blocks away from Eric and Steven's house. Man, I was tired of running out of people's houses!

As I approached the store front fear began to set in. Four grungy homeless men hung out near the entrance, with one sitting on the newspaper bin greeting each customer who entered with the smell of dirt, liquor and pure funk! All I could think of was, "If I were at home, I would be safe in my warm bed asleep." A phone booth sat a few feet from them on the other end of the building. As I headed in that direction, I could see headlights, multiple headlights entering and leaving the store. Some with men screaming out the window, "Hey baby where you going?"

"Where yo sexy ass going?" "You need ride baby?" Some of the cars played music so loud that I could feel the thumping beat through my chest.

Damn! I didn't have any money! How could I use the pay phone with no coins! Just as I turned away from the beat-up old booth. Candace pulled up behind me in her mom's car.

"Gina, girl what you doing? Why you run off like that?" Candace asked while catching her breath.

"Do you have a quarter?" I asked ignoring her question.

"Who you need to call? I need to get back home before my moms start tripping."

"I just need a quarter to make a quick phone call...please, I promise it won't take long." I said thinking to myself, "She wasn't worried about mama when she was bumping and grinding in the bedroom with Eric just minutes ago!"

"Damn...here," said Candace tossing me the coin.

I walked back to the booth and lifted the scarred black phone receiver off the large metal box to prepay for my call. I dropped the currency in the slot and the familiar tone blared in my ear to signal for me to dial.

After about the third ring I heard the familiar baritone voice respond, "Hello."

I said nothing.

"Hello!"

Still nothing, what's wrong with me? It's what you wanted. Speak up Gina, damn!

"Hey...can I speak to Jason?" I asked hesitantly, knowing full well it was him on the other line.

"What's up... this J, who dis?" asked Jason.

"Hey, this Gina...I was calling...I mean I just wanted to see if you were busy...and...I don't know...if you still mad at me?" Still not knowing what brought about his rage earlier. Just then a cherry red, 1982 Cutlass Supreme pulls up booming the song "I need love" by LL Cool J.

"Naw baby, I ain't...what's all that noise in the background? "Where you at?" Jason asked in an unusual serious tone.

"I'm at the corner store on W. Montgomery and Little York..."

"What the fuck you doing over there...it's almost 11 o'clock...your moms know where you at?"

"No, we got into it earlier after you dropped me off...she hit me and I left. I went to Candace house..."

"Candace Robinson...what you go to that freak house for?" Jason asked angrily.

"I...I...don't know...I thought you were mad or something and I got mad at my mama...so I ran straight to her house!" screaming over the loud music. Suddenly the horn from Candace's mom's car blew over the music from the car deafening my ears.

"Gina, come on girl I got to go!" Candace yelled.

"Ok...ok...look Jason, I got to go--Candace needs to take her mom back her car before she gets in trouble."

"You stay your ass right fucking there—I'm coming to get you," said Jason angrily.

"At the store... by myself...but I'm scarred. What if somebody mess with me?"

"Whatever, I'll be there in a few minutes...I'm on my way!" Click.

I slowly hung up the phone. Was he serious?

"Gina...I got to go...now!" Candace screamed out the car window waking me from my daze. I slowly made my way towards the dingy black Cadillac just noticing it was in desperate need of a wash.

"Go ahead and go..." I said slowly. "Someone is coming to get me..."

"Who Gina? Girl you crazy...it's late out here...what if somebody get you?" Bitch you better get your ass in this car and worry about a nigga later!" Candace exclaimed.

"No really, my moms is coming," I lied.

"So why don't you just have her get you from my house?" said Candace still aggravated by my decision. "Wait a minute...yall ain't even got a car! How yo mama pickin you up?"

"Candace... just go, Ima be okay!" I said getting agitated. I was not leaving, Jason said wait for him, "I'm waiting for him!" I was screaming in my head.

Candace gave me one last stare, "Okay girl, I got to go...be careful!" as she backed the filthy black vehicle out of the pot holed filled parking lot. She stopped abruptly shifting that last gear into drive and sped off into the night. Finally, she's gone! But as I looked around at my surrounding, I began to almost wish she was still there.

Cautiously scanning my surrounding, I began to walk back over to the broken pay phone. The once four grungy homeless men plastered up against the store entrance had been reduced to three. The six glaring eyes seemed to be observing my every move as if they were waiting for the right moment to approach me. Damn where was Jason! I was officially scared! The meow from a black and white fluffy cat startled me as it leaped from out of the bushes onto the booth. The brilliant glints of yellow gem stones seemed to gaze back at me as our eyes met in the dark. He then surged down to the pavement and sprinted out into the darkness before I could blink twice.

The bright headlights from a speeding vehicle turning abruptly into the lot hitting every hole that was in its path broke my observation. The familiar baritone voice screaming from the driver side window sent a surge of relief throughout my body. Finally, it was Jason!

"Gina!" he yelled out.

I scurried off towards the vehicle's passenger side, grabbed the door latch and jerked it open hopping into the seat as if my life depended on it. I could hear the dirty old men at the storefront screaming out to me, "Hey baby...where you going?" "You leaving us?" I closed the door, shut my eyes and let out a deep sigh of relief. It was over! But we hadn't moved yet...the car was still in park. I slowly opened my eye and looked to left, and our eyes met. His glaring eyes seemed to stare suspiciously into mine. Jason had the look of both anger and relief as he faced forward and began to slowly back up into the dark street. Silence was the only thing heard for the first few minutes of our travels.

"You okay?" Jason asked cautiously choosing his words wisely as if to not upset me. Which I thought was strange...wasn't he upset with me?

"I'm alright," I uttered, lying to him and myself. Truth be told I was not okay! I was far from being okay! This has been a day from hell! Steven aggressively trying to sex me up, my mom lashing me with the belt causing me to fall and bust my lip, and let's not forget the horrible sexual encounter with Jason that started everything earlier today!

Silence filled the car again. Jason just peered straight ahead, while periodically glancing at each mirror to check his surroundings as he continued to drive down the road approaching a red signal light.

"I...I don't want to go home," I said suddenly as he stopped the car acknowledging the traffic light.

"What...what you mean you don't want to go home...where you wanna go?" Anywhere but there was in my thoughts. I did not want to see my mother and have her continue her physical abuse from earlier. Hell, truth be told, I wanted to go with him and lay in his arms all night! But he was probably still upset from earlier...I wish I knew what it was I did to make him so mad.

"I guess I could go to my grandmother's house," I suggested hoping he would extend an invitation to join him at his house.

"Where does she live?" he asked while slowly taking off as the signal light changed to a bright forest green color.

"Way in Dobbin, Texas" I uttered in a low tone.

"In the country?" Jason exclaimed. "Man... I ain't going to no country this time of night...I ain't trying to get stuck in the back woods...them dark ass roads!"

"I don't want to go home!" I exclaimed abruptly crossing my arms like a spoiled child wanting her way. This unexpected behavior took Jason by surprise.

"Well... just come to my house for the night... my moms is with my aunties at my granny's house trying to get things in order for the funeral. And my pops was sleep when I left to come get you," uttered Jason. Damn! I forgot Jason's grandmother died today, I was thinking while slowly unfolding my arms. "You can spend the night with me, ain't nobody gonna come in my room anyway," he said turning to face me. "I don't want to sleep alone tonight anyway...I keep thinking about Grams and how I'm gonna miss her!" He turned and peered out the window. I thought for a quick minute...it's not like I'm not already out and in trouble! Plus, my mamma gets on my nerves...always wanting to swing first and ask questions later.

"Okay... I'll stay...but I need to call my grandma when I get there."

"Cool."

We continued down the road for approximately six minutes finally turning onto our street...Rolland St. As we passed my house, I could see a single light glaring from the side window of our small three-bedroom brick house with the large oak tree in the front. As we passed by, I couldn't help but wonder what everyone was doing inside. I know Reba and Rene were probably asleep. "What time is it?" I asked.

"Almost midnight," Jason replied while turning into his driveway.

As we entered his dark house, Jason gentle closed and locked the door behind us. The vague midnight streak that graced the floor was the only light we had, making it difficult to maneuver through the living spaces. As we carefully made our way down the short corridor... the faint scent of cigarette smoke and fried chicken filled my nostrils. Jason opened the door to his room and flipped on the light switch. Again, I felt the stench of tobacco and fried foods leaving my nostrils and replaced by the smell of feet and musty under arms; only this time the scent wasn't so light. Damn Jason, Lysol would come in handy right about now!

I sat on the twin bed on top of Superman's head, reached for the tan trim line phone on the nightstand and began to dial my nana's phone number. I watched Jason turn on the television set and begin watching the "Twilight Zone." This show always spooked me, especially right before the commercial break; the image of the tree in the midnight hour would appear accompanied by a short psychologically enhanced theme song that kept me horrified and afraid to go to sleep at night!

As the lights from the phone buttons clicked on and off with the pressing of each digit, a series of questions began to clutter my brain: What are you going to say? How are you going to explain your whereabouts to Nana? Did Nana already know what happened? What if my mom already told her I ran off, and she instantly takes her side? I quickly slam the phone down on its base making a loud ruckus that made Jason jump and turn my way.

"So...what's up...yo grandma answer?" Jason asked.

"I'm too scared!" I said staring down at the dingy grey wall to wall carpet on the floor.

"Well shid don't call then...you already in trouble," he uttered while scooting closer to me on the bed. "Hell, Ms. Deborah probably already told her what happened, so don't even worry about it till tomorrow when you go home."

But I have to call Nana and it's not that easy...and who the hell said I was going home! Nana loves me; she's the only one that cares about my well-being. I don't want her to be worried, plus she needs to know I am coming to her house to stay! I don't want to be at that house with my mom anymore, especially since her main goal in life is, To Kill Regina Jones, repeatedly. I will always be deemed as the weak species. But what's interesting is I'm seen as weak to a woman that thinks she's strong!

"No, I need to call her...she's going to be worried about me," I uttered as I picked up the phone and began to redial the number again. Jason turned away to finish watching the show while taking off his sneakers.

"Alright then, don't say I didn't tell you so!" he uttered bent over unlacing the black All-star Converse shoe.

"She did what!" Is all I could heard Nana say on the other end of the phone line.

"Where you at now?"

"At my friend's house a few blocks away; her mom is asleep, but she said she would bring me to you tomorrow."

"Your mamma got her damn nerves, why she wants to be hitting on somebody! Alright baby...well Nana going back to bed now...I'll call your mamma tomorrow; you call me if you need me. I'll see you in the morning. "said Nana before hanging up the phone.

"Yes ma'am," I uttered in relief as I replaced the receiver back on its base again. I turned around and faced the television set still a little dazed about all the happenings that day. All I wanted now was to experience a good night sleep, but the gentle touch of Jason's hand caressing my lower back signaled to me that the day was still not over.

"Come here," Jason said while his hand made its way past my back to my right side, pulling me towards him. "What your grandma say?"

I scooted towards him, not knowing exactly where his mind was, while suddenly reliving the car incident earlier today that ultimately lead to all of the events that occurred tonight. "She said she will see me in the morning." Jason scooted closer. I could feel the warmth of his breathe sprawl down on my left upper torso as he moved in for a kiss. Suddenly his tender lips were planted on my neck, accompanied by moisture from his tongue swirling around in circles with his lips lightly suctioning the outer layer of my skin.

"Good, that means you're mine tonight!" whispered Jason in between the sucking and kissing. He stood up and began to undress, peeling off one piece of clothing after another until he was completely nude. There he stood in front of me fully erected ready for play.

"Put it in your mouth," said Jason seductively.

"What...put what in my mouth?" I asked clueless to the fact. How dare he! He wanted me to suck his penis, after literally pounding me in the car from behind, with no explanation what so ever! The fucking nerve! I immediately jumped from the bed out of his proximity and headed to the other side of the room next to the bookcase. I hurried so swiftly that I stumbled on a pair of pants thrown on the floor, hitting a couple of the trophies that lined the shelves. A couple of them shook a little, performed a balancing act and took a nose dive unto the floor making a loud crashing noise upon impact. "Sorry!" I exclaimed as I kneeled down to collect the fallen awards.

"Jason...Jason what's wrong baby!" yelled the voice of a drowsy middle-aged female. Damn! I woke his parents up. "Jason you alright?" This time it was accompanied by a knock on his bedroom door.

"Shit!" Jason loudly whispered. "Shhhhh! don't say anything." He crept over to the door gesturing for me to stand out of sight. "Yeah ma...I'm alright, just tripped on some clothes on the floor and hit the bookshelf, I'm good though," he uttered.

I jumped as the doorknob suddenly began to rattle. "Shhhhh!" Jason gestured with his right index finger to his mouth.

"Baby, why is your door locked?" Jason's mother asked in her sweet motherly tone. Mrs. Monique Wallace, 40 years old, with cafe latte colored skin, long, silky, peanut butter brown hair and light brown eyes; she was beautiful. Many of the ladies on the street, including my mom said she was stuck up and not very "neighborly" whatever that meant. This is probably because she is so pretty and tall and pretty and dresses well and pretty! Of course, the men on the street had a different opinion about her. Every time they would see her coming, they acknowledge her by sending a kind greeting, yet their predatory stares indicated that they were secretly visualizing her naked.

"Oh, I must have accidently locked it when I came in..." Jason said in a slightly disrespectful tone. Man, if I talked to my mom like that, she would have kicked the door open with a 2x4 stick in hand swinging and swearing I was harboring boys in my room! "I thought you was with Aunt Lena and Aunt Earline?"

"I was baby...I was tired and came on home.... we go take care of everything else tomorrow...you sho you alright?" Mrs. Monique asked returning back to the previous conversation.

"Ma, I'm fine... I just don't feel like getting up to open the door!" Jason responded, still irritated and even more disrespectful this time.

"Alright baby, but I told you, you need to pick those clothes up off the floor," his mom said sounding less sleepy this time. "Good night baby, try not to make any more noise, you know your daddy had a long day and is asleep...I don't want to wake him up."

"Ma, alright," Jason...irritated.

"I love you!"

"Love you too!" he quickly exclaimed.

Jason stood at the door listening until he heard the door to his parent's room open then eventually close softly. He then grabbed my right hand gently with his left index finger to his mouth and began to pull me while walking backwards towards the bed. I followed his lead. I then noticed he had thrown on a pair of forest green athletic shorts with a white stripe outlining the outer parameters. He must have slipped them on when I turned to pick up the trophies.

He led me back to the bed and sat down, his butte covering Superman's legs and the lower part of his cape. He was trying to find the exact words to say that would not send me into another rage, he just stared at me.

"I want you to be my girlfriend Gina," Jason uttered.

The unexpected words hit me with great force. "Your girlfriend? Me" I whispered in a surprised and confused tone, trying to remember to keep the volume down.

"Hell yeah you!" he loudly whispered. "I want you all to myself, no lie Gina...why you think I got so mad earlier when I saw you talking to that nigga Steven!"

I definitely didn't see that coming! Wow he wants to go out with me and let the world know it! Now I see why he got so upset today...Steven...I am definitely not going to mention what happened at Steven's grandmother's house just a few hours ago.

"Come on baby, you can do stuff like this when you a couple," Jason said raising up off the bed just enough to pull his shorts down. There it was again, his penis, but this time it lay slumped over his testicles in sleep mode.

"Wait, don't you still talk to that girl Lisa? I know I saw her over here this summer."

"Man...I don't give a fuck about no Lisa!" almost forgetting he had to keep his voice down. Jason stood up... hovering his tall six-foot two frame over me, "I want you; I keep telling you this Gina! Damn, you thinking I'm playing!" He kissed me softly on the lips; then moved to my neck. I could feel his tongue briskly moving in a circular motion directly below my right ear lobe. The fire began to ignite, and I felt the moisture accumulating between my legs. "Come on baby, please...do it for me!" as he sat back down on the bed and pulled me down to my knees directly between his legs. I was now face to face with his fully erected Johnson.

"Jason...Jason wait, I ain't never did this before. You are the first and only guy I ever had sex with."

"Just grab it and massage it."

Hesitantly, I followed his instructions and with my right hand I grabbed his dick and held it like a broom stick. He put his hand on top of mine and began to slowly maneuver them both up and down. Each time he pulled down the foreskin, the inner pink portion of his sex organ would reveal itself getting longer and harder with each thrust. After about a minute he released my hand and hinted that I needed to continue this sex act on my own. He leaned back moaning,

"Ahhhhhh! Baby, go ahead and put your mouth on top...but don't stop jacking me off!" I slowly brought my mouth to the designated area and wrapped my lips around it. The salty, sweaty taste from a day of play made me gag! Then suddenly Jason placed his hand on my head and began to pump himself into my mouth. He held down my head with a tight grip, preventing me from any movement and would not let go. He continued to jab himself into my mouth and I gagged, I was choking...finally he pushed me away and my butte hit the floor. He immediately grabbed his penis and began to explode. He whimpered softly as the thick antique white fluid rushed out of his body. I sat watching him as his body jerked and trembled and his toes curled up.

"Hand me my shorts," was all he managed to utter to me. I picked up the green shorts and tossed them to him. They landed directly on his lap. He sat up slowly and proceeded to clean himself off with the clothing. "Damn girl, I almost shot you in the mouth! Come here!"

I slowly stood up thinking, what did he mean by that, shoot me in the mouth?

"Take off all them damn clothes and come lay down next to me." Not wanting to upset him, I followed his command removing all the clothes from my body down to my underwear. Jason scooted back in the bed to lay down leaving space for me to lie next to him. I immediately felt the warmth of his physique as I placed my body next to his. He turned me on my back, lifted my left leg and placed it on his hip to keep my lower limbs parted. He began to suck my left breast with intense force, stroking my nipples with his tongue. My vagina was running out of patience awaiting her turn to be pleasured, she became restless, antsy; with her lips silently screaming for some attention. Then suddenly, as if he heard her piercing cry, Jason began to run his fingers over the upper layers of my vagina until he found what he was in search of. And just like our very first encounter, he rubbed the area with his index finger with the perfect amount of aggression and gentleness until I exploded again with pure delight into his hands. I was in love!

The next morning Jason and I awoke bright and early before his parents got out of bed and he took me to my granny's house in Dobbin, Texas. I ended up staying there for three nights and on the fourth day my mother came to get me in her friend Dexter's car and took me home. We never talked about what happened that night, nor did she question my whereabouts after I stormed out of the house.

"You hungry?" my mom asked.

"Yes ma'am," I uttered in a low tone. I'm sure she didn't care one way or another, but I still politely responded. Then there was silence.

"I had to throw out some of your clothes; the hot water heater leaked out on your dirty clothes in the garage and that shit got mildewed!" said my mom carefully but in a firm, defensive tone.

"What! So, what am I going to do about clothes?" I said abruptly not realizing my tone.

"Calm down, my friend Dexter gave me a little cash so you can get you some more clothes...here now...take this." My mother opened the glove compartment and pulled out three $100 bills and handed them to me. My mouth dropped; this was totally unexpected, I was speechless. My mom had never given me more than five dollars at a time. Was she feeling alright? For the last few days, while at Nana's house, I've been preparing myself to face round two with Ms. Deborah Jones, what a pleasant surprise. I must admit, it felt good to not feel like the weaker species. She didn't feel the need to overpower me, to kill Regina Jones. Did she now want to protect Regina Jones, accept Regina Jones, and finally love Regina Jones?

The next few weeks at home were very similar also; I didn't have to clean up as much or babysit. My mom actually scolded Reba and Renee several times for leaving a mess, getting in my personal space and bothering my personal items! Wow, this felt like The Twilight Zone- a psychological twist to my mother's mood and demeanor. I just hoped the situation didn't eventually end tragically!

Chapter 7

month had already passed, and having sex with Jason became almost second nature to me. He would casually communicate to me his sexual desires either by note, a phone call or that sexy seductive look he gives me in passing. Our sexual encounters were not limited to the bedroom either. We discovered new and improved ways to mark our territory with our sex-capades. The world became our sexual playground. The back seat of his parent's crystal blue 1986 Caprice Classic, behind the old Maple tree near the dirt trail in the heavily wooded area outside our neighborhood, even the second level of the jungle gym at the community park became a regular setting for intercourse. Jason exposed me to so many sexual acts; of course, my being inexperienced did not sit straight with him, he wanted more and he wanted it now. After about the third time we made love the extreme pain of being stabbed in the vagina was replaced by strokes of pure ecstasy. He would turn me over and straddle my legs amidst his hips carefully placing his full erection inside me. Then his well-placed hands would cradle the thickness of my butt cheeks while guiding my movements to his specifications.

"That's it baby, ride me! Ride me baby!" yelled Jason. "You like that dick don't you? Yeah...you like that...ride me baby...DAMN!!!"

The more he talked the harder I worked, I was lost in his erotic language, seeking to reach one ultimate goal and that was to increase his pleasure. I wanted him to be happy; his happiness was my joy. And as he cried out at the release of his love exploding inside me.... I knew my goal was accomplished...I was in love!

The room seemed to spin in a slow rotation as my eyes opened to the sound of my alarm clock going off. I hit the top button twice, missing it the first time, as I attempted to end the annoying sound used to break and end a restful night sleep. There was however nothing restful about this morning; flips and summersaults in the deep pits of my stomach were being executed by the meatloaf and green beans my mom cooked the night before. Then suddenly without further notice my mouth began to well up with excess saliva, and before you know it, the food decided to change its direction and sprint up my esophagus in full speed passing through my mouth and landing on the cheap, turd brown dyed carpet on my bedroom floor.

The feeling was somewhat familiar like the upset stomach I had last Thanksgiving after sneaking a piece of my mom's half cooked turkey, even after she specifically said not too. "Gina watch this turkey while I run to the store to get more seasoning before I put it back in the oven to finish cooking. Don't touch it, it's not done!" But as soon as I heard the front door slam, I was sneaking a taste of the delicious golden-brown lump of poultry, without realizing the realness of salmonella poisoning! Oh yeah, it's real!

No sooner had the fresh vomit hit the floor, before I felt another round of gush forming inside my intestines. I instantly made a mad dash down the corridor to the bathroom, bumping into Reba as she was exiting from completing her early morning poop. The stench from her remains forced its way into my nostrils increasing the level of intensity of the contents within me, which were making its way back up my throat canal. I hugged the toilet, not at all concerned with the aroma of baby poo and human gas lurking out into the open. I repeatedly vomited into the commode until it was filled with the breakfast, lunch, dinner and a few snacks I had the previous day. This went on for about 20 minutes.

Totally exhausted, I sat back onto the floor and posted up against the bottom of the sink. I looked up at the light blue wallpaper with white flowers. The daisy prints seem to dance in the wind while the cleverly placed yellow spots in the center of each wall floral seem to follow my every move.

"What's going on in here?" my mother asked while standing in the doorway dressed in her dingy, off white, terry cloth bathrobe. Her hair was perfectly parted in three rows of pink sponge curl rollers with a mint green silk scarf tied around the edge of her head. With all the regurgitating, I hadn't even noticed her staring down at me.

"I don't feel good; I think the meatloaf last night made me sick!" I murmured.

"What you mean my meatloaf? Hell, ain't nobody else get sick!" Mama exclaimed, looking more annoyed than concerned about my sudden illness. "Look up there in the medicine cabinet and get that Pepto, then clean up this damn mess. Hurry up and get your ass up off that floor; you not missing school ... and go help your sisters get dressed for school! Mama having company this morning and I don't need no kids in my face while I'm tryin to get some money for that high ass light bill!" She exited the bathroom scooting across the floor in her worn, dingy grey house slippers, whose original color was white some nine years ago.

I slowly pulled myself up, holding on to the sink as if my life depended on it. As I leaned my body against the basin, I looked up at the mirrored door attached the medicine cabinet and began to stare at my reflection. "How am I going to make it through the day feeling like this! I reached for the silver knobs marked C and H, turned them clockwise and slowly placed my hands under the running stream of luke-water. I washed my face.

The ride on the school bus this morning seemed unbearable. It was hot, too hot, as if a blaze of heat had been ignited within the pores of my body ...I can't breathe! I wasn't perspiring or excreting moisture from my glands, nor did I see anyone else sitting uncomfortable in their seats on the yellow bus headed to school. It was a typical fall morning and the windows were half down as usual. I took out my notebook and began to fan myself, hoping that the rapid movement of air towards my face would give me comfort—it didn't. Suddenly the bus hit a large pot hole in the road and threw the passengers forwards in an upward bounce. Nausea. Again. I wanted to return home and crawl back into my warm bed to help relieve me of my symptoms. Then suddenly I felt sharp dull cramps ignite in the hollowness of my stomach, I was hungry, very hungry and ready to devour anything in sight.

Finally, just as the school bus made an immediate right into Eagle Drive, then down the ramp to release us eager leaners to our final destination, my stomach let out a loud snarling growl. The message was clearly received from my brain that my tummy was desperately seeking to be filled with nutrients. We all stood up in a single file line following the other to the one and only exit. Up the walk way and down the three steps, finally, fresh air!

I headed into the cafeteria towards my usual spot to place my belongings on the table. I didn't see Diana, but Freddy was seated in our usual spot talking to a couple of our female classmates. Knowing Freddy, he was probably gossiping!

"You alright?" Freddy asked me staring hard as I approached the table. "You look like you had a rough night baby doll."

"I'm good, just hungry." I murmured as I dropped my bag and notebook on the nearest seat next to him. "Watch my stuff...be right back!"

"Girl, where you going in a rush?" he yelled out to me.

"I'll be right back!" I shrieked.

"Oh, she must be hungry yall!" I heard Freddy say to the girls laughing out loud.

Ignoring him, I hurried towards the tray line to get breakfast. DAMN!! A line! Teenagers of various ages, heights and grade levels occupied the first 16 slots in line. As I waited my turn, the raging bull in my belly was in attack mode, aggressively and loudly terrorizing the inner linings of my abdomen!

The line swiftly moved as the cafeteria workers quickly placed a round flat sausage patty, three golden brown French toast sticks and one scoop of imitation eggs, on the beige, six compartment serving tray. Once filled, they placed each tray on top of the glass window protecting the food. I reached out to grab the next durable, shallow, container filled with food, noticing the light surface scratches on the tray from its frequent usage by students. The surface scars seemed to surround the food in each compartment. I grabbed an apple juice and white milk to complete the meal and scooted towards the cashier. She was a large Black lady sitting on a tall black stool wearing a white uniform, white apron and a hair net covering her reddish-brown curly hair. Her single focus was on scanning lunch cards, compliments of the free and reduced lunch program for students of low-income families in the state of Texas. I handed her my card when it was my turn, she scanned it and handed it back. "Thank you," I said, rushing out the door towards my table to devour the food.

As I approached the table, I noticed Diana seated next to my belongings and the females talking to Freddy were walking away.

"Hey girl, what's up?" Diana asked as I took my seat.

"Nothing, just hungry as hell!" I said as I began to remove the clear wrapper around the plastic spork, knife, napkin and straw. I headed straight for the French toast first and didn't come up for air until the raging animal inside me was satisfied!

"DAMN girl! Your mama don't feed you at home? You swallowed that shit like it was your first meal in days!" Diana said laughing.

"I told you she rushed off to get that food like the school was going to run out of that nasty shit before she made it in the line!" said Freddy in his very elaborate tone. "You better than me, can't pay me to eat that mess!"

"Whatever...I was hungry!" I murmured. My mom cooked meatloaf last night and that shit made me sick to my stomach! I was throwing up all morning!"

"Well, you might as well get ready for round two, cause I don't see that nasty shit you just ate staying down either!" laughed Freddy giving Diana a high five.

"Boy you crazy!" laughed Diana.

I chuckled a little as I pushed the tray to the side and picked up my purse to re-apply my makeup and get ready for the school day. I proceeded to open my round, mirrored compact that housed the mahogany color powdered foundation and applied it to my face with the enclosed sponge. While carefully rubbing the contents on each cheek, nose, chin and forehead I listened and eventually joined in the conversation Freddy and Diana was having about a few of our classmates and school. Then suddenly the loud solemn bell releasing us to homeroom rang. My friends and I slowly rose from our seats laughing, talking and gathering our belongings all at the same time, continuing our conversations as we exited into the hallways headed to our lockers.

The hall was filled with eager students scrambling to get to their destination, teachers monitoring the halls to ensure their safety and administrators on alert in case their security and well-being was compromised. Red tops, black t-shirts, yellow and white dresses, blue hair bows, denim shorts and jeans. All the colors of the rainbow seemed to run together in an intense speed ultimately turning into a large color coated blur. Why was everyone moving so fast? Slow down! My head began to slowly spin on its axis, leaving me feeling like I had just jumped off the merry-go-round in the park near my house. The spinning grew faster and faster causing me to feel lightheaded. Then without further notice, everything went dark.

"Regina.... Regina...Regina! Can you hear me? Regina!" I heard Mrs. Barlow, the school nurse screaming my name as I slowly opened my eyelids. The short portly lady, dressed in an all-white cotton dress, thick white panty hose and white, heavy soled, laced up, orthopedic shoes, was on her knees over me. She was on my right side holding my right hand with her thumb pressed down on the middle of my wrist. She used her right hand to apply a cool wet towel to my forehead.

Once my eyes were completely opened, I noticed the rest of the individuals towering over, our principal Mr. Rickson, an assistant principal Mrs, Malory, my favorite teacher Mrs. Ringold and a couple other adults staff members that I wasn't familiar with.

"What happened?" I asked slowly raising up, still feeling a little woozy from the lack of blood circulation in my brain captivity.

"Slow down honey," said Mrs. Barlow. "You wouldn't want to rush getting up and pass out again."

"Regina dear, do you know where you are?" said the familiar voice. An English teacher, Mrs. Ringold had come closer to me and comfortably sat next to me on her knees. She wore a beautiful long sleeve, silk, button down, lavender top with black polyester trouser pants and black, low heel pumps. She smelled of fresh powder and lilacs with a hint of eau de toilette.

I met her last year as a sophomore, when I was assigned the locker right next to her classroom. I was bent down at the lower locker turning the dial three times to the right, back two times to the left...when the beautiful Caucasian lady with her short blonde bob hairdo and ocean blue eyes stepped out of her room and began to stare directly at me. I slowly turned her way with curiosity lurking within my mind, wondering why is she staring? And just when I was about to question her actions she says, "Sweetheart, is that blouse supposed to be worn like that?"

I looked down at the lime green off the shoulder knit sweater and noticed the seams on the outer lining of the blouse-- when they should have been on the inside! "Oh crap!" I exclaimed. The lights were out at our house due to non-payment and I had to do my best to get myself, Reba and Rene dressed for school that morning. Mama said she was going to pay the utility bill that morning. Apparently, her friend gave her some cash to take care of it when he left that morning, which was before I got up to get dress. But what was more ironic is that Freddy and Diana talked to me the entire morning during breakfast in the cafeteria and they said nothing!

"Come in my class and fix your shirt," Mrs. Ringold suggested. "None of my students have made it to class yet...you have a minute."

I quickly closed my locker door, hurried into the classroom. Mrs. Ringold quickly closed and locked the door behind me and waited patiently on the other side of the hard-framed panel. She stood outside the door directly in front of the small fitted rectangular glass window just above the knob to ensure no one attempted to enter. "Just knock when you are finished!" she yelled from the other side.

The shirt quickly went over my head and I turned it on the right side. As I pulled the shirt back on the correct side, I noticed her podium centered in front of the classroom in front of the chalkboard. It had several pictures of gold rings. How interesting was my first thoughts! She must have a thing for golden colored rings?

I knocked twice at the door to be let out of the room. Mrs. Ringold turned around at the sight of me in front of the window she was guarding.

"You all done?" Mrs. Ringold asked with a smile.

"Yes ma'am," I responded while crossing the threshold into the hallway. Several students had already began lining up at the door waiting for her permission to enter. "Thank you for letting me use your room." I said politely with appreciation as I made my way pass her students down the hall to class. Every day after that she would go out of her way to speak to me and render me a compliment of some sort. Then one day I stayed after school to finish a project for history class and was supposed to ride home with Rachel and her mom, but Rachel ended up going home early instead. So of course, I was stranded at school, not knowing how I was getting home. It was 5:35 in the evening and the sun was already setting in the west. I sat on the iron, three-seater bench in the front of the building to gather my thoughts and devise a plan that could get me to mi casa at a decent time, without my mom jumping to conclusions about where she thinks I might have been. Then out walks Mrs. Ringold and two other teachers headed towards the parking lot to their vehicles with the look of exhaustion plastered across their faces.

"Regina darling, you okay?" asked Mrs. Ringold. She was looking lovely as ever in her ocean blue turtle neck sweater that matched her eyes; she was always so flawless, even after a long day at work. She headed towards me with her black fitted cotton stir-up pants tucked neatly in her black leather riding boots--just stunning!

"Yes, ma'am," I replied, not wanting her to know my current dilemma.

"Well, why are you just sitting here? Is someone picking you up, it's getting dark and there aren't any administrators left in the building," said Mrs. Ringold with a genuine concern. "Do you need a ride?"

"No ma'am," I replied.

"So what time are they picking you up?" she continued to probe.

"Um...well they should be here soon...."

"Who is they? Your mom? Dad?" Mrs. Ringold asked, not allowing me to let my pride stand in the way of me safely getting home.

"My friend Rachel left earlier and she was my ride home," I finally confessed. "She lives on my street and was supposed to stay after school too, but she went home early and didn't let me know. Now I'm stuck here with no ride!" I was frustrated.

"Where are your parents? Are they able to come get you?" With what, was all I could think, we don't have a car!! Public transportation, our feet and my mom's male friends got my family where we needed to go!

"My mom doesn't have a car." I said while looking at the ground, another confession.

"Well honey I can take you home. Is it near here? Will your mother mind? You can go back into the school and call her to make sure it's okay?" Mrs. Ringold asked in a nurturing motherly tone.

"She won't mind..." I murmured. I just needed to get home.

"Well come on...my car is over there."

I followed her to a beautiful bright white Lincoln Town car with dark tinted windows. Wow! This car was beautiful! Mrs. Ringold walked to the other side of the car and inserted the factory key into the driver side keyhole to release the switch that unlocked the doors. I opened the door to the luxury vehicle and got in. It was like heaven sitting on the soft leather gray seats. She placed her purse in the backseat, got in and started the car. I remember the soft purr of the engine being so light and whimsical that the car seemed to float like a cloud as we rolled down Antoine Drive.

She asked me several questions about school including what was my favorite subject? I guess it was **Reading, since I read a lot.** As we proceeded down the street through the twists and turns, she told me she had two sons, one was an adult already out of school and her youngest, Brice, was a 16-year-old junior and went to school there with us. She had been married for 22 years and been teaching for 16 years, ten of those years were at Eisenhower.

When she finally pulled up in front of my house, I thanked her for bringing me home. I wasn't just grateful for the ride, but also for her caring concerned spirit towards me. It was what I needed and desired, I never received this type of attention from my own mom. I appreciated her persistence and concerned for my well-being. I still remember watching her drive off, wishing my own mother could be more like her, professional, loving, nurturing, caring.......

With Mrs. Ringold and Mrs. Barlow's assistance and Mr. Rickson standing near for support, I was lifted off the ground to my feet. I stumbled twice before catching my balance. "You need to come to my office and lie **down**; we can call your parents," said Nurse Barlow.

"No, I'm fine, I just need something to drink,"

"No young lady, we're not giving you that **option**; go ahead and head down to the nurse's office so you **can lie** down. The paramedics are on the way to check you out," said Mr. Rickson in his deep baritone voice. "Ladies, please make sure she gets looked at and her parents are contacted; I need to make my meeting. Regina, I will be checking on you later. Thanks everyone for your help!" he exclaimed while heading down the hallway. The six-foot five school leader made his way back to his office addressing a few students in the halls that were out of area, while cheerfully speaking to the staff members in his path.

"Come on young lady," murmured Nurse Barlow as she and Mrs. Ringold lead me down the hall holding my arms. I'm glad they were there to guide me; I was still dizzy!

The paramedics came and after my pulse, temperature and blood pressure was checked, I was declared okay. The nurse insisted on calling my mother to inform her of the incident and recommended that I follow-up with my private doctor in the next couple of days. My mother was not at home to receive this information, but it didn't matter, unless I was damn near dead, she wasn't taking me to see a doctor based on their recommendations. However, I still promised the medical team I would relay the information to her. A few hours later I was released from the nurse's office to go to class. Thank goodness it was almost time for lunch—I was hungry!

Chapter 8

"**G**irl you pregnant!" yelled Diana through the telephone receiver.

"Pregnant? Are you serious? How...why...what?! I'm not pregnant!" I loudly whispered back, making sure my mom didn't hear me from the other room.

"You had yo period this month?"

Well, now that she mentioned it, my cycle had not come yet, but its irregular and never comes on the same day every month. "Diana hush, I ain't having no babies...at least not now anyway!" I continued to whisper loudly.

"Gina please, the way you say you and Jason be humping... bumping and grinding, and I know yall not using any condoms!" Diana still yelling. "I'm bringing you a pregnancy test to school tomorrow and you gonna take it before school during breakfast."

"Girl please, you trippin! Why are you jumping to conclusions and why before school?"

"Because morning urine is the best urine sample to take; its most accurate. When was your last period, Gina?"

"I don't know," embarrassed to admit. I didn't know, I never kept track of it, never felt the need to.

"You don't know? Girl! Well... did you have one this month?"

Didn't know the answer to that question either! It was already close to the end of October, and I literally didn't remember having a period this month. DAMN! Jason and I hadn't used any condoms and I don't take birth control! Oh DAMN!! What if I am pregnant? My mom? School? My MOM? Oh shit! What would Jason say? How would he feel? It's his senior year in school; he has college recruits waiting to scout and watch him when basketball season begins! Oh man, what have I done? How did I get to this point without being cautious? Wait, I'm jumping the gun! What if I'm not pregnant? Just because I vomited a little doesn't mean I'm with child!

"I don't know Dee," I replied worriedly. "I don't want to jump the gun but...I'll take the test in the morning...just don't forget to bring it to school with you."

"Oh, I won't...but, what if you are pregnant Gina? You already know how Jason is... that bastard ain't looking to have no babies! And you already know yo mama go trip!!" said Diana in an equally aggravated concern tone. "I mean...if you are...you know...having a baby.... girl look, you have choices," she said delicately, as if the words she spoke were going to cause me bodily harm if spoken incorrectly. And she was right, I did have options, but what option should I choose? I guess I will deal with that after I receive the results.

The bathroom was swarming with teenager girls prepping for the new day. Each of the four wall mirrors were occupied with two to three girls applying lip stick, lip gloss, eye shadow, eye liner. Hair was being combed, brushed and plucked, while clothes were being rearranged and changed. Each girl underwent metamorphosis, transforming from their parent's innocent babies to the naughty school girls.

"There goes an empty stall over there Gina," Diana said while handing me the blue and purple colored Clearblue Easy pregnancy test kit.

As I headed to the first available bathroom stall to prepare to ace my exam, I began recalling the directions inside the box I read just 20 minutes earlier at the table during breakfast. "Pee on the stick enclosed, blue if you are pregnant, pink if you're not. I am not pregnant, I am not pregnant," thinking out loud. I drank several cups of juice this morning to ensure there was enough urine to successfully complete the assessment. At this point my bladder was screaming for me to release the fluids within. I opened the box and removed the contents inside, what is lateral flow technology? A plastic stick? I pee on this instrument and wait three minutes for the results. I'm so glad this is not like the pregnancy tests I've seen my mom use every time mother nature decided to delay her monthly arrival. She would leave cups of urine on the top shelf in the bathroom while at work and call me at home to get the results! Her desire to be pregnant at her age and for the tired old bums she brought home was beyond me!

I raised up my dark denim blue skirt to my waist and slid down my pink cotton underwear. I was too nervous, small drops of urine decided to exit my vaginal area and run down my leg. I quickly decided to continue pulling my panties down past my feet until they were completely off and in my hands. I hung them on the door hook to protect them from any splashing or unnecessary moisture that missed the commode and made its way to the floor. I immediately extended my legs apart, backed up and squatted down over the toilet bowl. The pee was coming, fast. I quickly held the stick under the stream catching the flow before my bladder had completely emptied itself into the bowl. I sat the stick on the tissue container, wiped off, and put my underwear back on. Blue plus sign if you're pregnant, pink negative sign if you're not. I pulled down my skirt and unlatched the door to exit the stall. "Now we wait," I said replying to Diana's curious staring eyes.

I lay in bed wrapped up in my multi colored patchwork quilt my grandma made me a few years ago. I wanted this day to end! As I lay in the moon lit room staring at the ceiling in deep thought about my results, my eyes began to well up with tears. "A baby!" was all I could think of at this point in time. Hoping the images of blue plus signs and infants in blankets sucking bottles of milk would simply go away, I closed my eyes as tightly as I could. They didn't. They wouldn't, I was pregnant--with Jason's baby!

The sounds of little hands knocking on the door pulled me out of my trance. I heard the knob turning and suddenly the door was opened and the light switch was turned on. "Sister...what you doing?" asked my 8-year-old baby sister Reba while sucking her thumb.

"I'm sleep Reba," I managed to say while wiping my eyes. "Turn off my light and go back in the living room and watch t.v. with Rene," I said sternly. I simply didn't want to be bothered right now.

"I'm hungry," Reba said in her sweet baby voice, simply ignoring my request. DAMN! I didn't feel like getting up to cook, but my mom would kill me if she knew I didn't feed them while she was at work. Plus, Reba was the baby, my baby, my cocoa colored princess. She was quiet, sweet and very timid at times. I always felt the need to protect her, as if I had given birth to her myself. Almost immediately after she was born and eventually released from the hospital, my mom had to go back to work and her daddy Ricky simply disappeared. Therefore, she didn't get all the attention and breast feeding that Renee received as an infant. So, at the tender age of ten, I made her bottles, changed her soiled linen, bathed and fed her every night before I went to bed. My brother Raymond, who was supposed to be watching us all at age 12, was always outside playing with the other kids on the street was not at all concerned about feeding and changing a baby.

"Alright, go back in the living room with Rene, I'll be there in a minute to cook." I murmured.

"Ooookay," as she exited the room.

I unwrapped myself from the blanket and sat up on the edge of the bed and wiped away the tears from my face and eyes. I had to pull it together in front of my sisters and definitely before my mother came home from work. I was not ready to face her with my dilemma, not now, not ever if it were up to me!

"Come get these toys off this floor Ree and Nae!" I yelled as I walked slowly down the hallway making my way to the kitchen. Toys were scattered everywhere! Jump rope, dolls, doll clothes, crayons and books! The books were definitely Reba's- the school teacher, or at least that's what she thought she was. At any given Saturday or Sunday morning, you could definitely catch her teaching in an imaginary classroom, reading to imaginary students and yelling at an imaginary boy that keeps disturbing the class with his mischievous behaviors! "OUCH!" I felt the sudden sting of the sharp object piercing through the skin of the bottom of my foot. "Rene, come get these damn jacks!" I screamed furiously in my mother's voice.

"Oooooo, Ima tell mama you cuss!" cried Rene while picking up her things.

"I don't care, tell mama! And I'm gonna tell her you poured out all her nail polish on the bed the other day!" I yelled in anger. She hushed. "So, if I get in trouble, you get in trouble!" They cleaned up the mess and went back in the living room to continue watching television. That damn Rene, always wanting to tell on somebody as if she did no wrong. That's why I couldn't stand her and every chance I could I would let her know! She was lighter than the rest of us, even though she and Reba had the same dad. Her skin complexion was beiger than the rich cocoa brown like Reba, milk chocolate like me, or deep dark chocolate like my brother Ray. Leave it to my mom, Ms. Deborah Rochelle Jones, to have one child out of four who didn't match! Three mochas and one latte!

Chili cheese hot dogs, that's easy enough! I pulled an old small grey pot out of the cabinet, filled it with water and placed it top of the old white General Electric stove. I reached on top of the refrigerator for the large box of wooden matches to light the burner. I opened the eight pack of wieners and dumped them into the water to boil.

As I stirred the chili, I realized I hadn't talked to Jason at all today. I wondered where he was? The yellow analog clock hanging on the kitchen wall read 6:15. I made my way to the front of the house out the front door and stepped outside into the cool breezy fall weather to look and see if the blue Chevrolet was there; it was. That's interesting. I usually get a call from him by now, but I got nothing, no call, no note, no nothing?

I made my way back inside and headed straight to the phone in my bedroom. I lifted the receiver to the curly corded, pink, plastic, trimline phone and began to dial Jason's number on the rotary turn. I dialed each number waiting patiently each time for the numerical wheel to return to its original position. It rang twice... "Hello," said Jason's mom, Mrs. Monique. I paused. "Hello," she repeated almost instantly.

"Hi Mrs. Monique, may I please speak to Jason?" I murmured, finally able to speak.

"Whose speaking?" she asked. I never understood why she always asked this, especially since I called so much.

"It's Regina from down the street."

"Well baby, he a little busy right now, I'll have him call you back."

"Yes ma'am," I said in a low disappointing tone. Busy?

"How is your mom?" Mrs. Monique managed to sneak in just before I released the phone receiver to its base.

"She's fine, at work right now."

"Well tell her I said hello."

"Yes ma'am," disappointed but still trying to sound as polite as I could. I hung up. Busy? Doing what? I saw him earlier today before he went to basketball practice; he told me he would call me as soon as he got home.

"Da food burning!" yelled Renee with her right hand on her right hip. I jumped up and ran to the kitchen. DAMN!! The chilli was badly scorched, however, I managed to save enough to make Reba and Renee one and me, at least three. I was always hungry. And after reading my results from this morning I now know why. Just hoped the food didn't travel up and land where I currently stood, but instead stayed down and eventually made its journey down into the commode!

After dinner was eaten, dishes were washed and the girls in their room getting ready to go to bed, I called Jason again, but this time there was no answer. I looked at the clock for the millionth time that night and it was 8:48. My mom got off work at 9:00, so I had about 30 minutes to complete my mission. I threw on a light wind breaker jacket and white cloth canvas shoes before checking on the girls. They were lying down almost asleep, well at least Reba was asleep, that damn Renee, still up dressing her doll! What is this fashion night? Go to sleep already! I softly closed the door before she could see me then yelled, "Renee go to sleep, NOW! And turn off that light!" I waited by the door for a few more minutes waiting for her to rebel, but the lights finally went out without an argument. Good girl Renee!

Feeling the cool breeze from the wind beat my face with every step, I made my way down the street. I began to slow down when I noticed a small red Toyota Corolla pull up in front of Jason's house. Then out of the house walked Jason, accompanied by a female! Well, maybe it's a cousin or something, but when he walked her to the parked car, she turned to face him and their lips met with a deep tongue induced kiss that was accompanied by a long loving hug. Was that Lisa? The hell! Is this why he was too busy to talk to me earlier? I felt steam brewing from heat being generated in my head as I became more and more angry!

He finally released her from his tight hold, and she proceeded to the passenger side of the small sedan and opened the door to get in. I picked up my pace, the fury building up increased my momentum as I began to speed walk to my destination. Just before I could reach their location, Lisa put her right leg in and the female driver of the vehicle slowly pulled off when the door shut.

"Jason!" I yelled. Startled by my sudden outburst, he turned and looked in my direction.

"Aw...Fuck!" said Jason before turning to go back inside his house.

"So, you with Lisa? I've been calling you and your moms said you were busy...what you too busy fucking Lisa?"

"Girl, don't come down here with all that drama...she was just here to get her book for class tomorrow so she can do her homework," said Jason defensively taking a step backwards first staring at me, then at the ground.

"But you kissed her, you hugged her! Why would you kiss and hug a girl you don't like? And why was she in your house? And why haven't you called me all day…if she just came by to get a book?" I yelled in rage.

He slowly took two steps towards me, "I done told you about hollering at me girl! I ain't no fuckin child! I said she was just here to get her book…shit! Deal with it! But you can turn around and go back home with all that clowning! Nobody trying to hear all that!" Jason yelled as his anger began to fume. He gave me a final look of rage, turned around and headed towards his house. I followed behind him trying to talk, but he wouldn't stop to listen to me, so I reached out to grab his muscular arm. He instantly jerked away from me, knocking me off balance. I fell hard in the dirt mud on the ground.

"See, look what you made me do!" Jason yelled. "You need to get up and go home before you make me mad!" he said turning to head towards the door again.

"You mad?" I said slowly getting up off the ground without his assistance. "I see you down here kissing and hugging a girl you claim you can't stand…but you're the one that's mad? I can't even believe this shit!" I exclaimed.

"Go home Gina, before your mama come home, catch you down here and whoop your ass! I'm tired, I'll call you tomorrow when I think you calmed down," Jason said walking away nonchalantly, as if my words and feelings didn't matter.

"Go home? What's up with that Jason? I thought you loved me?" I murmured walking up behind him. "Jason!" I screamed once again grabbing his arm wanting his undivided attention. And then without warning the sharp force from the back of his hand made its landing on the right corner of my mouth sending me into a delirious state of confusion. I stumbled back again, but this time I landed on the hood of his parent's blue Chevy. I held on to the car to keep from falling to the ground. The porch light of his house came on and this time Jason rushed over to grab me to keep me from falling. "I just came to tell you that I'm pregnant Jason..." I jerked away from him and hurried home.

"What's going on out here?" was all I could hear from Jason's dad Lester Wallace as I began to run, releasing from my eyes tear after tear as they flew freely in the cool night air. I no longer felt acceptance, protection or love. I was once again a mockingbird, I'm weak and lack power and everyone I come in contact with sees this lack of strength in my personality and feels the need to overpower me. To Kill Regina Jones.

Chapter 9

"Lie back and place your feet in the stirrups," said the medical assistant as she turned around facing the table to get the instruments ready for the physician to successfully complete the process. I did what I was told and slowly lay back, carefully fitting each heel in the cold metal loops attached to the examination table. I searched my surroundings, observing every inch of the room; it was cold and dreary! White walls, grey tiled floors, egg white cabinets with silver hardware attached to each door.

"I'm cold," I murmured in a low voice. The young female walked over to the side of the table, open the attached drawer, pulled out the white linen and handed it to me. I unfolded the sheet, careful not to disrupt the IV needle and line that was placed in the fold of my right arm. I covered my entire upper body, purposely omitting my feet since they were spread too far apart for the rectangular piece of cloth to cover. I slowly lay back down, uneasy, and began to think about Jason's reaction to my having our baby or not having our baby, just a little over two weeks ago. An infant at our age was simply out of the question and after that night I saw Lisa leaving his house and he hit me, his main goal at that point was to get rid of the fetus growing inside me. Of course, he claims he would never violently touch me, "Gina, you ran up on me and I reacted, then you fell back on the car!" I could still hear Jason yelling back on the phone that night once I made it home. "We too young to have kids! FUCK!! I'm going to college on a basketball scholarship next year, I can't be no daddy!" was all I heard from Jason coming through the phone receiver.

I had no voice, no say so in the situation. My opinion, my suggestions, my decision didn't count. The answer was "No!" NO baby! Not now...not ever...as far as Jason was concerned. I cried myself to sleep that night knowing full well Jason was right. I was 16 years-old and in the 11th grade, what can I possibly do with a baby. But at that point I didn't care about a baby; my heart ached and was broken in a million pieces! Why was Jason with Lisa that night? What did I do to him? Why didn't he love me anymore? Did he love Lisa now? And now he is mad at me for being pregnant!

"The anesthesiologist will be here in a few minutes to give you an injection. Then the doctor will be in shortly to start the procedure," said the assistant awakening me from my flashback.

"Okay", I managed a weak response. "How long will it take...I'm kinda scared."

"Just relax, it's been a very busy morning and it may take a little while since we are a little behind. Dr. Grey had to respond to an emergency earlier this morning and that put all her appointments behind schedule, but she will be in as soon as she can. Do you need anything while you wait?" the assistant asked while heading towards the door and reaching for the knob.

"Something to drink..." I said knowing full well the instructions clearly stated I was not to have anything to eat or drink after midnight last night. Diana called to make sure I did not have anything last night or this morning while I was in route to the clinic.

"Now Ms. Jones, you know you can't have anything until afterwards," the assistant responded amused. "I meant, would you like a pillow or another sheet to cover up with before I leave?"

"Naw, I'm good." I really wasn't good at all...I was hurt, scared, nervous and very tired from lack of sleep last night. I kept tossing and turning wondering what Jason was doing and wishing he was there with me. I needed him to hold me in his arms, comfort me, gently kissing my forehead and whispering in my ear that everything will be okay. But that was simply not the case with Jason. Our last conversation last night, if that's what you want to call it, consisted of him telling me to make sure I was up early so he can drop me off at the clinic on his way to school.

"Make sure you out front when I pick you up later after I get out of school," Jason exclaimed while pulling up in front of the facility this morning. "I don't want to be looking for you in no clinic!"

Jason handed me a roll of money to finance the entire procedure. I stared down at the large wad of mostly $20 bills and thought, "Is this all our child is worth?" I slowly stepped out of the car, and Jason drove off. I was alone. Diana insisted on going with me, but Jason wouldn't hear of it. He wanted to keep the entire ordeal a secret, even though he knew she already knew about the pregnancy and possibly the termination. I think he wanted to escape the guilt driven stares from my best friend indicating she did not approve of his actions thus far. And she didn't!

"Girl, how you let that bastard talk you into having an abortion? And why he don't want your mama to know? Why he not going with you? And since he not going to support you, especially since this was mainly his decision, why he don't want me to go with you?" Diana exclaimed. "That fool is crazy! He makes me so fucking sick!! Sorry ass!" Telling Diana about Lisa and his pushing me sent her fuming! His not wanting to accompany me today drove her fury over the edge. Jason was dead to her!

Hearing the door close as the medical aide exited the room startled me, sending my heart racing into an unnecessary panic mode. Relax Gina...RELAX! I couldn't! I wanted to cry, but I was all cried out. I began recalling the words to the popular ballad performed by Lisa Lisa and Full Force. "I was all alone on a Tuesday morning." and even though it wasn't raining outside, but inside I was slowly dying...and Jason, he left me so confused. Now I'm all cried out...over you..."

I was awakened by the sound of the door opening, it was the anesthesiologist entering my room to administer medication for pain. "Ms. Regina Jones?" asked the young, handsome, Caucasian doctor. His youthful look almost made him look too young to wear the title doctor.

"Yes sir," I responded drowsily.

Extending his hand out for me to shake, he asked with a smile, "How are you today? I'm Dr. Drew Stevenson and I'm here to administer you pain meds for your procedure."

"Hi," I manage to say while wiping the drool from my lip with my left hand and shaking his hand with my right. As I grasped his hand in the brief up and down movement, I couldn't help but notice his friendly, deep ocean blue eyes that briefly gazed upon me. He was beautiful, like a human Ken doll waiting to take Barbie out on a dream date in their dream car, have their dream wedding and live happily ever after in their dream house.

"The anesthesia will begin to kick in...around 5 to 10 minutes after I inject it into your IV port. It will make you extremely drowsy, will someone be here to drive you home?" Dr. Stevenson asked while running his fingers through the golden blonde highlights embedded within the layers of his hair strands.

"No... I mean... yes, someone will drive me home. I...I just don't...I mean...no one is here with me now." I murmured.

"Good deal, as long as you have a responsible individual readily available to transport you home safely, everything should be fine." Dr, Stevenson said with a reassuring smile. He began gathering the contents needed to fill the tube connected to the needle he used to inject the medication into my IV. "You will feel a little warmth inside, but don't be alarmed it's just the medication flowing through." I then closed my eyes as I saw the needle pitch its way through the small IV port taped to my arm. "Alright Ms. Jones, all done! Are you okay?" asked the handsome doctor. Waves upon waves of warmth began to invade my entire body. My anatomy began to fall in an extreme state of relaxation. The medication was taking effect immediately, ready or not here it comes!

Then just as I was about to respond I heard voices on the other side of the door and shortly afterwards it opened and in walked the doctor and her assistant to begin the procedure. The process used to perform the vacuum aspiration to remove the fetus from my womb was explained to me by the consultant at the clinic a few days ago. And prior to that the doctor at Ben Taub Teen clinic explained to me the entire fertilization process last week when Diana and I went in to finalize the results we already knew. We skipped school, rode three buses to the Medical Center for the doctor to inform me that I was five weeks pregnant. Jason's sperm penetrated my egg, which passed through my fallopian tubes and is now resting peacefully in my uterus, waiting to undergo its various stages of development. My baby's heart, lungs, and stomach were already starting to develop. Now it was time for the abortion doctor to abduct my unborn fetus from my body. I silently shed a tear and then another and another. My thoughts now were, who's going to explain to me how to cope with knowing I deliberately ended my early pregnancy on a medical table that is similar to the ones used to deliver a mother's infant while in labor. I'm literally ending a life on a table that also welcomes a new life into the world!

"Morning Dr, Gray."

"Hello Dr. Stevenson, is Ms. Jones ready?" was the last statement I heard before falling asleep.

Then suddenly I awoke to the strong humming noise from the vacuum suction; I felt the cold airy plastic tube that was placed over my vaginal area. "MAMA!" was all I could cry out as my soul was being ripped from my body. I whimpered silently and fell asleep again.

When my eyes reopened, I saw the young medical assistant disposing of, what I can assume, the materials used to successfully complete my procedure. She was the only one there in my room. I glared at the digital clock on the wall and it read 12:11 p.m. The procedure was complete, but Jason wasn't going to be there until after 3:00 when school let out! "Ms. Jones...Ms. Jones, are you awake?" the assistant asked as she slowly made her way to the medical table bed, I was lying on. "It's time to get you dressed so you can go home."

Still very drowsy I slowly rose up. I could feel the pressure and throbbing in my eyes from all the crying. "Yes, I'm woke."

"Well, it's important that you follow the post abortion guideline that the consultant reviewed with you the other day such as no sex for at least two weeks. And remember you will have some light abdominal pains and vaginal bleeding...which are all normal side effects. But if both become severe and accompanied by fever and chills, you need to go to the nearest emergency room," the young assistant explained. "How do you feel?"

"Sleepy! And a little sore!" I exclaimed.

"Well, that's to be expected, but don't worry... with rest and time, both will eventually wear off. Now, I need to remove your IV so you can get dressed. We need this room for another patient." She removed the needle and port from my arm and replaced it with a bandage and additional stretch wrap for reinforcement to make sure the bandage stayed in place. "There you go, now let's get you dressed!"

Once dressed, the medical assistant pushed me down to the lobby area in a wheelchair. I had my paperwork that included a prescription for pain medication and my purse in hand. "What time is it?" I asked as we made our way down the long corridor to the lobby area.

"It's about 12:56 p.m. Is your ride here?" she asked.

"Not yet, he should be here around three," I murmured.

"Ms. Jones, you knew what time the procedure was to end; someone should have been here waiting to take you home," exclaimed the assistant sounding a little disturbed. I explained to her the situation and she agreed to leave me there in the lobby and come check on me from time to time to make sure I was okay. She helped me out of the wheelchair into a seat next to a table. Still very drowsy, I slowly transitioned from one seat to another. "You take care Ms. Jones. Good luck!" she stated as she walked away pushing the empty chair. I lay my head on the table saddened from the earlier events, feeling as if my heart had been ripped from the very depths of my soul. I began to cry thinking once again, I am a mockingbird, I'm weak and lack power and everyone I come in contact with sees this lack of strength in my personality and feels the need to overpower me. To Kill Regina Jones. To Kill Regina Jones' baby.

Chapter 10

"Gina...Gina, girl wake up!" I felt the strong tugs and heard the deep voice yelling my name. "Gina, you alright?" Jason exclaimed while continuing to shake my upper body.

"I'm woke...I'm woke," I said startled from being awakened so abruptly.

"Man! I thought something was wrong with you! Come on so we can go."

Again, I slowly stood up with Jason's assistance, and we headed towards the exit that would eventually lead us to his car. As we approached the door, I read the analog clock on the wall, it was 4:45 p.m.

The cool breezy fall air felt good when it hit my face and body as I exited the clinic. Jason walked at a slow pace holding my right arm as if his life was depended upon my getting to his parent's car. The powder blue Caprice Classic was illegally parked in front of the building awaiting our arrival. After carefully placing me in the car and closing the door behind me, Jason quickly jumped into the driver's seat.

"You alright?" Jason asked before starting the ignition. "You want me to let the seat back?"

"I'm fine," I replied, almost shocked by his kind demeanor towards me. Jason gave me one more quick look before turning the ignition key and putting the car in drive. We proceeded down the street in total silence with Jason avoiding any and all eye or physical contact with me. Why was I not surprised?

Of course, since it took Jason so long to pick me up from the clinic, I wasn't home to get Reba and Rene off the school bus. Therefore, while in route, I asked him to pull over to a phonebooth so I could make a call to the one person who could help me in this situation. He willingly did what I asked after I explained to him the situation with my mom. He pulled up to a Wendy's restaurant and parked. There was a pay phone sitting on the outer edges of the parking lot, next to a full-service Shell gas station. He then surprised me and jumped out of the vehicle and hurriedly made his way to my side of the car, opened the passenger side door, reached for my hand and actually helped me out of the car, then accompanied me to my destination.

"You alright?" Jason asked again in a sincere voice.

"I'm good, just a little sore and sleepy from all that medicine." I murmured. I reached for my purse for change, and before I could put my hands on the imitation leather bag, Jason stopped me.

"I got it, you need change, right?" Jason asked.

"Yes." He reached in his right pocket and handed me the large, circular, silver coin.

"I'm gonna run in Wendy's while you on the phone and get us something to eat. What you want, a burger with cheese and some fries...a drink?" Jason asked, staring at me with his deep light brown eyes, which displayed a mixture of concern, guilt and sympathy.

"Uh...yeah, that's fine," I said, a little surprised at his offering to buy me something to eat. It wasn't that I felt he had a problem with financing my lunch, it's just that, I simply can't remember ever going out to eat with him. As a matter of fact, now that I think about it, I can't recall engaging in any type of social event with him other than sex!

"Cheese... no onions...and a coke. Thanks Jason," I murmured. I was hungry and in need of food...soon!

"No prob. Be right back!" he murmured as he walked off heading towards the small food chain. He hurried pass the cars parked in the lot with light blue denim Girbaud Jeans and his black letterman jacket with "Wallace" spelled out across his back. I continued to watch him until he finally disappeared behind the glass door into the restaurant. What's got into him? He was being a regular "Mr. Nice guy" a totally different guy than I was used to dealing with! He was kind, considerate and thoughtful! Wow! If God could just find it in his heart to make this Jason Wallace's personality last forever, I would be utterly grateful!

I dropped the silver coin in the designated slot and proceeded to punch the seven digits on the numerical key pad that connected me to my desired local destination. After the third ring chime the familiar voice yelled back out of breath, "Hello!" Yes!! It was Diana and luckily, she was at home.

"Hey D! Its me." I managed to say in my weak state.

"Girl, its after 5 o'clock! Where you at? Your mom called me looking for you twice! I had to lie!" Diana exclaimed, still out of breath.

"I know, Jason didn't pick me up until 4:45 and I asked him to stop at a pay phone to call you, cause I ain't going home right now.

What did my mom say? She sound mad?" I asked knowing full well I already knew the answer to that question.

"Girl please, hell yeah she was mad! I just told her you probably had to stay after school to finish a project. I didn't know what to tell her; she was yelling at your sisters in the background and asking me questions at the same time! You okay?" I began to explain to Diana what happened as Jason walked up. The fried, fatty delicacies in the bag he carried began to fill my nostrils, reminding me of my hunger! I finished my conversation with Diana and placed the receiver back on its mount.

I asked Jason to drop me off at Diana's house instead of mine, so I could temporarily avoid dealing with my mom and her abuse. My goal was to avoid any and all of her physical and verbal mistreatment all together. My best friend told me to come to her house and rest until her dad came home from work. Her plans were to use his old, green Ford pickup truck to take me home. Thoughts of me trying to climb into the half ton pick-up, when just a few hours prior I had my pregnancy terminated, started to plague my mind. Oh well, I guess I will cross that bridge when the time comes.

It was after five o'clock when we arrived at Diana's subdivision Heather Glen. I could never remember the name of her street; I just knew how to get there from the main street, Ella Blvd. You make a right on the first street off Ella, go all the way to the end of the road and it's the last house on the left. We pulled up in front of the peach colored, one story brick home. It had a large car port that covered a four-car cement driveway; it led to a large trifold window which was once a garage door. On the other side of the window used to be a garage, but had been converted to a family room some years ago when Diana was a little girl. Diana was the only one home. Her mom Mrs. Tina Walters had just left for work a couple hours ago to work her evening shift at St. Joseph Hospital downtown. Her dad Frank worked for the City of Houston. He got off work at five and was on his way home.

Neither of Diana's parents went to college; they just held down very decent jobs so their family was able to live very decent lives. They had attended Wheatley High School on the northeast side of town together and eventually become high school sweethearts who married young. Approximately one year after graduation when Mrs. Tina became pregnant with Diana's older brother Damon. Diana would often recall her memories of them living in an apartment until she was 8 years old; then they moved into their current house in Northwest Houston. I often found myself being envious of Diana and her family life. Her family lived the life I often wished I could have had. They ate out once a week as a family, held regular family functions at their home and went on a vacation to a beach every year. Her mom Mrs. Tina said their summer breaks started off small when they were little, just to Galveston and back home. But this past summer after Damon graduated high school, the entire family went to Disney World in Orlando, Florida. Diana would tell us about how it rained the entire trip, but it didn't stop them and the other tourists from visiting the world-famous parks and touring the city. They simply bought rain ponchos and kept it moving.

Diana's brother Damon, was 18 years old just like my brother Raymond; however, age is their only similarity! While Damon was graduating high school this past May, Raymond was fighting a court case against him! When Damon was scoring touchdowns at Friday night football games, Raymond was stealing cars in parking lots! When Damon was hanging out with friends at social events, Raymond was getting high with thugs in an alley in the hood! Damon was entering his freshman year at Prairie View A&M University; Raymond was being sentenced to prison for breaking and entering! While Diana's parents were planning and saving for tuition, my mom was always scrambling to scrape up bail money!

Jason or "Mr. Nice Guy" helped me out of the car and to the door. Diana was already standing in the entryway with a look of concern on her face as she watched me get out of the car. When she finally looked annoyingly at Jason as we made our way up the walk way, he didn't dare say a word!

"Come on Gina, I got you," Diana said as she approached me and took over helping me into the house.

"I'll call you later when I think you made it home," Jason said while handing me my food from Wendy's and avoided making eye contact with Diana.

"Alright." I said, still a little woozy. He turned and walked off towards the driveway, and we walked inside and closed the door behind us. Diana lead me straight to her room, so I could eat and lay down for a little before her dad made it home.

Diana's room was layered in her favorite colors, pink and purple. Pink and purple sheer curtains on her windows. Light purple walls, pink lamp and comforter and a large pink shaggy rug with huge purple flower prints on the floor.

"Come on Gina girl, you can lay in my bed," Diana said as she closed the door. I walked in slowly, still feeling the stench and soreness from earlier. I first sat down on the covered mattress and sat my bag of half eaten food on the floor next to me. "How you feel? You need me to get you something? Did Jason buy this food? It's the least he can do...sorry ass!" she asked not taking a breath and raising her voice simultaneously.

"I'm a little sore and sleepy from the anesthesia...but other than that I'm okay...and yeah, he bought it. He was being so nice to me...I guess he feels bad," I said sighing.

"Well hell, he should, he did knock you up and made you get rid of yall baby! And he talking to that Bitch Lisa!" Diana exclaimed getting upset again. "Oh yeah girl, I forgot to tell you, Sandra in my

Chemistry class said Jason and Lisa are a couple. She saw them together with his parents at Red Lobster two Sundays ago with their church clothes on!"

WHAT!!! Jason was with Lisa, again? So, they a couple now? So, he does want her, "Damn!" My eyes began to wail with disappointment and sadness again. What did I do to him to make him want to get back with his ex? When he called, I came, willing and ready to submit to his every request, not caring about the consequences that I could possibly encounter with my mom if she knew I was sneaking off to have sex with a boy! The hell with that; I was pissed!

Diana went on to tell about her additional findings about Jason and Lisa. Their trips to the mall, hanging out at the Taco Bell on Antione Drive after the varsity football and basketball games.

Diana eventually switched gears and began talking about what happened at school and how her *boyfriend Tay* made her mad at lunch today, but, at that point I had completely tuned her out. My exhausted mind had rested on thoughts of my relationship with Jason versus Jason's relationship with Lisa. But who was I kidding, Jason and I have only been sexing since the beginning of the school year. There was no dating, hanging out with other classmates, going to dinner and church with his parents! We had sex, and that's it! The few times we did engage in intercourse at his house, his parents were either not at home or not aware of my presence there. And now it was almost Thanksgiving and Lisa has gained love, happiness and a lasting relationship, while my gains included hatred, sadness and loneliness. I have suffered losses that can never be regained, my virginity, my baby, and soon my sanity. This was not what I had in mind for a happily ever after!

Diana's dad finally made it home, and Diana helped me into the large half ton pickup to take me home. I was actually looking forward to getting in my bed and resting. My early morning procedure and the events thereafter had really taken a toll on me, I was exhausted and sore. I made it home around 7:30p.m. that evening which was not good. My mom was there, waiting for an explanation with the leather rawhide strap in hand. She was ready to swing and strike her focus target, and I was her focus target. I made up a lie about why I was late coming home and limping in with Diana's assistance. I told her I **tripped and hurt my ankle, while running to try and catch the bus to get me home from school, but that I ended up missing anyway. I told her I had to start walking home, and Diana came looking for me based on their phone conversation earlier.**

"I was walking down West Little York when she saw me and picked me up," I said, hoping the lie was believable.

"Well, go get some ice or something to put on it! And get them DAMN sisters of yours! Its Friday...and I'm going out tonight!" my mom yelled as she walked towards her bedroom. She left me alone, thank God!

I struggled in the kitchen having to stand for a long period of time while slowly preparing dinner for my young siblings. Of course, Rene worked my nerves asking me tons of questions while Reba played with her doll and watched me fry the chicken wings. After dinner, I ordered the girls to take **a bath and get ready for bed; it was almost 10:00 pm. And my mom had already left to go to the café. At this point pure exhaustion and severe abdominal pain had taken over my body. I didn't know how long I could take all the movement, I needed to get settled soon. Then after a fairly short warm shower, which were the doctor's orders, I was ready to go to bed! I checked and secured the front door lock and then turned the lights off on the girls in their room. I finally made it to my room, closed the door and literally collapsed into my bed.**

I lay down on my back in bed staring at the ceiling, reflecting on today's events, while the pains seemed to consistently beat my lower stomach like bombs being dropped in a war zone.

Jason and Lisa? Lisa and Jason? No, it should be Jason and I. Jason should be in love with me, not Lisa. As far as I was concerned Lisa was the enemy sent to destroy her opponent, me. But, unlike the others, I was not going to let her Kill Regina Jones!

Chapter 11

"You don't have to keep calling him honey," Mrs. Monique exclaimed in an annoyed tone. "I will let Jason know you called, he just a little busy right now...he'll call you when he gets a chance."

"Yes ma'am." I placed the phone back on its jack and slowly lay down on my bed. I didn't cry. I won't cry, not anymore. It has been three days since Jason dropped me off at Diana's house, and I haven't heard from him since. Even though I did notice his parent's blue Caprice Classic was parked in the student parking lot, I don't recall seeing him at school today and trust me I looked! I even skipped my fourth period class and attended D-lunch with all the athletes, and he wasn't there either. It was almost as if he were purposely trying to avoid me! Did he not want to be in my presence? It's not like we've ever presented ourselves as a couple to the general public. Almost all of our interactions were behind the scenes, after the curtains have closed to ensure the viewing audience was unable to sneak a peek of our show. Our relationship development has been almost entirely behind the scenes, lacking stage directions and clearly written instructions from the director for a successful production and assurance his spectators are delighted. We had no audience, no spectators, no group of admires and haters to view our performance and give feedback! So how could they critique work done in secret and out of the public's view?

"Fuck this!" I jumped up out of the bed and my drowning sorrow and put on my dingy, beat up, white cloth canvas shoes. I walked straight to the front door hurriedly, bypassing Reba and Rene playing in their room hoping neither of them saw me. Luckily, they were so focused on their activities that they didn't notice me pass by. I reached the door, unfastened the latches, turned the copper colored knob and pulled it open. The cold crisp winter breeze forcibly struck my face and neck as I took my first glimpse outside in the direction of Jason's house. There was that damn red Toyota Corolla parked directly in front of his house! No wonder Miss Monique was telling me he was busy; he was busy alright, busy loving on Lisa! Anger and rage began to take over my mind, body and spirit. The cold air turned to steam as it bounced off me and back into the atmosphere as I began to reflect on my recent loss less than a week ago at the clinic. Is this why he wanted to abort our child, so he can be with his precious Lisa? Who in the fuck does he think he is?

"Put on your shoes and a jacket!"

"Where we going?" asked Rene raising herself up off the floor and placing her right hand on her hip.

"We walking down the street to Rachel house; I need to borrow her shirt for school tomorrow," I politely answered, trying not to sound annoyed, hoping this was enough of explanation for her probing question! I checked the time, it was 7:23, and my mom wasn't getting off work for at least another two hours. That was at least three and a half hours to see what I needed to see, hurry back home and get the girls bathed and to bed!

"Okay!" Renee said shrugging her shoulders, implying that the answer given to her would suffice. "Come on Reba, get your shoes so we can go with Gina!" They quickly threw on their pink sneakers that flashed a red flare of light with every step and pink Care Bear jackets. I grabbed some crayons and a couple coloring books to keep them occupied while we were at Rachel's house. I needed reinforcement to ensure both girls were out of my hair while I planned my next move.

We were finally off and headed down the street to Rachel's house in the cold air. Rachel's stuck up ass lived right next door to Jason. My plan was to go to her house and convince her to come outside so we could hold a conversation on her porch about her favorite subject, Rachel! I could eavesdrop on Jason's house and see who came out, and when they did come out, I planned to go straight into attack mode, conquering all that lay in my pathway. I will no longer be the weaker species; they will no longer Kill Regina Jones.

As the girls and I headed down the street, a bright head light from behind suddenly appeared out of nowhere, beaming directly on us. The heavy beam of light created a dark image of our bodies that positioned itself on the dark gravel road in front as we walked. I used my hand to direct Reba and Rene to walk in front of me on the side of the street so that the upcoming traffic could pass. As we walked, the roaring sound of the exhaust system seemed to move slower and slower as it approached us. DAMN, I hope this wasn't my mom getting home from work early. It was just like her to come and ruin my plans! The car slowed all the way down and finally came to a roaring halt once it was right next to us. Naw, this was not my mom! Ms. Deborah Rochelle Jones would never ride along in a car with an individual that felt the need to rev up their engine like this! Nope, not my mother!

"What's up Gina?" the familiar voice exclaimed. The window went down along with the gas pedal, while the vehicle remained in park mode. The light smoke from marijuana began to escape the inside of the car and fill our nostrils before disappearing into the night air "What you doing out here... its cold girl?" I looked at the red two door sports car and recognized the individual inside; it was Steven. "Who dis, yo lil sisters?" Steven asked.

"Oh...hey," I said timidly, wondering why he was driving on my street this late in the evening. "What you doing over here?"

"I was coming to see my homie Trent...I saw your sexy ass image in the dark and stopped! Shiiittt, I recognize that ass from anywhere!" Steven said with a sly grin, revealing the shiny gold tooth centered around his perfect white teeth. I blushed. Steven was really handsome-in a thug like way.

He opened the driver side door and stepped out dressed in all black, ready to steal away the moon like a thief in the night! Black leather jacket, black t-shirt underneath, dark jeans and all black K-Swiss sneakers. He wore a thick gold chain around his neck, gold watch on his wrist and of course the gold tooth, which reflected off his milk chocolate colored skin. This was the same jewelry I saw him in that day at the store, then later that same night at his grandmother's house.

What was he doing? Why is he getting out the car? Making sure I had them guarded under my wing, I grabbed both Reba and Rene's hands and pulled them both closer. I had two things to see and two people to do! I had no time to stand here and entertain this meaningless conversation! And I hoped he didn't think we are going to have another reenactment of what happened almost two months ago. We were on my street, in my neck of the woods, where I had the upper hand. We were standing on my turf, where foul play would not be tolerated or he would be dealt with! I began to stare in his direction with glaring, annoyed eyes, hoping that my look would prompt him to be on his way. It didn't work! He just stood there staring at me even harder.

"So, who is this, lil Gina one and lil Gina two?" Steven asked while reaching out to touch Renee's right arm. I pulled her back before he could make contact.

"These my little sisters," I murmured, looking down and around deciding at that very moment that avoiding eye contact with him would probably be best. I took a deep breath and sighed, **loudly.** Enough already! "So...what's up? Trent's house is right there." I said pointing directly at the red brick house with brown panels connected to the windows, two doors down from mine.

"I know where he stay... nigga can't holla at you for a minute?

"I guess so," I said timidly shrugging my shoulders.

"Gina, I'm cold," said a chattering Reba pulling on my jacket sleeve to get my attention.

"I'm ready to go!" yelled Renee pulling at my other sleeve. Ordinarily I would be upset, but their demands couldn't have come at a better time.

"Alright lil lady, I just wanted to talk to your sister for a minute, Steven said amused by Renee's cockiness. He then reached into his pocket and pulled out a handful of cash. After looking down and separating the bills, he gave both Reba and Rene a $5 bill each! Both girls stared at the money in amazement. "Yall alright now?" There was no response from either; both were still mesmerized by their sudden small fortune.

"So what's up? You know I been wanting to hook up with you," said Steven looking back at me, satisfied with the girls' response to his generous gesture. "When can I come see you?"

"Come see me? Boy, my mom don't let me have no boy company!" I exclaimed in amusement. Me have company! Yeah right! Not at Ms. Deborah Rochelle Jones' house!

"Damn, you mama be trippin like that? Well...can I call you?" Suddenly I saw head lights from a distance coming from Jason's house. DAMN! I didn't see who came outside and got in the car! However, could see that it was the red Corolla Lisa was in that night. I looked harder at the scene from down the street, I could see a male figure looking down the street at us while bent over talking to someone through the driver side window. It was Jason, wearing his letterman jacket with his hands in his pocket. My vision wasn't the best, but I was sure of it.

"You want to call me?" I slowly asked still focused on the car, the lights, Jason and the inactivity going on down the street.

"Yeah girl, I told you that last time I saw you I wanted to holla at you. You still talking to ol' boy Jason?"

"Jason? Down the street? Naw, we just friends," I responded while my eyes were still fixated on Jason talking through the window of the vehicle and staring hard in our direction at the same time. "That day you saw us at the store, I was just riding to the store with him," I said, lying.

"So, what's up, can a nigga get yo number?" Steven asked again. Just when I was about to respond, I saw Jason immediately walk to the passenger side of the red Toyota, open the door and get inside. Once the door closed, the car took off slowly in our direction and with one click the semi dull lights became large spot lights beaming directly on us as we stood off on the side of the road near Steven's Mustang. As the car approached us, it slowed down then came to a complete stop. "Who dat?" asked Steven as the small sedan approached us and stopped just past the trunk of Steven's car. Just as I was about to answer, Jason poked his head out the window

"What's up man?" asked Jason while manually rolling down the window. Steven began to reach behind his jacket, into the back part of his jeans, underneath his belt, in preparation for the unknown as he looked into the car at the face of the person talking to him.

"Say cuz...I didn't know who this was rolling up on me like that," exclaimed Steven, bringing his hand from behind his back and under his jacket. "What's up Jay? What you up to bruh?"

"My badd man!" said Jason, getting out of the car giving Steven some dab, or well-known homeboy handshake practiced in the hood.

"Nothing much man... just out here...tryna holla at your girl. I saw her walking when I turned on the street on the way to go holla at Trent."

"Oh...what's up Gina?" asked Jason, finally acknowledging my presence.

"Nothing," I responded quietly looking down at Reba. He stared. "I was just walking to Rachel's house to get my book from her. I need to do my homework," now looking past everyone. Jason continuing to gaze intently, as if to unravel the mystery of why Steven and I were carrying on a conversation in the middle of the street this late in the evening. He didn't appear to care about the other individuals amongst us.

"You know...Trent live down there," said Jason, the second person to point out the red **brick house with brown panels on the window.**

"Yeah I know, I'm about to head that way in a minute," Steven replied.

I looked inside the red Toyota Jason stepped **out of and noticed** the young female seated inside. Yes, it was definitely Lisa! She was wearing a pink knit hat and sitting in the driver seat of the vehicle with, both hands positioned carefully on the steering wheel. From the looks of it she was moving and twitching in the seat, trying to get a clear glance at who we were and what was being discussed. She too was probably wondering what was going on since Jason made no attempt to hide his bold gaze at me.

"So what's up man? Gina told me yall was just friends. When I saw yall at the store awhile back, I just assumed she was your gal...but I guess yall just cool," said Steven suddenly breaking his awkward moment of silence. "Who dat over there in the car? Is that you man? That's your gal?"

"Huh...oh yeah...yeah that's my gal Lisa, she taking me to get some Taco Bell real quick," Jason responded, finally coming out of his trance. "Oh yeah, me and Gina...we cool...right Gina?" **Hell NO!! WE NOT COOL-- were my thoughts. You push me down, convince me to kill our baby and then ignored me for a week! And now we are s**upposed to be cool?

"Yeah...we cool." I finally managed to spit the words out, looking at him in pure disgust! He finally admitted to being with Lisa, now that his back was to the wall. I began to pull at both Reba and Rene's hand and walk towards Rachel's house. "Look yall, I got to go before my moms get home from work, I see yall later."

"Wait a minute girl, you not gonna holla at your boy? What's up?" asked Steven while following us.

I paused from my walk, "Oh...that's right...my phone number...you have a pen?" I turned to wait for a response.

"Hold on a minute, let me look in my car." I impatiently waited as Steven rummaged through the glove compartment in his vehicle.

"Jason, come on baby I got to get home!" Lisa yelled from inside the Corolla.

I looked up and Jason was looking at me in a state of shock! Was he **jealous? The thought of me surrendering my telephone number to another guy appears to be sending him into an emotional mental state of jealousy. He didn't move, he didn't blink, he didn't say a** mumbling word awaiting the outcome to my exchanging numerical phone digits with another guy!

"Here you go baby," Steven said while handing me a torn slip of paper he found in his car and a pen. "Write your number on this." I grabbed the pen and paper and proceeded to scribble my name and number down, then pass the slip back to Steven. Jason's mouth dropped in shear amazement; he was stunned! He still continued to stare in disbelief until the loud horn from the Corolla broke him out of his hypnotic trance.

"Jason baby, I really have to go," said Lisa in a loud yet careful tone. "I have to pick my sister up from work on **time,** or she won't let me use her car again." Lisa continued, feeling the need to render an explanation for being impatient. Frequently looking back at Steven and I, Jason slowly turned in the direction of the red Toyota. Steven and I continued to hold a conversation about his calling me and us eventually getting together soon, while Jason proceeded to the car with his head held low in defeat, no longer wanting to witness his opponent claim the winning prize. This was the same reward that he claimed just months ago and kept tucked away in hopes to prevent others from wanting to compete for it, but now the opposition has been given a chance to claim the trophy. The passenger side door of the car slammed without a single goodbye uttered. The vehicle then took off and eventually disappeared in the dark of the night.

"I guess we made your boy mad! I guess that fool thinks he supposed to have all the women! Shiiitt...he better think again!" Steven moved closer to me and my sisters. "So, when can I call you...Ms. Gina?" asked Steven, looking down at the paper then back up at me, smiling and grinning with no regards to Jason and his sudden departure.

"I...I guess tonight...tonight is fine. I mean don't call too late, my mom be trippin," I murmured, finally realizing what was happening.

I just gave another guy my number in front of the guy I love! Now Jason is going to really be upset with me. But the real unexplained phenomenon was the feeling of satisfaction that has overcome me after seeing Jason's unexpected reaction to the entire ordeal. "Look Steven, I really have to go before my moms pull up," I said, suddenly realizing how late it had become.

"That's cool baby, I got what I wanted," said Steven smiling in good spirits, the gold from his teeth seem to twinkle in the moonlight. "Can I at least get a hug?"

"Oh...yeah, that's fine." I stepped forward and extended my right arm out and wrapped it around the middle part of his back. Steven returned the gesture by extending both of his arms out and wrapping them on the lower part of my back, placing me in a close tight hold that forced my face to become buried in his solid muscular chest. After about five seconds of eternity, I pulled slowly back noticing a set of bright headlights turning on the street. Nervous, I stepped back and grabbed both of my sisters' hands hoping and praying it was not my mom. Whew! It was just Mr. Campbell from down the street. He rode by in his royal blue, two door El Camino stirring up the cold air. As I thanked God for the answered prayer, I told Steven goodbye and pulled my sisters in the direction of our house walking at a hurried pace. As I stepped into my driveway, I turned around to see Steven; he was leaning on the hood of his car watching my every move.

"Bye sexy!" he said as he waved. I blushed. I turned around continuing to pick up my pace until I reached my destination, the front door to my house. As I searched my pocket for the key, I heard Steven's car door open, then close. By the time I turned the key, the red Mustang was driving away.

"Hurry up and take off your jacket and clothes and get in the tub so you can take a bath before mama get home!" I yelled. Both girls followed my orders and ran into their rooms, removing their clothing articles piece by piece. I went to my room to take off my jacket and shoes and returned to their room to check on their progress. It was almost 9:00 pm and my mom was on her way home.

"I like your friend, he go give us some mo money sister?" Reba asked as **I bathed her little body in the tub.**

"Yeah Gina...he nice!" exclaimed Renee in the tub with Reba bathing her arms. "Ima buy me some candy wit my money!"

"He alright, but make sure yall don't tell mama or he not gonna ever come back and give you nothing...ever!" I said, lying to ensure my mom never finds out about tonight. Both girls pause, Renee looked at me and Reba looked down at the water.

"Okay sister," murmured Reba, swaying her hands back and forth in the water.

"Okay, but when he gonna come back and give us some mo money?" asked Renee--of course.

"If you tell mama, he ain't never coming back!" I exclaimed looking Rene straight in her eyes, showing her, I meant business! I grabbed a towel "Come on and get out and get ready for bed!"

Chapter 12

It was 10:36 pm and my mom was still not home. The girls were in bed asleep, and I was finally under the covers myself, waiting to fall into a deep coma-like sleep. However, it was hard to relax after what happened earlier tonight. Jason had the actual audacity to come down to my end of the street to be nosey!! And to add insult to injury, he was with Lisa, his girlfriend! Jason was actually jealous of Steven?

Then suddenly, the sound of the front door slamming startled me.

"Gina...bring yo ass here!" yelled my mom from the living room. My mother, Ms. Deborah Rochelle Jones, 36-years-young, with four kids, two baby daddies, and a mouth so bad she could put pirates to shame.

"Baby, calm down," said an unfamiliar male voice.

"I ain't calming down; she know damn well I don't play that outside at night when I'm not home SHIT!! And she had my damn babies out there too! Gina, bring yo black ass here now!" she yelled again. "Ouch...shit!" mom exclaimed bumping her knee on a table next to the couch trying to get to the hallway that lead to my room.

"Baby, you alright?" the unfamiliar male voice again. I quickly jumped out of bed in my t-shirt and threw on some shorts, then ran into the living room. My mom was hunched over rubbing her right leg.

"Why in the hell did you have my babies outside this time of night hugged up with some damn boy!" mama exclaimed. Before I could mumble a single word in response to her claims, she came rushing towards me with her hands up at chest level shoving my body as she screamed at me. The strong force sent my body rushing to the other side of the living room, causing me to hit the solid oak china cabinet in the corner that housed antique collectables from over the years. "I done told yo bitch-ass not to be running around with these manish... no good ass boys around here!" And before I could catch my balance, she was headed toward me still limping and began throwing blows, hitting me any and everywhere she could. Even though the sudden unexpected violence exerted upon me left me weak and speechless, I managed to quickly squat down on the floor using my arms to cover my head for protection against any other unexpected induced act of abuse from Deborah Jones.

"Deborah baby...STOP!!! That's enough!" the still unfamiliar man yelled, attempting to pull my mom away from me! "Give her a chance to explain!" he continued to scream while holding her around the waist with such a tight grip that she had no choice but to surrender to his masculinity. I continued to guard my head and face a while longer, still amazed at the physical strength the 36-year-old woman still had.

"I'm sick and tired of this shit! She won't be satisfied until her ass is walking around here pregnant! And I ain't taking care of no bastard ass kids!!" mom continued to scream.

"I was on my way to Rachel's house...I needed my book for school," I slowly spoke

while peeking around my arm to ensure it was safe to come out of my shell.

"Well, why the hell Mr. Campbell just passed by and said he saw you out there with some boy with a red sports car?" Ms. Deborah Rochelle Jones asked while pulling away from her friend and adjusting her clothing. The short, sleeveless, purple, polyester dress had jumbled up on her when her friend put her in the tight grip; it revealed her beige slip and upper thigh.

"This boy...he was looking for Trent's house...he used to go to Eisenhower last year with us," I manage to quickly say, still a little timid but slowly putting down my arms anyway. "He musta seen me walking and asked me for help," I lied, hoping it would diffuse the situation. My mother paused and looked down at the ground, then slowly walked over to the wing backed, cream colored couch covered with large deep brown leaves. She slowly sat down to gather her thoughts.

"Well...why the hell was Bee and Nae out there with you in all that cold air?" my mom asked finally breaking her silence; she looked me straight in the eyes. My mom never addressed Rene and Reba by their full names.

"I didn't want to leave them in the house alone, so I took them with me," I said speaking in a low sad tone. I slowly raised my head and looked in her direction. Her male friend sat down next to her, with one hand on her shoulder and the other rubbing her leg consoling her. He was a fair skinned man with silky black curly hair cut down low. He didn't look like the typical man she usually brought home; he actually looked fairly young, like he could be in his late 20s or very early 30s. Judging from his white K-Swiss sneakers, acid washed jeans and leather jacket, I'd say he was about 28 or 29 years old!

"Go get your ass in the bed girl! I'll talk to you in the morning," said mom in a more solemn tone. I jumped up hurriedly and ran to my room and got back in bed. It was almost midnight, and I had to go to school the next day. I got underneath the blankets and sheets, relieved to be out of harm's way. Having to endure the wrath of Deborah Jones was never an easy task!

I couldn't sleep; I lay there in bed, again thinking about Jason! What did he see in that Lisa girl? Yeah, she was pretty, I guess! Maybe I should call him and see if I could come by his house when his parents were out like I used to. I could wear my little, black, denim shorts that he likes to see me in. We could have sex anyway he wants; he could have me anyway he wants to have me! I know Lisa doesn't please him. He already told me before that's why he left her alone, because she didn't please him sexually. "That bitch can't fuck right! I like sexing yo sexy ass Gina!" Jason would always say!

As I began to dose off, bringing this night and its events to a close, I began thinking about the last time Jason and I had sex. I became deeply aroused as I drifted off to a sleep like coma. I felt Jason's touch, caressing my thighs and hips so soft and sweet. He began kissing my thighs slowly heading in an upward direction towards my secret garden. He slowly spread open my legs ready to take a bite from my forbidden fruits!

"Jason? Jason, you've never did this before!" I said rubbing his head and running my hands through his silky hair.

"Just relax baby, I want to make you feel good," said the deep baritone voice. "Jason?" I asked, awakening from my sleep.

"Shhhhh!" said the voice again, "we don't want your mom to hear us." This was not Jason's voice, his hair or his touch! His warm breath tickled the hairs on my prairie when I finally realized it wasn't Jason and I was no longer asleep or dreaming! I jumped out of the bed and ran to the light switch and flipped it on, it was my mom's friend in my room on my bed!

"What the fuck!" I said, shaken and confused.

"Now hold on, just be cool," he said while slowly standing up. "I just came in to check on you while your mom was in the tub. I didn't mean to scare you."

"It's dark and you were in my bed about to put your mouth on my cat!" I yelled. "How the hell is that checking on me?"

"Okay...okay, just calm down," the unknown man said in a loud whisper. "You know your mama a little crazy! Neither one of us wants her to come in here tripping and going off like she did in the living room earlier. I ain't never seen no shit like that...a parent knocking their kids to the ground with no remorse...no regrets...that shit was wild!"

"Why you in my room? Why you not with my mama in the front room waiting for her to get out the tub?" I stood there staring at him awaiting a response. I was wearing only a t-shirt; no bra, no panties, only a t-shirt. This was too peculiar; he had no reason to be in my room...at all! "You were under the covers ready to go all the way until I stopped you! What's up with that?" I said placing one of my hands over my loose breasts and the other on the bottom of my t-shirt. I kept pulling it down to keep it from coming up and revealing my precious jewel, the same gem he attempted to draw his tongue over and strike repeatedly.

"Look, I don't even really know your moms...I just met her at this bar tonight getting drunk with her coworkers. She approached me and started asking me questions about my age and what I do for a living, then eventually my name. She seemed alright...but she 10 years older than me and not really my type...but she asked me to bring her home. Man...your moms is wild, she was all over me in the car telling me what she could do to me if I just gave her a chance," he said chuckling out of curiosity. "But when we got here and she started attacking you, I was turned off! You seem so sweet; I was feeling really bad for you. So, I came in and checked on you!" He stood up to head my way. "But when I came in....and saw you looking so damn sexy and chocolate...laying in that bed!! Dam-it girl!" he said looking me up and down biting his bottom lip.

"If she 10 years older than you...that means I'm 10 years younger than you!" I whispered even louder, listening at the door for the water to stop in the shower. Thank God my mom likes long baths!

"DAMN! You just 16, with a body like that! I thought you looked pretty young...but that body!" He continued to stare at my partially naked body.

"Look, you need to leave before my mama gets out the tub!" I said moving away from the door. "She about to be done with her shower!" The water suddenly went off. "Go, get out, the water just shut off!"

"Alright then." He hurried to the door and turned the knob, but before exiting he paused, "this just between you and me...right? You know your moms is crazy!"

"Yeah...whatever...just go!" I said pushing him out and turning off the light. I gently closed the door and jumped back in bed. My heart was racing, my body was shivering, my nerves were shot! I began to mentally prepare myself for the worst; my mom would simply go off on her friend and put him out after seeing him leave my room! Then, she'd make her way to my bedroom to continue her rage. I slowly took long deep breaths to calm my spirit in preparation for what was about to happen. But how do you prepare for a person who continues to ignite uncontrolled anger on her young. I used the security of my blanket by wrapping myself up in it tightly, holding my body, crossing my legs. I didn't want any more surprises.

I suddenly heard loud laughter and talking coming from the front room. Happiness...not anger? Pleasantries...not wretchedness?

The conversation and giggles slowly faded as they moved to another room...my mother's room I could only assume. I began to relax; the last thing I needed was for my mother, Ms. Deborah Rochelle Jones, to come in my domain accusing me of wanting her man...again! About 20 minutes later I heard loud moaning and the head board crashing into the wall, indicating that her sexual encounter with the unknown guy who was just trying to freak me less than an hour ago, had begun.

I just wanted to go to sleep, but instead I began to think about all the times my mother accused me of acting inappropriate around her men. In her mental rolodex inappropriate behavior could be defined as wearing shorts that were to my thighs instead of my knees, getting up late at night to go to the bathroom when she had company, or sitting in the family room watching television too long when her company arrives. I remember a few years ago, I guess I was about 12-years-old when my mom's current lover, Walter Mitchell, came over to our house while she was at work. I remember it like it was yesterday, Mr. Walter was what we called him. He came over bearing gifts for my siblings and me, including Raymond, who was about 15-years old at the time. I remember being in the kitchen cooking dinner for Reba and Rene while watching their every move. They were both toddlers at the time and were frequently involved in daily toddler activities. The 58-year-old man sat patiently on the couch watching the show *"Bonanza"* in the living room and never said a word. Finally, after an hour had gone by, I heard loud coughing, so I went and asked him if he needed something to drink. Of course, the middle-aged portly man only nodded "yes", revealing his receding hairline and baldness on top of his head, unable to speak. While he continued to expel the air from his lungs, I rushed back into the kitchen and poured him a glass of cold water. The coughing seemed to calm as I made it back with his drink. After several long gulps, the water and the cough were gone.

"Thank you young lady," Mr. Walter murmured while clearing throat. "I really appreciated that!" As he handed me the glass, the front door opened and in walks my mother, Ms. Deborah Rochelle Jones, 36-years-young, with four kids, two baby daddies, and a mouth so bad she could put pirates to shame!

"What the hell going on in here?" she exclaimed, staring at me first, then Mr. Walter; her eyes were filled with suspicion.

"What you mean what's going on? Hell, your sweet daughter brought me a drink; you know I have asthma!" he yelled back.

As the bickering increased between the two, I managed to sneak out of the room quickly without being noticed. I went back to the kitchen to finish preparing dinner and didn't dare leave again! The arguing eventually stopped, and Mr. Walter ended up spending the night which was good for me, I most definitely--did not want to deal with her accusations and abuse. However, two days later she took me to the clinic to have the doctor examine me to see if I had had sex! I remember the medical team being reluctant to do the exam because of my age, but she told them some lie about her catching me in bed with a boy and she was afraid that I might have a STD. "MAMA!!" was all I could cry out as the doctor placed the cold metal instrument inside my vagina!

They didn't understand, the doctors, nurses or Mr. Walter, that I am a mockingbird, I'm weak and lack power and everyone I come in contact with sees this lack of strength in my personality and feels the need to overpower me. But my mom understood, and all she wanted was To Kill Regina Jones.

Chapter 13

"Steven who?" asked Diana while simultaneously scooping a spoonful of Frosted Flakes cereal from her breakfast bowl to eat.

"Steven...ummmm...he went here...I guess last year but dropped out...I guess," I answered, also munching on the sugary cornflakes. "All I know is he didn't come back to school this year. Remember, he had gold teeth and now he be out there hustling dope."

"Oh...that guy you ran from when you were at Candace house!" she exclaimed excitedly, happy to finally have some remembrance of him. "Wait...why was he on your street? And where were you going with the girls? Did your mama catch you?" asked Diana. She began bombarding me with a series of questions in between each bite of her cereal.

"Okay...one question at a time please! First off he was looking for Trent's house when I was on my way to Rachel's house to spy on

Jason" DAMN, that was not supposed to come out! I was thinking while regretting the last response.

"Spy on Jason!! Geeeennaaaa...why?!!! Leave his sorry ass alone!" said Diana in an uproar almost spilling the milk remains from the finished cereal.

"Calm down, I never even made it down there when he stepped outside to walk Lisa to her car..."

"He walked Lisa to her car?!! That fool got some nerve! Low down dirty..."

"He saw us talking down the street and got in the car and came down where we were. He stood there and watched while I gave Steven my number." I said while applying a high shine gloss to my lips. "...and he wouldn't stop staring until Lisa finally called his name and said she had to go!" Suddenly the loud deafening chime dismissing us from breakfast to class rang. "I guess he got mad...I guess...he just stood there in the street staring at us," I said while standing to gather my things.

"Did he say something...what did he say...where was Lisa? What did she say?" asked Diana inquisitively. She too began collecting her belongings. We both proceeded towards the cafeteria doors that exited into the hallway.

"Girl, Lisa was sitting in the car the whole time looking dumb! Finally, she yelled for Jason to come on. You could tell she was getting mad...but was trying to stay calm!" I chuckled at the thought of her reacting to Steven and Jason watching me and her watching Jason and Steven follow my every move that night. "Jason didn't say nothing!"

"Girl please, he was probably scared of what Steven might do to him if he did speak a mumbling word!" We both laughed. "So...you go...talk to him...Steven?" asked Diana, walking through the large golden double doors.

"I don't know," I answered shrugging my shoulders. "He seems a little crazy...plus...I still...well you know I..."

"Girl...if you say you love Jason, we gonna fight!" I didn't respond. "Gina...Jason sorry ass...is sorry! That bastard doesn't care about you! I still don't understand why you were sneaking around with him in the first place!" I began to look down at the linoleum floors that paved the hallways of Eisenhower High School, counting each chiseled dot design embedded in each tile that lined the ground. Why do I still love Jason, after everything he did to me, the unexpected violence, the abortion, and his being with Lisa. Shouldn't this all be enough? I looked up and stared at the wall...my wall of shame...shame because deep down I knew all of Jason's negative actions towards me were probably not going to be enough for me to stop loving him.

"I think you should talk to him..."

"Really?" I responded shocked at her statement. "But you hate Jason!"

"I'm not talking about Jason!" exclaimed Diane, stopping dead in her tracks to give me a dirty look. "You should talk to Steven; he must really like you...chasing you down the street trying to get your booty!" We both laughed as we headed down the hall to our lockers and eventually to our first class of the day.

I debated on whether or not I wanted to tell her about my mom's friend in my room. I really wanted to forget the whole incident and act as if nothing happened. After hearing the head board rapidly pounding the wall last night when I went to the bathroom, I knew I was home free!

"Remind me to tell you about my mama's new friend she brought home last night when we go to lunch." I murmured as we headed down the hall.

"Damn, your mama be gettin' it! Didn't she just bring home some old dude not too long ago?" Diana asked while heading in the direction of her class. "Okay, I'll remind you...let me get down this hall to class...you know Mr. Brooks be trippin when you late to his boring ass class! I don't need to know nothing about dissecting frogs in the real world!" We both laughed as we went our separate ways.

"See you at lunch!" I murmured as I continued Speech class with Miss Rizzo, who got on my last nerves.

As I walked, I instantly felt my bladder waking up and shooting hints to my brain it needed to be relieved of the urine I had been collecting since I left home this morning. So, I headed straight for the girl's bathroom at the end of the 700 hall. Before I could grab the large brushed nickel handle attached to the massive door, it swung open from the inside releasing several females who obviously had the same thought in mind, pee before class! The warning bell chimed indicating we had two minutes left before our first class started. I immediately pushed through the entrance past all the exiting ladies who had been smart enough to head straight to the bathroom right after breakfast. I chose one of the many now empty stalls and went inside to pee. While relieving myself, I could hear the last of the feet scurrying out into the hallway, rushing to class. After thoroughly cleaning, I flushed, pulled up my acid washed jeans to button and buckled my belt. As I unlatched the door to the small compartment, the final bell chimed loudly, and the bathroom was completely empty. First period had officially begun, and I still needed to wash my hands! I pushed the button on the metal box on the wall next to the mirror to release the cheap liquid soap into my hands, lathered and rinsed. I grabbed a paper towel, took a quick glance at my clothes and makeup, I was good. I headed towards the exit and pulled the large metal handle. Then, out of nowhere Jason appeared in front of me, sandwiching me between him and the bathroom door.

"What's up?" asked Jason in the deep baritone voice, his tall frame hovering over me.

"Nothing...." I replied, a little shaken from his sudden appearance. He continued to move in closer and closer until finally my back was pressed tight against the solid barrier. I was barricaded between the door, its handle and Jason, I couldn't move. The sweet smell of his warm breath showered down on my forehead.

"So...what's up with you and Steve? You talking to that nigga now?" Jason asked taking one very small step back in order to view my response. The smell of Irish Spring soap and a hint of Cool Water cologne began to fill my nostrils.

"No...I mean...he asked me for my number...I gave it to him," I responded looking down.

"Why you giving him your number? You don't want me no more?" Jason lifted my chin forcing me to give him eye contact. His gaze was deep and seductive yet seriously searching for answers to unanswered questions. I simply shrugged my shoulders. Why did I give Steven my number when my heart obviously belonged to Jason? But what about Lisa?

"What about Lisa; you don't love me no more?" I boldly stated, a little shocked at my own bluntness. "Why is she always at your house now?" I stared straight into his deep brown eyes, now wanting my questions answered. He began looking around to avoid looking in my direction at this point.

"Look...my moms likes her... and so she comes over to help me with Pre-Cal. You know that shit hard!" Jason said, fishing for any answer that would meet my satisfaction. "So...she be coming over sometimes...I mean she cool and all...but you know I'm crazy about you girl!" My chocolate cheeks became cherry red as I began to blush from his statement.

"Meet me afterschool today at my house. I'm skipping practice and going straight home today," he said moving back in closer. Suddenly a powerful surge shot throughout my body and vagina fluids were released into the seat of my panties.

"Okay," was all I could utter. Jason released me from his hold and allowed me to remove myself from his presence. I could feel his stares as I made my way down the hallway to Ms. Rizzo's class. I took one last look back; Jason was gone. I hurried to first period hoping my teacher hadn't marked me absent.

"Damon Charles, sit your butt down now or you will be put off this bus!" yelled Ms. Parker, our middle-aged school bus driver. Damon, 14-year-old, ninth grader known for causing a disturbance on the large passenger vehicle while in route to take students home. This was the third time she had shouted for him to take his seat since we left the school. Ridiculous! But this silly freshman was not going to spoil my mood. I was going to be with Jason! I just couldn't wait to make it home so we could be together and rekindle our relationship with some much-needed love making. I gazed out the window at the scenery deep in thought about him being so close to me this morning when I walked out of the bathroom at school. It was a reminder of how much I missed his smell, his touch, his manhood! Oh DAMN! What about my sisters? DAMN! DAMN! DAMN! In my Florida Evans voice. Well Gina, what are you going to do about the girls while you are at Jason's house getting some loving? I could do what I used to do, and that's make them a snack to eat, make them lay down and leave the house once they were asleep napping. Mom told me not to commit this act anymore since it interfered with them wanting to go to sleep at night. But desperate times called for desperate measures! I needed to desperately be with Jason!

We finally arrived at our destination. I was the only one getting off at my stop today. I guess the other kids on the street either got a ride home or stayed after for extracurricular activities. Reba and Rene were my extra-curricular activities. I hurried up the aisle then down the three steps, onto the slate grey gravel road. The cool breezy fall air gently slapped my face while the sun hovered over me at the same time, Houston has such peculiar early December weather. "Bye Ms. Parker," I murmured.

"Have a good evening baby," the aging woman replied as she yanked the iron handle that closed the metal shutter doors. The flashing red lights went off and the bus took off down Desoto street with a trail of smoke on its tail. As I made my way to down the street to my place of refuge, I couldn't help but notice the empty driveway at Jason's house down the street. I guess he hadn't made it home yet. I glanced down at my watch, Reba and Rene would be getting off the bus in about 30 minutes, which gave me just enough time to get in the house and make them something to eat before nap time. Hurrying past the first three brick houses on the street, I continued walking towards my home, and just as I was about to turn into my yard, I heard a familiar sound of a vehicle revving up as it turned the corner onto my street. The sound became louder and when the car eventually came to a roaring halt right next to me, I knew exactly who it was without even looking up!

"What's up sexy? How was school?" Steven asked through his passenger side window.

"Uh...what...what are you doing? What are you doing here?" I asked in total disbelief. I began to scan the area; no adults in sight! Thank God my neighbors all worked during the day! I needed no snitching on me about unannounced guests popping up in front of my home to chat!

"Shit, I came to see you!" he said grinning, revealing his gold tooth.

"Steven look, my moms be tripping! She don't let me have company! She was mad last night after the neighbor told her I was out here talking to you with my sisters."

"What neighbor?" Steven opened the door and stepped out of the car with his large gold chain resting peacefully on his white Gucci sweatshirt.

I pointed to the Campbell's cream-colored brick house across the street, "over there...remember last night he passed by us in an old El Camino...he just not home right now." He turned and glanced at the house then back at me. I never noticed the neatness of his hair, so freshly cut and faded on the sides and edged up in the front and back with about a half inch of hair on top.

"Well I guess we have to be more careful then," he murmured as he walked around the car revealing the light-colored acid washed Girbaud jeans and black and white Adidas sneakers. Damn he was always so nicely dressed, but I guess it's easy to dress nicely when you have money. He continued towards me, "Damn! I see ya looking good in those jeans! Can I get a hug?" Steven stood directly in my proximity with his arms extended. He wasn't as tall as Jason, I guess about 5'11, but still towered over my 5'3 frame. I leaned into his chest barely bringing my right arm around his lower back area. Before I knew it, both of his arms were wrapped around my mid-section. He held me in a firm, affectionate hold that made me feel so desired and loved. For a second, I was completely and utterly lost in his romantic embrace. His body smelled like Cool Water cologne and baby powder; I was almost in heaven until I realized this was not Jason. Oh DAMN! Jason! I pulled back immediately.

"So...what you about to do? Want to go get something to eat?" Steven asked while analyzing my body up and down. I started looking around to avoid his stares.

"Naw, I have to get...." Just as I was about to finish my statement, Jason's parent's powder blue Caprice Classic turned onto the street and came rolling by Steven and me. DAMN! I hid behind Steven and acted as if I didn't see him, and I guess it worked because he surprisingly kept rolling up the road to his house. "I have to get my sisters...they about to get off the school bus in a minute." I glanced at my grandmother's old digital Timex watch she gave me last year; it was already 3:38 pm! "But I guess you can call me or something, I have to watch them cause my mama at work." Steven's eyes were still locked on me.

"So...when they get off the bus, I'll take all of yall to eat...hell I know they hungry! So what's up?" Steven asked, still staring and unwilling to take no for an answer. "What time yo moms make it home? I can have yall back before she gets home. I'll just pay yo sisters off...they'll be down for food and money!" he said chuckling.

The faint sound of multiple car doors closing made me turn around and look in the direction of Jason's house and I counted not one, but two bodies walking towards his front door. Undeniably, the first body was Jason, I'd know his body frame from anywhere! But the other person, I couldn't quite make out until she came from around the other side of the vehicle. Lisa! That no good bastard told me to meet him at his house and he brings home another woman! No wonder he hurried past us so fast without stopping! I continued to stare until they both went inside, I notice Jason pausing and looking my way, even after Lisa entered his home.

Just then the large yellow motorbus pulls up at the stop in front of the street and spits out several hyper elementary students including my two sisters. Each one leaping off the last step and running in different directions holding and dropping important papers that I'm sure needed to go home to their parents. Rene and Reba were no exception to the rule, both girls sprang off the bus and raced over to where Steven and I were standing.

"What's up lil ladies?" Steven asked, finally focusing his attention on someone other than me. Neither one of them spoke back; instead both girls gathered around me each one grabbing one of my hands clinging to either side of me as if their life depended on it. "Yall want something to eat?"

"Sister, I'm hungry..." my sweet Reba said in her whispery soft voice. I glanced down at Jason's house one last time, but he had disappeared inside with Lisa.

"Yall, go in the house and put your bags up; we gonna go get some food with my friend." I boldly said without giving a second thought to the possible consequences that might come from me leaving with a boy and taking my young siblings along for the ride. But I didn't really care at the moment; my insides were fuming from disgust. How dare he claim to miss me, be so crazy about me and invite me to his house, but brings home the girl he'd been spending all his time with! Then claims to not like her, but instead like me! Fuck it! I'll chance an ass whooping from my mom to get away from all of this, even if it is for a short while!

"We going with my friend to eat some good food yall...okay?" Reba simply nodded in agreement displaying her big brown puppy dog eyes. But Rene...

"Is he gonna give us some more money?" asking with her hand on her hip.

"Yeah, I guess, but you can't tell mama, or he not giving you nothing! And you gonna get a whooping!" I exclaimed, absolutely annoyed by her question.

After putting the girl's belongings in the house and swearing them to secrecy, we loaded up in Steven's red Mustang and headed to our destination. Because the Mustang was a stick shift, we jerked slightly with each gear change. He didn't talk much, just constantly looked out the window as if he was searching for something or someone. It almost seemed as if he were going out of his way to be seen by any and everybody who noticed. The radio was blasting "My Posse's on Broadway" by the rapper, Sir Mix A-Lot as we continued down the road, and sure enough as we rode, I noticed people walking and passengers riding in other motor vehicles looking at us as we passed them in the street. Many continued watching even after we were long gone down the road. As we approached our destination, Steven decided to turned into a Shell gas station.

"I need to get some gas...yall want something?" Steven asked after lowering the volume on the radio. I noticed that the only time he turned the music down was to ask a question or make a statement.

"No..." I responded.

"We want some candy!" yelled Rene before I could finish my response.

"Yall wanna come in?" Steven asked letting down the seat so they could get out. "Come on and get what you want." The girls hopped out the backseat of the car and followed Steven inside.

I continued to sit in the passenger seat watching the traffic flow on the main street, Antione Dr. The Metro City Bus pulled up and released passengers on one corner. Then, a couple of them ran across the street to catch the same public transportation, just going in another direction. Across the street, a small white sports car slowed down to turn into the parking lot of a Bank of America and was almost hit from behind by a large dark brown Cadillac, because the driver wasn't paying attention. Next, a series of honking horns and curse words being exchanged by the individuals in the vehicles, filled the air.

I sat back in the seat and tried to relax, but the thought that I'd be caught by one of my neighbors or my mom's friends frightened me. I continued to fidget, shifting from side to side, unable to rest easy in the seat.

"Sister, look what I got?" Reba said standing at the window holding a box of Nerds and two sour apple Blow Pops. Startled, I jumped.

"That's good...where is Rene?" I asked looking at the entrance to the store. Rene was walking out and heading our way with a small paper bag in one hand and opening a pack of Now-n-Laters in the other, not even paying attention to where she was going. She simply walked slowly, head down, with only one agenda, opening the candy and popping one of the squares in her mouth. Steven came out next; he was putting his change back into his pocket. Checking his surroundings, he constantly looked around.

"Rene, hurry up!" I yelled. I opened the car door to get out and let them in. While Steven pumped the gas, I could hear the girls giggling and candy paper rattling.

"I like him Ree...he give us money and candy!" Renee muttered to Reba in a low tone thinking I didn't hear her.

"Yall eat Grandy's?" Steven asked while getting in the car. He looked at me then back at the girls.

"Grandy's? What they sell?" asked Rene, with a mouthful of candy, before I could respond.

"Sit back and be quiet...they sell chicken." I responded. My mom never took us out to eat, but I remembered Diana's parents taking us there after church one Sunday. "That's fine, we can go there..."

"I don't want no chicken!! We want pizza!" yelled Rene.

"Rene, shut up!" I yelled, tired of her obnoxious behavior! She really got on my nerves!

"We can go to Show Biz Pizza, over there across the street," Steven said exhibiting those perfect teeth with the single gold covering on one.

"Yaaaayyyy!" yelled the girls from the back seat. They continued to scream and jump with excitement in the back seat of the Mustang.

"That way, while they play I can get to know yo sexy azz!" he said, still smiling.

I shrugged my shoulders, "Okay...girls...stop all that noise!" They settled down, and we drove off. I really didn't care where we went; I just didn't want to be at home to see Jason and Lisa--together! So, as long as we made it back by six o'clock before that crazy mama of mine got home, I was good!

After the girls ate their pizza, Steven gave them each a handful of change he had gotten from the cashier to play games. "Make sure yall stay together...and if you act up, fight or cry...we leaving!" I said, mainly focused on Rene, the main culprit.

"Okay sister," said Reba, giving me a kiss on the cheek before running off to play. And out of nowhere, Rene hugs my neck! I watched them run off together to play in the ball pit.

"So, what's up? he asked.

"So, what's up? I asked.

"You know what's up...you know I been tryin to holla at you, ever since I saw you at the store with ol' boy! Nigga just want to get to know you better. How old are you, about 18?" Steven asked. He scooted closer to me, placing his left arm over the booth around me.

"I'm 16."

"Damn girl, I thought that sexy ass was at least legal!" he chuckled.

"What's that supposed to mean, what you saying...I look old?" I asked, a little offended.

"Naw...not older, you just mature...with the body of a grown woman! How you get so damn fine? I need to meet yo mama and see if you get it from her?"

"Naw...you don't need to meet my mama; she mean as hell! If she knew I was here with you, she would lose her mind and try to beat me out of this place."

"Oh, shit...beat you? Naw...we can't have that!" he said looking at me a little concerned. "I'll make sure you home on time, and if I have too, I'll talk to moms...I usually have that "mama magic" they always like me." Who was he supposed to be, King Midas, and every mama he touched turned to gold? Trust me, I know my mama, and no boys means just that, NO BOYS!

"So what you like doing for fun? You ever go to the beach?"

I shrugged my shoulders again, "I don't know...sometimes my best friend and I go skating when I go to her house. But most of the time I'm at home with my sisters." I said watching Steven take a sip of his Coke. "I don't really go nowhere...my mama strict! Plus, she ain't never at home! My brother Ray Ray in jail...so I have to always be there with them," I said pointing at my sisters as I watched them riding a spaceship ride in the middle of the arcade room.

"Ray Ray...Raymond Jones? He yo brother?"

"Yeah..."

"Man, I know Ray, we used to slang together, but I didn't know he had a sister or sisters! Man it's a small world!"

We continued to talk about my life, our mutual friends and why he dropped out of school. He said he had gotten into some trouble a couple of years ago with some friends who stole a car at the bowling alley. He was caught joyriding with them and was given probation for the felony act; however, he never reported to his probation officer. When a warrant was sent out for his arrest, he stopped attending school thinking law authorities would arrest him there. He was eventually arrested at his home and later served a year in a juvenile detention center.

I was surprised at how easy he was to talk too. He listened to me talk about my sisters and how Rene worked my nerves and Reba was my baby. He even told me about how he and his cousin Eric came to live with their grandmother. Eric's dad and Steven's mom were siblings and Eric's dad was shot and killed in a café when Eric was 12 years old. His dad had been sleeping around with another man's wife. The man followed his wife to the café one night and caught him with her. They got into a scuffle, and he was shot three times in the chest. After the funeral, Eric was sent to Atlanta to live with his mom. She had moved there after divorcing Eric's dad, but had left him in Houston until she got settled about three years prior to the deadly assault. When Eric turned 18, he decided to move back to

Houston and live with their grandmother. Steven was 14 at the time. Although he was very open to discussing the events in Eric's life, he wasn't very forthcoming about his past.

"Sister look, I bought me a ring and bracelet with the tickets I won!" said an excited Reba as she flashed the hot pink rubber bracelet and matching plastic ring with pride.

"That's pretty...uh, where is Rene?" I asked looking around.

"Over there," she said pointing at the prize counter. Rene was holding a ton of tickets, leaning on the display case while choosing the prizes she could afford. I looked at my Timex; it was already 5:45p.m. Man, time had just flown by!

"We need to go, its almost 6:00 and my mom will be home soon." I began to get up grabbing Reba's hand and pulling her towards Rene. Time was of the essence; we had to make our departure now!

Night time had already formed a blanket over the city by the time we made it to our destination from the family funplex. I asked Steven to keep the music low as we approached my home. I then suggested that he drop us off on the corner of my street and the main road, instead of in front of my house--I wanted no surprises from my mother tonight. When the car came to a stop on the corner of Rolland Street and Desoto, I released the latch to open the door.

"Hold up...you need anything?" Steven asked while grabbing my left arm.

"No, I'm good. Come on girls." I pulled the seat up and one by one they got out. "I'll talk to you later," closing the passenger door.

"Wait!" He reached into his right front pockets and pulled out paper bills, went through a few and chose one and handed over to me. I just stared at it. "Here, take it!" I slowly grabbed money and looked at a $20.00 bill. My jaw dropped; but nothing came out. I was speechless! "Good night sexy!" Steven drove off with his radio blasting a new track, "Boyz in the Hood" by NWA.

Chapter 14

an unfamiliar black, two door Toyota truck was parked at my house in the driveway. I forgot it was Wednesday and mom's off day. She must have company over which was music to my ears because I'm sure she was on her way out, just probably waiting for me to get home and let me know what I already know, "Gina, make sure you get your sisters cleaned up and cook them something to eat...don't have my babies here hungry! And clean my DAMN house--especially that DAMN bathroom! Don't be sitting your ass in here on that DAMN phone all night!" I can already hear her stern words leaping out of her mouth past her lips and bouncing from wall to wall until the message lands in one of my ears and runs out the other. Oh, will you shut up already! News flash Ms. Deborah Rochelle Jones, I know how to take care of your kids and your house, I'm sure, better than you can!

I'm sure upon entering into the house I will witness my mom supplying comfort and pleasure to yet another one of her male friends for monetary gains! It was funny how she could cook, cater and commence to being everything to a man but couldn't seem to find time to care for her daughters and only son. I know my older brother Raymond is and has always been problematic, but what do you expect when you have a mother who goes through men like a box of tissue during flu season. And every time a new fellow comes along, you allow the new guy to chastise your son in his own personal way, because you claim your eldest is "out of control" and you "don't know what to do with him anymore." Time and time again I would see her comrades inject their personal form of discipline on Ray and every time seemed more extreme than the last. Like Jimmy Dixon who would tie his arms to the bed post to beat him with a large leather strap, claiming that this was the only way to keep him from running away from him. But the worst was Melvin Tate, he made us both soak in a tub of cold water before disciplining us with a belt. I always made sure I walked a straight line, so I didn't get in nearly as much trouble as Ray. However, about three years ago before Raymond went to jail, he came home holding a man's shoe in one hand and a ripped plaid shirt in the other. He apparently saw Melvin at the corner store buying a six pack of beer.

"Gina, that fool started asking about moms and you, then had the nerve to tell me how bad I was as a kid! I whooped his ass!" Ray continued bragging in detail about how he repeatedly struck him violently with enough force to render him unconscious. "I made sure that nigga wasn't going no-where no-time soon!" Ray exclaimed holding up the old shirt and dingy shoe.

As I entered into our humble abode expecting to hear and see my mom's new man sitting in front of the television watching "Rawhide" or "Bonanza." She of course would be prancing around back and forth from the kitchen to her room and back into the living room seeking his attention, catering to his every need by serving him drinks and food, with one ultimate goal in mind, to obtain as much money as she could get out of him. My mother, Ms. Deborah Rochelle Jones, 36-years-young, with four kids, two baby daddies, and a mouth so bad she could put pirates to shame. She wanted a partner in life and love, but would definitely trade it all for a man with some money.

The scene, however, was different. The opening of the front door revealed a living room that was dark and apparently untouched that day. I walked into the oddly silent house and was about to head to my room when I heard the toilet flush. I re-routed my steps and began to walk towards the kitchen. While looking down the hallway I noticed the door to my mother's room was open. I could hear faint snoring coming from that direction and as I passed her room I looked inside and there she lay spread eagle on the bed, on top of the covers completely naked and sound asleep. I could smell the sex in the air, mixed with beer and fast food! "What the fuck!" I was in total disgust! Who wants to witness the remains of their single parent's sexual intercourse? I leaned into the room quietly to reach for the door knob and closed the door softly as to not disturb her resting from too much dick intake. Just as I shut her bedroom door, the bathroom door opens and there stood before me, my mom's young guy friend from the other night completely naked.

He was about average height for a guy, 5"10 or 5"11, no more than six feet tall with a very fair skin tone and deep curly hair, almost as if he were mixed race or something. But his penis, which was lying in the midst of his natural wooded forest was, large, dark and still semi erected from his recent sexual encounter.

"Oh, my bad pretty lady...I'm just trying to get back to your moms! Didn't mean to give you a peep show," he said with a sly devilish grin on his face. To avoid the already awkward situation, he should have quickly bypassed me in the hallway back to my mother's bedroom with very little interaction. But instead, he insisted on adding an extra bounce or two to his stride as he came towards me. This encouraged his Johnson to swing and sway from left to right with each step.

"Is your moms still sleep?" asked the 20 something year old man while his penis was still dancing. I still couldn't believe my mom was seeing a man closer to my age than her own!

"Once I finished laying down the pipe...man...she was out like a light! Your moms can get pretty wild for a woman her age!" he chuckled shaking his head.

I tried looking away from him...I needed to focus on something else...like at the four-legged creature sprinting up the interior wall...or the leftover dirt remains hiding in the deep crevices of the corner floor, which was a direct result of the girls' half cleaning the floor. But it didn't work, my eyes wondered back to his mid-section, and there it was again, now slightly limp dangling down past his genital balls. The naked man continued to walk my way with his Johnson bouncing around with every move he made, and he proceeded with the pretense of passing by me, but he didn't. Instead he paused stopping directly in front of me- I didn't know what to say, I couldn't move as his eyes met mine. He then gently caressed my right cheek with the back of his hands and asked, "Have you been thinking about me since that night?"

NO!! Was my next thought! I then quickly ran into the bathroom closing and locking the door behind me. Hell, the only thing I was thinking about was him leaving me alone!! I placed the toilet seat down, indicating a man had just peed and neglected to place the seat in its normal setting. I pulled down my jeans and panties and sat on the commode. As I emptied my bladder, I could vaguely hear an interior door close. I rushed to finish emptying my bladder into the toilet. I just needed to get to my bedroom and stay there until it was time for me to get Reba and Rene off the bus. I wiped myself clean, pulled up my pants and washed my hands all in the same minute. I headed back to the door and peaked in the hallway; the coast was clear. I then made a mad dash pass my mom's room, to my bedroom where I was safe...hopefully!

I gazed down at my watch, 3:30, I needed to get out of here to get the girls off the school bus. The loud ringing from the phone made me jump. I lifted the receiver up just as the second ring ended, making sure the bell chiming did not disturb my mother and her young man.

"Hello."

"Hey there sexy...you miss me?" said the familiar voice on the other end of the line. This voice had become synonymous with joy and excitement and hearing this person speak had become a part of my daily norm.

"Hey Steven," I murmured in happiness. "I was just about to leave out to get my sisters off the bus."

"Yall down for going somewhere; we can roll out to the park or something?"

"Naw...I can't, my mama home! She not gonna let me go out with no boy!" I exclaimed. It probably didn't matter since she was preoccupied with company of her own, laid up in bed in a sleep like coma, buck-ass naked for the world to view, while her nameless boy toy pranced around our house flirting and flashing **his colossal dick for me** to see!

"Damn yo moms be trippin!" Steven replied, chuckling with disappointment.

"I know, but she should be at work tomorrow when I get home."

"Let me pick you up from school then? Matter of fact, don't go to school. **Let me pick** you up in the morning, and you can spend the day with me."

"Not go to school...I..I...can't do that...what if I get caught? What if the school calls my mama?" I replied in shock from his request.

"They not gonna call for just one day! Come on baby.... we always have your sisters...cause I know you have to keep them...but...shiiittt...I wanna spend a little time with you ...alone!" Steven exclaimed, not taking NO for an answer!

"Uh...well...let me think about it," I simply replied, not knowing how to respond. Me miss school? Well, it's not like she's ever home to answer the phone! My mom hasn't even signed my report card since I was in the 8th grade! Staying in school and getting an education was not a priority in this house; not getting pregnant and not sneaking around with boys was! "Let me go get my sisters...I'll call you back."

"Alright sexy, hit me back!"

I dashed out of the house without even glancing in the direction of my mother's room. It was a very chilly December afternoon, and I was in such a rush that I left my jacket on the bed. Oh well, not going back there until I have the girls with me! Just as I made it out of the yard, the yellow school bus pulled up and spit out the antsy elementary school students. Once the bus ejected its last kid, it made a final roar and pulled off down the dark asphalt street.

"We going to Showbiz today?" asked Rene, as she and Reba ran towards me holding worksheets in their hands because they didn't have a backpack to carry their belongings.

"Naw, not to....." Just as I was about to answer her, the door to our home opened and the unknown man stepped out with my mom standing in the doorway unable to go any further because she was wrapped in a housecoat.

"Sister who is that man walking to the truck in our yard?" asked Reba.

"I guess that's mama new friend," I murmured.

"Ah man! Mama at home? That means we can't go nowhere!" exclaimed Rene.

"Shhhhh, remember, don't say nothing around mama. We going somewhere tomorrow, Steven called and told me before I came out here to get yall off the bus."

"Yaaayyyy!!" both girls screamed in pure delight as we headed towards the house. I looked up and saw the young man open his truck door to get in while my mom waved to him goodbye.

"There go my babies!" my mom said as we approached the porch looking at Reba and Rene. I then looked back at the truck when I heard the loud roar of the ignition starting and the man staring directly at me. Just as I was about to look away, he winked and blew me a kiss. He put the truck in gear, looked over his right shoulder, backed up and drove away. Wow!! This guy was unbelievable! He's probably been sexing my mother all day before I came home and still feels the need to flirt with me! The nerve! Where the hell does my mom find these men? And when she finds them, what does she see in them? This man was clearly a wolf in sheep's clothing, a walking creep! And if I were to tell her about his sexual advances towards me...she wouldn't believe me and would probably continue to see him.

"Mama...who was that man?" Rene asked in a sassy manner as she watched the truck turn off our street unto the main intersection and drive away. I was waiting for a, "none of your business or don't worry about who that is, that's my business not yours!" But instead my mom laughed and responded gleefully.

"Rene, that was the insurance man," my mom responded.

"What's an insurance man?" asked Rene, still probing.

"He is the man that's going to make sure yall alright if something happens to me."

"What's gonna happen to you mama?" asked a concerned Reba.

"Nothing my baby," mama responded and kissed them both on the forehead. "Come on yall, let's go in the house. Mama making her babies **some chili dogs tonight!** Gina baby can you walk to the **store** and get your mama a loaf of bread?"

"Yes ma'am."

"Go get my purse baby so I can give you some money." I hurried in the house to her room to get her large black handbag sitting in the gold colored velvet arm chair in the corner. As I headed back out of her bedroom, I noticed her bed was still a mess! Damn, they didn't even bother to clean up after themselves!

I handed my mother her bag, and she reached inside and pulled out a five-dollar bill. "Get a two-liter bottle of soda too and cookies," my mom instructed as she handed me the bill.

"Yaaaayyyy!!" exclaimed the girls as I ran to my room for my jacket and headed out the door. My mother was clearly in a sexual bliss, and walking on cloud nine to insist on buying us treats to go along with our dinner! I must say, her sudden acts of kindness were quite nice. It didn't happen very often, so when it did...I took full advantage of it!

I headed down the opposite end of the street towards the large red and white sign that warned us that the bayou was just ahead. I traveled across the extra-large ditch **to a street called Carver Rd,** which was the same street the store was on. It was a short cut to the store, but I had to pass Jason's house to get to the ditch. Well luckily, I didn't see his parent's powder blue Caprice Classic parked in the driveway, indicating he wasn't home yet. Good! I was all clear to cross over the pathway that lead to the trail that brought me to Carver Road, and from there it took me about 15 minutes to get to the store. It sickened me to have to pass the local winos and drunks hanging out on the side of the building, just to get to the store's entrance. The smell alone made me want to gag! The mixture of malt liquor, cigarettes, musty under arms and pure funk made my nostrils flare! I located all the items and paid the Chinese clerk for the goods and headed back home. I was about ten minutes into my walk when

I felt the warmth of a vehicle behind me. I turned around…. Jason! Damn, where did he come from?

"You want a ride?" Jason asked yelling from the driver side.

"Yeah…I guess.." I slowly walked to the passenger door, almost reluctant to get in.

"What's wrong, you act like I'm gonna do something to you!" he said staring me up and down. "I know you cold…come on girl, I won't tell your man I gave you a ride."

"I don't have a man; Steven is just my friend…you're the one with a woman! Are you **sure it's okay for me** to get in with you? Wouldn't want you to get in trouble!" I said sarcastically as I got in the car and closed the door.

"Oh, you got jokes!" Jason laughed as he began to drive. "So…if yall not together, why haven't I seen you?"

"You have a girlfriend!" I exclaimed, highly annoyed. "Last week you invited me over to your house…but then pull up to your house with Lisa!" I said still annoyed and apparently a little upset. He had some nerve.

"Well when I saw you with ol' boy Steve, shiiittt, I just left it alone!"

"You already had her with you when you came home…. or did you forget that part?" Jason looked straight ahead smirking a little admitting his wrongdoing in the situation. "Look, I finally get it…Lisa is your girl and that's who you want. I just have to deal with it," I said feeling heartbroken as the words spilled out of my mouth. Silence filled the car. Jason began to drive slower and slower as if to prolong our time in the vehicle together. His pace had decreased so drastically that at one point I think the pedestrians walking on the pavement outside were surpassing us. As a matter of fact, if we went any slower, we would probably be going backwards!

"Can you drop me off by the Big Ditch at the trail? I don't want my mama to see me getting out of the car with you…I'll walk the rest of the way," I asked.

"Yeah…I know how Ms. Deborah be trippin!" Jason responded, finally breaking his silence. **When we finally reached the trail, he pulled off the road and came to a complete stop, placing the car's gear shift in park. This seemed** a little extreme to just let me out, but I just went with it. Just as I reached for the door latch, Jason grabbed my arm to stop me and put on his hazard lights.

"Look, I do talk to Lisa…but why we can't still chill together? I mean…she cool and all…. and my moms like her…but I still like you." He clutched my arm holding it tighter to keep me from exiting the vehicle. I looked down at his muscular right hand wrapped around my left forearm, suddenly realizing he had no intentions on letting me go until I gave him the response he was looking for.

"So…what do you want to do…?" I asked as I sat in semi restraint looking at the door latch and back at his strong hold. I understood now that the wrong response could ignite the evil forces of Mr. Hyde. So instead of reacting to his aggression, I stayed calm, cool and collected so that the good Dr. Jekyll would stay in our presence.

"I want to see you…tonight!" Jason murmured, still fairly calm.

"Well…I could come by your house later…" I replied, quickly thinking of an exit strategy with no real intentions of meeting up with him at all! It wasn't because I wasn't still in love with him, but instead, I was mainly just tired of being let down. Plus, **I was really liking the direction my relationship with Steven was going. "You know how my mama usually do…she goes out after we eat…I could come to your house once the girls go to sleep."** I lied.

Jason slowly loosen his grip, "Alright…we can do it like we used to."

"Okay…so let me go home and take this stuff to my mom before she gets to wondering where I am, and end up not leaving at all." I continued to add to my false statement, hoping my deceiving him would grant me freedom from his confinement. Jason stared at me with his deep brown eyes, as if he were searching for any hint of deception.

"Alright baby," he said, finally releasing my arm. "I'll see you in a little bit." He then leaned over and kissed me twice on the cheek and then on the lips. He then did something that was pretty unusual for him; he placed his right arm around me and embraced me in a hug. It was loving and endearing, as opposed to his usual misleading seductive hugs to entice me into doing what he wanted. Finally, he slowly let go.

"Okay...I'll call you when I'm on the way," I said as I pulled the door latch and jumped out of the car. I headed to the trail that lead to the small bayou at the end of my street and walked halfway up the dirt path. I turned to **look back; Jason was still parked and staring through the passenger window at me. I waved-- to him it was a goodbye** for **now--** but for me, it was a final farewell.

Jason flew pass my house as I made it to the front door and turned the knob to let myself in. He blew, I waved, I went inside and closed the door. The girls were watching cartoons in the living room area while my mom was on the phone in the kitchen. She still had on her raggedy old purple house coat, and from the sound of her conversation, she was making arrangements to go out later. She had already began boiling a pack of Oscar Meyer wieners with the cheese fill. She was opening a can of Wolf brand chili by juggling the can opener and can with both hands and the phone receiver wedged between her tilted up left shoulder and bent head so that her ear could listen. I put the soda in the refrigerator and laid the bread and cookies on the counter, then headed back into the living room to watch "Woody Woodpecker" with the girls. It wasn't like I wanted to spend time with them, I was trying to see if Steven had called while I was out. I guess there was no call since neither of the girls looked up from the television when I returned. Trust me, if he had called, they would have told me.

We later ate our hotdogs and cookies while watching more television. "The Cosby Show" had just ended and "A Different World" was about to come on when the phone rang. I answered on the second ring but was sadly disappointed! "Hey baby, where your mama at?" asked my mom's friend Ms. Gloria on the other line.

"Hi Ms. Gloria, hold on let me get her." They talked for a brief minute confirming her pickup time, the hung up the phone.

"Alright girls, I want yall in bed by 9!" she said still in good spirits.

"Yes ma'am," we all replied. My mother headed back in the kitchen to finish cleaning it so she could get ready to leave for the night with her girlfriend. At 8:30 when "Night Court" began to play on NBC, I made the girls take a bath and get ready for bed. By the time nine p.m. rolled around, we were in bed, and my mom had left for the evening to hang out with friends. I couldn't sleep, so once my mom left the house I got out of bed, I decided to continue to watch more television. I sat in the living room watching "Hill Street Blues" or at least it was watching me as I watched the phone. I wanted Steven to call, since I wasn't able to communicate with him earlier today. I guess I had gotten so accustomed to our meetings this past week and a half, I just wanted to hear his voice before I went to sleep. I wanted to finish our conversation from earlier, but I know his usual nightly routine lead him to the streets to hustle. That was his way of life, how he made his money. The life of a street hustler.

The loud laughter from the live audience on "The Tonight Show" combined with the ringing of the telephone, woke me up. I scrambled to reach for the receiver "Hello?" I answered groggily.

"What's up sexy? I almost didn't call thinking your moms was going to answer the phone. You sleep? Can you talk?"

I got up to turn the volume down on Johnny Carson delivering his jokes to his spectators and television viewers. "Steven? Hey...naw

I was up watching t.v." I answered, glad that he had finally called. "Where you at?"

"Shiittt, I'm at the house, about to lay it down. I just wanted to see if you could talk?"

"Yeah, I can talk, my mom went out with her friends, I'm just here with my sisters...but they sleep though."

"So... what's up? You want me come through there for awhile?"

"Boy...no! I don't know when she coming home! I told you she crazy!" I said letting out a chuckle. "But I'm glad you called...you still wanna pick me up tomorrow? I thought about it, and I guess I could leave school after second period..."

"Alright cool, what time second period end...about 9:30?" Steven asked.

"I think it's about 9:35...I will just come out by the gym area and meet you by the tennis courts."

"Alright...bet! I got plans for you sexy lady!"

We continued our conversation until well after midnight, talking about life, his life, my life, my sisters and everything in between. **You could tell he needed and wanted to talk, and I loved our conversations. I was learning so much about him** and his life, and I liked it! Probably because it took my mind off of the non-existing relationship I had with Jason. I can't recall having any meaningful discussions with him, except when he confided in me about his grandmother's passing. Other than that, our only conversations were sex talks. To Kill Regina Jones.

After about two hours, our conversation was forced to come to a close. The bright headlights were beaming into the window and that could mean only one thing...mom's home! Steven and I said our good byes until tomorrow, and I went to bed before Ms. Deborah Rochelle Jones made it to the porch to unlock the front door.

Chapter 15

I still can hear Diana in my ear this morning at breakfast. "You skipping school to be with a damn tennis shoe hustler? Girl, you really trippin now!" I could sense she was slightly annoyed with me because of my poor choices and sudden mishaps lately. She didn't have a problem with me talking to Steven, but she did express her disapproval for Steven wanting me to miss class to hang out with him. "Look Gina, you my girl and I'm here for you...but DAMN! I hate to see you lose yourself in this nigga like you did Jason! He ain't worth it just like Jason wasn't worth it...and you see what happened with that!" Diana exclaimed.

"I know...but..."

"And what makes you think you going to get away with skippin?" Diana asked cutting me off. You know damn well attendance call home!" Mrs. Dunlap be waiting for a kid to slip up and not go to class or be tardy so she can call they mama and daddy!"

"I know Dee...I..."

"If you know, then why you letting this dude convince you that it's okay to get in trouble? Hell, he not gonna take that ass whooping for you when your moms finds out!"

"Dee...please!! I know my mama crazy...and will whoop my ass if she finds out...but what if she doesn't find out! She never found out about Jason," I said in my defense. I knew she meant well, but she knows as well as anybody, I'm going to do what I want to do! She knows how my mother is, Ms. Deborah Rochelle Jones, always ready to accuse me of something I didn't do and issue an extreme consequence in the end. So, I figure I can proceed with committing my preferred crimes, which is sneaking out of the house to be with Jason or skipping class to hang out with Steven. These mischievous behaviors I never get caught doing! And—like always—I will continue to suffer consequences for offenses not committed, like I usually do.

"Ugh...Jason! Don't remind me!" she said in pure disgust.

"Oh yeah, I was walking home from the store yesterday and made the mistake of letting him give me a ride home! Girl, he tried to hold me in the car by grabbing my arm and not let me out until I agreed to come to his house later that night after my mom went out with her friends!"

"I know DAMN WELL...all this time we been talking...you just now decided to tell me you went to see Jason last night!" Diana exclaimed; this time sounding more aggravated then the last time.

"Girl please!!! I just told him that so he could let me go! You know that fool is violent! And I didn't want to set his ig-nant ass off!!" I said chuckling a little as I drank my white milk from the small, individual carton. "When my mama left, I got on the phone with Steven and talked to him until mama came back! I ain't even thinking about no Jason!

"What's up with you and Jason?" said the familiar, flamboyant male voice. It was Freddy, just walking up to the breakfast table where we were seated in the cafeteria. I hadn't seen him much lately, since he's been riding to school with his friend Nikki, who has her own car. They usually get to school late and have to run straight to class in the mornings.

"Oh...boy where you been?" I asked, shocked at his presence.

"Yeah, where you been? You haven't been here for breakfast in a minute! What happened...you lost your free ride?" Diana asked as we both broke out into a loud laugh.

"Hell naw, I still gots my free ride dear! Nikki mama said she was gonna take her car if we make it to school late one more time!" Freddy answered, amused as he pulled out a seat and sat down. "So, I will be on time from here on out!" he stated with his famous hand snap. He was so gay! We all laughed. "Well...what about Jason...you know that fool talk back to Lisa!"

"I know! Trust me!" I quickly responded with attitude. "Ain't nobody worried about no Jason!" I made sure I chose my words correctly with Freddy because he was notorious for talking a person's business to others! And because of that I didn't tell him anything about the relationship I had with Jason, the abortion or Steven!

"We were just talking about how I was surprised he gave me a ride home from the store yesterday; you know his ass don't do nothing for nobody!" I said lightly kicking Diana under the table to get her attention so she wouldn't say anything else to Freddy. This conversation went on for a little while until the bell rang, and we were released to our first period class. By the end of second period, I was ready to leave campus to meet with Steven. He promised to be on Eagle Dr. behind the tennis courts by 9:35. So, my plans were to exit the building down by the gym area after the tardy bell rings and everyone is in class. I will just hang out in the girl's locker room, and when they leave out from getting dressed, I will leave too.

When the release bell rang, I went straight to my locker, making sure I avoided Mrs. Ringold; I did not want to have to lie to her, but I didn't want to take anything with me, no books and no bag! I even left my purse at home; everything I needed to get me through the day was in my pocket. My lunch card, lip gloss, and $10 from some of the money Steven had been giving me since last week. I had more money at home, but this was the smallest bill I had. Steven left me at least $20 after every visit last week. However, the last time we met, Steven stopped to get burgers from Burger King, then took us to T.C. Jester Park, which was about 12 miles from our house, outside of Acres Homes. This location was a perfect spot for my sisters to run around and play on the playground without having to worry about our nosey neighbors or my mom's friends catching us away from home.

Well, before Steven dropped us off that evening, he slid me $50, two twenties and one ten-dollar bill.

The bell rang and I was the first student to jump out of my desk and head to the exit before the other kids in class. I hurried down the hall making it to my locker just as Mrs. Grainey was headed out of her classroom. She was following another teacher with whom she was in deep conversation with, down the hall towards the teacher's lounge. Good, the coast was clear! I threw my books and bag in my locker and was off. I made my way through the back hallway down the stairs to the girl's locker room just before the tardy bell rang. I then waited in one of the toilet stalls until all the girls finish dressing, so they can head outside to the track to run laps. Ugh! I hate running laps on the track! Glad I wouldn't be in gym today!

To make sure I was discreet, I blended in with the rest of the loud chattery young ladies complaining about their upcoming one-mile run, I was the last one out of the locker room. I began to linger back as we made our way to the exit door that lead to the football field. I fell all the way back from the crowd and ducked into the nearby bathroom to wait for the athletic hallway to clear. Finally, after a minute or two of silence, I pulled the door open just slightly to peak outside to see if the coast was clear. Suddenly, a strong thrust from the outside of the door sent me back in the bathroom slamming my back side up against the wall that separated the entryway from the sink; I hit it hard, sliding down a bit from losing my balance. Once I re-adjusted my equilibrium, I looked up at the tall familiar male figure standing over me.

"Where you going? Why you trying to sneak out? Who you hiding from?" asked Jason.

"What the fuck! Why are you in here?" I asked, not sure if I was shocked to see him or his presence in the girl's bathroom.

"Naw... answer my questions," he said moving in closer. "Where you sneaking off too?"

"I'm going to class!" I exclaimed. "Why you in the girl's bathroom? And how did you know I was in here?" I asked angrily. I didn't care about his getting mad or possibly displaying his aggression to scare me. I wanted and needed to get pass him and outside to meet Steven.

"I been following you since you left class! I know yo schedule, and you ain't supposed to be down here now... you don't have gym until later." He moved into my immediate proximity, putting himself directly in my face. "So why you down here peeking out of bathrooms?"

I didn't respond; instead I tried moving a little to the right so I could run to the door and escape. It didn't work; he pushed me in the corner behind the door. "Look Jason, I got to go to class." I tried pushing past him; he wouldn't bulge.

"Why you stand me up last night?" he asked with both hands on the wall on either side of me. I was caged in like a prisoner, and he was the guard. "I was waiting for you to come by...and you never did. You know I wanted some lovin from you!"

"My mama didn't leave like I thought she was...her ride never came," I lied thinking of the best deceitful statement I could think of, but it didn't work.

"I saw Ms. Deborah leave in a car last night around nine o'clock...so why you lying?" Jason moved in and was pressing up against me so tight that I could feel the cold from the stone walls through my pink cotton shirt dress. I was sandwiched between the wall and him.

"Damn...you watching my house now?" I asked in disgust. "Well, if you would have kept watching, you would have seen her come back 30 minutes later because she only went to the store," I continued, still angry but still attempting to create a believable lie. "So, I couldn't come." He paused, staring down at me...hard, breathing his warm breath on the edges of my forehead. My heart beat was rapid. I wasn't sure if I wanted to be angry at him for keeping me there or scared at what he might do. One thing was for sure, I had to get out of this bathroom!

"I still want my lovin you promised me yesterday!" Jason murmured. He removed his right hand from the wall and placed it on my left breast and began to caress it with slight aggression. I pushed his hand away with my left hand, feeling very irritated by his touch. He then put the same arm around my waist and yanked me closer and proceeded to kiss my neck. I pulled away, but this made his hold stronger-- he then kissed my neck. As his lips made its way down my chest, he removed his other hand from the wall to undo the buttons on the top part of my dress.

"Jason...stop...I got to go to class." I tried to remain as calm as possible but couldn't help the extreme agitation that was continuing to build up inside. He wouldn't stop but instead, he resumed his course of action with more aggression at an accelerated pace. Then, suddenly the door swung open hitting Jason in the back. He jumped and turned around while releasing me from his hold. It was one of the female students that had been outside running laps. She came in to use the bathroom and caught Jason where he wasn't supposed to be. However, Jason was relieved to see that it was just a student and not an adult; the penalties for a boy being in the girl's bathroom making out with a female could mean expulsion!

"What's going on in here?" asked the young, pretty, blonde freshman or sophomore. I didn't know her, but I knew the current gym class was all ninth and tenth graders.

"Nothing!" I exclaimed pushing away from Jason. I headed straight out the door, thankful and taking full advantage of the sudden interruption. I looked around and the halls were still clear, so I ran straight ahead to the exit that lead to the tennis courts. I pushed the steel handle that unlatched the door that locked automatically once you exited the building to the outside, this kept intruders from getting in. Once outside I spotted the familiar red sports car on the other side of the tennis courts just as we had discussed. I looked around, still no one in sight, so I released the door and headed towards the vehicle at a super-fast pace. I was half way through the court when I heard someone yelling.

"HEY!!" I turned around; it was Jason! He had followed me out the building and was running to catch up with me. Just as I was about to start running, he caught me and grabbed my left bicep and yanked me around. "Where the hell you going!" Jason exclaimed.

"Jason, let me the FUCK go!" I yelled, pulling away from his grasp. He grabbed me again, and this time I began to fight back swinging my fists in hopes that the punches landed where it would hurt him the most. I continued to swing and apparently it was working because he let me go and I fell to the ground, face first in the dirt. Ouch! But I had to get up quickly before he started again. As I regained consciousness, I could hear tussling in the background.

I finally looked up and it was Steven and Jason, battling on the same sidewalk, in the same spot Jason and I were just fighting on. I apparently missed the very beginning of the physical conflict, because once I focused my eyes, Jason was already on the ground being kicked by Steven in the abdomen repeatedly.

"You keep yo mother fucking hands to yo-self nigga!" yelled Steven as he continued the blows with his foot to Jason's stomach area. Jason began to ball up against the fence that housed the tennis courts, looking helpless as a baby.

I finally jumped up and ran to Steven and grabbed his arm, "Come on Steven, let's go!" I tugged him until he followed my lead. "We got to go before someone comes!"

"Don't ever let me see you put yo mother fucking hands on her again!" Steven yelled in rage as we walked off. He then looked around grabbed my right hand and began to hurry to the car, this time pulling me. "Come on baby...you alright?"

A weak, "yeah" was all I could say. I couldn't believe what just happened, Jason and Steven...fighting? Steven defending me the way he did. WOW! No one had ever fought for me, well except for my mom, but never a guy. I kept seeing an image of Jason balled up against the fence gasping for air from the repeated blows to his mid-section, and I did feel some sympathy for him and his well-being—but not much. Yes, this was who I loved, the guy I lost my virginity to just before school started, the young man who fertilized the egg that I carried in the walls of my womb for eight weeks. So why didn't I feel the compassion for him I once felt not too long ago? I guess my lack of sympathy towards his demise was because I knew Jason would no longer be able *To Kill Regina Jones.*

Steven and I climbed inside the car and headed towards West Gulf Bank. He didn't stop until we passed Garden City apartments and made it to West Montgomery Rd. "How long this nigga been putting his fucking hands on you?" Steven asked as he came to a complete stop at the intersection, still in a rage. He looked down at the steering wheel waiting for me to respond.

"He only did it one other time...a month or so ago," I replied, still sore from the push and fall.

He turned to look at me, "Well, once was one time too many!" Steven said in a very serious tone. "One thing I can't stand is a nigga fighting on an innocent female!" But that's okay, I got some heat for that fool if he tries that shit again!" He opened up his glove compartment to reveal a small black steel gun. The sight of the firearm sent chills down my spine.

We continued to ride down West Montgomery until we got to the West Little York Rd. The light turned red at the intersection, and Steven pulled into the left turn lane and stopped. He then turned and looked at me again.

"Look, before we go any further...I need to know...you still got feelings for that fool? I ain't got time to be fighting no worthless battle!" His tone was firm and serious, "if you want to be with that nigga...just let me know now!" The traffic light changed, and Steven made a left. We passed by the same convenient store I ran to that night when Jason came to pick me up. Now today, I'm riding with the same guy I was trying to get away from!

"I don't like him like that anymore," I murmured. "We weren't really a couple, he just...I mean, I just..."

"That nigga just wanted to hit and go, get you all in love! Now you don't want his ass...nigga can't handle it!" Steven exclaimed, trying to keep his calm. "You ain't got to tell me no more, I know the game! Just as long as you ain't tryin to get back with him, we cool." He pulled up in front of the same white shotgun house sitting on bricks piers with the large porch and white columns in front. "Come on, you need to get cleaned up." I looked down at my clothing; I was a mess!

I followed him into the house; we went pass the living area into the hallway to the bathroom. He opened the door and flipped on the light switch and led me inside. The bathroom walls were covered with a sky-blue wallpaper with images of brown sea shells. Steven opened the cabinet door under the sink and handed me a white wash towel. "I'll be in the other room waiting for you," he said managing a smile with his gold tooth finally making its appearance for me to adore. As he turned and walked away and closed the door behind him, I couldn't help but admire his clothing attire. As always, he was dressed very sharply in a red and white stripe t-shirt with Guess jeans and red and white Nike tennis shoes.

I turned on the water and proceeded to saturate the towel. While the water ran, I looked up in the mirror at my reflection and realized I looked horrible! There was dirt in my hair, on my face and neck and on my dress! After about 20 minutes of wiping and patting and dusting off, I finally looked at least presentable. "This is just going to have to do for now," I said staring in the mirror, holding the white towel that wasn't white anymore. I opened the door holding the soiled cloth and made my way across the hall to the only open door with a light on. Steven was sitting on the bed reading the newspaper, listening to a large radio sitting on top of a brown chest in the other corner of the room.

"You read the newspaper?" I asked in amazement.

"What, you don't think a nigga could read?" I just be trying to stay enlighten on current events...plus I just like to read." Steven said folding up the Houston Chronicle circular. "You good? You look better," he said while standing up to turn down the radio. He walked over to me and took the dirty towel from my hand and threw it in white dirty clothes hamper next to the dresser. On the other side of the brown five drawer chest was several pairs of name brand sneakers, all lined up neatly against the wall.

"I didn't say you couldn't read; I just don't see many guys our age reading newspapers...hell I barely see them reading text books!" I said laughing. Steven walked over to me and gave me a hug. It was nice and sincere and definitely something I wasn't used to—but something was missing

"Wanna sit down?" Steven asked.

"Uh...I guess..." I said nervously. I wasn't expecting to come to his house, let alone stay and get comfortable. I wasn't even sure if anyone was here. Oh, damn Gina!! You've managed to do it to yourself again! You're at the home of a man you know, but still know little about, and anything can happen! With all the excitement from all the earlier events, it just dawned on me that I have, again, put myself in a very vulnerable situation.

"Its okay sexy lady, I won't bite," he said chuckling a little. I sat down on the dark brown bed spread like a church lady at Sunday service crossing my legs, with my hands placed politely on my lap. "You want something to drink? I know we got soda."

"That's fine," I murmured. He left. While he was gone, I looked around at the images on the wall. There were several posters of the basketball player, Majic Johnson on the wall, as a matter of fact, he had the same poster Jason had on his wall. I guess that was his favorite player too. I also noticed a framed picture of a woman holding a child on her hip. The boy was laughing and full of joy in the young woman's arms. He looked to be about two or three years old.

"Here you go," I jumped a little as Steven returned to the bedroom and handed me a can of Coca Cola. He then shut the door and turned the small latch on the knob to lock the door. My heart began to race...I didn't know what he was thinking, but I was not having sex with him! I was ready to go!

"Thanks." I peeled the tab back, pulled it off and took several sips of the drink. "So, who is that on the picture?" I asked, sitting the can on the floor, pointing to the framed photograph on his nightstand.

Steven walked over to the nightstand and picked up the picture. He paused as if to be reminiscing, "That's my moms and me when I was almost three years old. My grandma said she took the picture of us here. I think she was tickling me or something cause I wouldn't stop laughing. Grandmama said she had to take the picture cause we looked so happy." He sat the picture back down.

"You never told me...you never said anything about her...your mama, you only talked about Eric's daddy."

"I know." Steven spoke and that was the end of that. He walked over and sat down next to me on the bed. He put his milk chocolate colored hand on my knee. "So what you feel like doing today?"

"I don't know," I shrugged my shoulders shyly, looking down afraid to make eye contact. "I was just about to ask you that?"

He starred at me and rubbed my left cheek with his free hand. "You hungry?"

"A little...well yeah...I am." I took a deep breath, trying to hide my nervousness; it didn't work.

"Why you so nervous? You should be used to me by now...all this time we been hanging out." Steven continued to stare at me, and eventually lifted my head up so I could stare back at him. He licked his perfectly crafted lips seductively. "I want to kiss you."

"Uh...okay..." I puckered up my lips and closed my eyes. His lips met mine; it was a very soft, sweet peck. He then just stopped and continued to gently rub my left cheek. I opened my eyes, and they were reunited with his deep dark brown eyes.

"That was nice...but those aren't the only lips I want to kiss," he said rubbing my thighs. "Can I put a smile on your face by kissing your other lips?"

"Huh?" I was confused...what other lips? "What other lips?" I asked, puzzled.

"Lay back." Steven gave a direct command while continuing to rub my thighs. Oh! I thought, those lips! But I was not ready to take our relationship there! I was still trying to get Jason and how he felt inside me off my mind. No, absolutely not, this was too fast.

"Steven...no, I don't want to have sex with you...it's too soon...I barely know you!" I made an attempt to get up but instead became lost in his gentle, soothing massage to my upper leg, so the rest of my body wouldn't allow it. He began to suck on my neck; it felt good! He needed to stop; therefore, I tried to push his hand away, but the kryptonite in his fingers caused me to lose power. I slowly lay back on the bed and he followed my lead by lying right next to me, looking into my eyes and kissing me again. His hands began to move down south and made its way under my dress landing directly on top of my panties that housed my vagina.

"I want to kiss these lips." Steven's index finger began to circle the top of my prairie, which was still hidden by my underwear. Steven whispered in my ear, "Can I kiss on these lips?"

"What...you want to eat my cat?" I asked. I didn't like saying the word pussy, it just seemed so unladylike to talk this way.

"Naw sexy, I want to kiss your lips!" He began to kiss my neck, then my chest, then my thighs. He raised my dress up and kissed the top of my pink undies. Then, he rubbed his chin and mouth on the prickly hairs busting through the cotton cloth as if to relieve an itch that was waiting to be scratched. He raised his body while down below and removed my cotton panties and tossed them on the floor. Steven rested his knees on the floor and gently straddled my legs up on the bed between his head. He then placed my right leg on his left shoulder and my left leg on his right shoulder putting his face directly at the point of no return. He blew his warm breath on my forbidden prairie, causing my click to stiffen and my hairs to sway.

"Steven...wait!" I put my hand on his head and attempted to push him back, but instead he gently grabbed my hand and placed it on the back of his head.

"Just enjoy the ride baby!" he murmured, returning to his intended activity. And I did enjoy this journey to ecstasy. He gently kissed my click several times and then used his tongue to repeatedly stroke the inner realms of my vagina. I exploded in ecstasy and tried to pull away, but he gripped my legs in a tight hold and continued to indulge in my delicacies until my body released its final burst of pleasure, I then fell limp, weak and unable to move. Steven planted one more final kiss to my right thigh and stood up. He closed my legs, push my frail body to the middle of the bed and walked out of the room closing the door behind him. I took a few more deep breaths and finally was starting to regain my strength when he returned, holding a warm, wet washcloth in his hand. He laid down next to me and whispered, "how you feel?" His breath smelled liked cool mint and Listerine.

"I'm...I feel good..." I managed to utter.

"Here you go sexy; let me help you clean yourself." Steven spread my legs again and proceeded to wipe clean all the fluids I just recently released from my body. Wow! How sweet! Jason never did anything like this for me! He reached on the floor and positioned my legs so that he could put my panties back on. "So, what you want to do today?" He asked as he pulled my undies up over my booty and vagina.

"I...I don't care," I answered raising up, he held my hand to assist me.

"You ready to go?"

"Aw...yeah...okay" still shocked at his not wanting anything from me in return.

Steven took me downtown to a restaurant called the *Spaghetti Warehouse* to eat since he remembered my favorite dish was lasagna from my telling him the other day during one of our many conversations. I had never been to a restaurant this nice! The waitress brought us everything Steven requested including my homemade lasagna. It wasn't as good as my grandmother's but it was still delicious, with the warm bread that was complimentary with our meal. We left the restaurant and went to Garden Oaks movie theater to see the movie *"Harlem Nights"* with my favorite comedians, Eddie Murphy, Richard Pryor and Redd Foxx. He bought a large bucket of buttery popcorn and large drinks. It was nice to be in his company and treated so special, without my sisters tagging along and Jason on my mind!

Later on that same day after leaving the movies, we waited for my sisters to get out of school and took them to Pancho's Mexican Buffet. I laughed thinking about how both girls got a kick out of raising the flag to signal the waitress they wanted more food from the buffet line. Before we knew it, there were several unfinished plates of tacos, taquitos and flautas covering the table. When we got up to leave, the young, Latino busboy gave us a quick look of disgust, let out a long sigh and began to clear and clean the table.

"Gina...Gina...can we get some candy?" Rene kept insisting loudly while yanking on my right hand as we approached the gumball machine near the exit door. Steven reached in his pocket and pulled out a hand full of loose change and handed the coins to both girls. After wrestling with the machine and watching the round colorful balls dispense from the machine, we exited the building to Steven's red sports car and headed home. This time when Steven dropped us off, he walked us to the door. I instructed the girls to go inside and start getting ready for their bath. Once we were alone, he leaned in towards my face and kissed me passionately in the mouth, allowing our tongues to intertwine. As our tongues danced and danced in the realms of our mouths, our arms began to lock one another into a loving brace, while our hands repeatedly moved slowly, up and down the backs of each other's torso.

"Reach in my pocket," Steven whispered, pausing briefly from our moments of passion. I reached down into his left denim jean pocket and pulled out folded paper and looked down at it. It was a 100-dollar bill! I stood there shocked at the face of Benjamin Franklin staring back at me on the printed currency.

"This for me?" I asked, staring up at him, eyes wide open!

"Hell yea!"

"Uhhh...thank...thank.. you..." I said slowly, almost speechless.

"You welcome sexy...let me let you go before you moms get home!" Steven kissed me one more time gently on the lips and turned to walk away. As I watched him make his way back to the car, I looked down the street; the blue Caprice Classic was not parked in its owner's driveway. I looked down at my digital Timex; it was 6:18 p.m. and my mother had not made it home yet.

Steven blew his loud horn as he sped off booming the song, "I need Love" by L.L. Cool J. I waved my hand, pushed the $100 into my bra, using my left breast to protect it. I looked one final time at the empty parking spot down the street and wondered, "where was Jason."

Chapter 16

Finally, school was out for the Christmas break! And as much I loved being on campus away from home, I was ready for a break, I was ready to spend more time with Steven. I mean, he was no Jason, but he did make a girl feel special. I now saw what people meant when they said. "Once you get a taste of the good life you can't go back to foolish living. Why settle for jello when crème brulee is constantly being bestowed on you? With Steven, I've had a chance to savor a taste of the good life. Money, new clothes, eating out all the time, and riding in a fancy sports car. What more could a girl ask for? With Steven, life was good! He provided me with a certain touch of excellence, that was totally undeniable! Jason who?

It was just a few weeks ago that Steven took my sisters and I to Showbiz Pizza to eat and play games. Just a little under a month ago he gave me my first cash bill, just because… just because…because he just didn't want to see his girl broke.

"Your sexy ass should always have cash in your pockets. And I'm just the man to make sure you always do," he said later that same night on the phone. It was just last week he laid me down and granted me great sexual pleasure without me having to return the favor; he simply wanted to please me. This was so different from anything I had ever experienced with anyone; no one ever wanted to just please me and make me happy!

It was early Christmas Eve morning, around 9:20 a.m. My eyes popped open at the conclusion of my long night of dreaming. I leaped from the bed to head to the bathroom before I peed in my pants. As I sat on the commode relieving myself, I couldn't help but notice the quietness that filled the house. Like every year, my sisters were picked up yesterday by their dad's parents to spend Christmas with them. And my mom left this morning at 8:30 to work her annual double shift so she can be off tomorrow on Christmas Day. I had the entire house, the entire day to myself! I brushed my teeth, washed my face and made my way to the kitchen to begin preparing for myself a hearty breakfast of buttery toast, eggs, pan sausage and grits. Just as I was filling the small sauce pan with water for the grits, the telephone rang. It was Steven; he wanted to make arrangements for us to meet up so he could give me my Christmas gift. Although I was excited about receiving one of his fabulous gifts, my mom was very clear about me not leaving home at any time while she was at work. "You bet not let me call and yo ass don't answer the phone!" was the last statement she made before exiting my bedroom last night. So, I knew my usual outings with Steven would not be happening today! My mother knew I was at home alone with no Reba and Rene to keep me occupied, which can be loosely translated into, no kids to watch and report what I was doing!

"Well...since you can't leave; let me come over there?" Steven asked in a raspy voice, sounding like he just woke up. When I thought about it, I guess the best solution to this problem would be for him to come here. He could park his car down at Trent's house and come in through the back door so none of our nosey neighbors could see him entering the house and report their findings to my mother. Lately my mom, Ms. Deborah Rochelle Jones, has been in very good spirits because she was still dating the young guy. This same young man that was still flirting with me and I still continued to avoid at all costs. Obviously, mother is still not aware of what's going on and I planned to keep it that way as long as possible. My hopes are that he--like the rest of the men in her past--will simply make an exit out of her life before this situation comes to a head and explodes!

"Uh...okay." I responded, still a little unsure, but willing to take the chance. I told Steven what to do when he arrived and informed him of the hearty breakfast I was preparing.

"Damn girl! Yo sexy ass can cook too? I'll be there in an hour!" Steven exclaimed, no longer sounding as if he had just woken up.

After a little over an hour had past, I tidied up the not so dirty house then changed into some warm ups and a t-shirt. I had just about finished cooking when I heard loud music blaring from a car's speakers, so I decided to go look out the front door. I stepped out into the wintery air and looked down the street to the first place I always look, and no, the blue Caprice Classic wasn't in the driveway, I guess Jason wasn't at home. I then looked to the right and saw the red sports car parking in Trent's paved driveway. The chill of the winter morning left my teeth chattering, so I came back inside and closed the door to prevent more cold air from filling the house. I returned to the kitchen to finish cooking the last of the scrambled eggs. As I stirred the slimy yellow fluid in the hot, buttery coated frying pan until it formed a fluffy yellow solid, I began to think about Jason and how he had totally avoided me these last few weeks since the incident at school. If he was driving and saw me walking down the street, he would turn his head in the opposite direction and keep driving by without stopping, speaking or blowing his horn. At school, if I saw him, he turned and went in the opposite direction to avoid any possible contact with me. One day last week, he was walking through the cafeteria with other student athletes laughing and talking and didn't realize I was walking his way until I was right next to him. I purposely bumped him to see how he would respond, and all I got were several apologies in return and an assurance that it would never happen again! Wow, was all I could utter as he continued his conversation and walked off with his friends. My flashback was interrupted by a knock on the back door, Steven!

"What's up sexy," he asked as he entered into my home. His smile was bright and the gold tooth sparkled.

"Hey there," responding with a hug as he approached me. I was still holding the spatula used to cook the eggs in my right hand, a few pieces of the yellow scrambled eggs fell on his nylon Adidas jacket. "Oh... my bad, I got food on you," I said lifting the contents off his clothing and tossing it in the trash.

"I'm good sexy! Damn girl...you got it smelling good in here!"

"You want to eat? I made sausage, eggs, toast and my famous grits!"

"Hell yeah!" Steven exclaimed rubbing his hands together. Steven sat down at the kitchen table as I reached into the cabinet to get plates so I could serve breakfast for two. As we devoured the hearty breakfast, we talked about how we both planned to spend Christmas day with our families, or at least I talked in detail about my mom and me going to my grandmother's house in Dobbin, Texas, the country. My uncle Lonnie, his current wife Aunt Gwen and their kids, my twin cousins Lonnie Jr. and Connie, who were 10, Brandon, 13 and Craig, 15. My uncle was older than mom, but his kids were younger than my brother Raymond and I. Also, my great Aunt Hattie, great uncle Lester and great uncle Earl, my grandmother's sister and brothers, and their families should be there also. I went on and on about my relatives and their crazy antics over the years at past family functions; then suddenly, I realized I was the only one doing the talking. When I tried to ask him questions about his family and plans, he just simply replied, "Me, Eric and granny go do our thang tomorrow." Not sure what that meant, but I eventually just left it alone.

After we finished eating, Steven took off his jacket and helped me clean the kitchen, how very sweet! As we began to wash the dishes the phone rang. I stared at the yellow phone mounted on the kitchen wall and already knew who was calling, Ms. Deborah Rochelle Jones!

"What you doing? Is my house clean? Anybody called me?" And of course, her favorite,

"don't have nobody in my damn house!"

"Yes ma'am." is what I finally uttered before replacing the phone receiver back on the latch.

After the dishes were done, Steven and I headed to the living room to watch a little television. However, before we sat down to relax on the plush brown flower print couch with the pointed, wooden, brown arm rests, I headed to the window to look for any signs of my mother, my mom's friends or nosey ass neighbor's snooping around for evidence of wrongdoing on my part, to share with Ms. Deborah Jones! There were a few neighborhood kids riding their bikes on the street. Other than that there was no one else around this early afternoon. I pulled the heavy dark drapes closed tight and headed over to the television to turn the knob to power on the floor model set. "What you want to watch?" I asked, standing in front of the television turning the dial.

"Don't matter to me," Steven responded. "Mind if I take my shoes off?"

"That's fine," I shrugged my shoulders, continuing to turn the dial while he unlaced his white Adidas sneakers with the black stripes on the side. I eventually paused at the sight of my favorite holiday movie, *It's a Wonderful Life*. "Let's watch this...it's my favorite Christmas movie!"

"That movie look old as Hell! DAMN, ain't no color?" he asked laughing a little at my movie choice. I sat down next to him on the couch ignoring his silly comments. I watch this movie every year on television during the holidays. Although it's my favorite, I could never understand why the main character George Bailey was so adamant about ending his life because of the direction it was going. Hell, in my opinion his life was ten times better than mine! He had a loving family, home and he touched so many lives throughout his life, but he wanted to end it because of a bank mix-up.

I doubt it if anyone would have ever noticed if I were never born. Like what if the baby the lady had at the hospital would have made it and I had died. Would my mother cry like the other mother who suffered the loss? I didn't save anyone's life, I didn't prevent the pharmacist from accidently administering poison to a customer, and I'm sure I wouldn't have anything to do with leading a financial institution to finance homes for hundreds of families, I'm not that smart! George Bailey had a lot to live for, I simply did not. I'm sure my existence or non-existence wouldn't have mattered to anyone.

"What's this?" I asked touching the rectangular imprint in his pants pocket.

"Oh shit!" Steven exclaimed, slightly raising up to reach into the pocket of the nylon Adidas jogger pants. He pulled out a narrow gold gift box and handed it to me. "This your Christmas gift." I slowly grabbed the box and lifted the top lid off. Inside was a beautiful yellow gold herringbone chain necklace. I was speechless! This gift tops any gift I've ever received in my life! "WOW!" was all I could utter.

"Turn around, let me put it on you," he said while reaching for the necklace and taking it out of the box. I slowly turned around, still in disbelief as he placed and fastened the beautiful chain around my neck. "There you go sexy!" I jumped up off the couch and ran to the nearest mirror to admire the chain of gold around my neck. As I stared at my reflection in the mirror, I gently touched the chain, totally mesmerized by its beauty as it lay against my chocolaty skin. After several poses and a few blown kisses from me to me, Steven walked over and hugged me from behind breaking me out of my narcissistic behavior. "You look good sexy!" Steven began kissing and sucking my neck and ear repeatedly.

"Thank you so much Steven...but I didn't get you anything," I turned around, embracing him in a hug and kissed him on the lips. He continued to hold me and make contact with my mouth.

"I never got a gift this nice before!" I exclaimed while pulling from his embrace to continue admiring the necklace in the mirror. I wasn't sure why I didn't like staying in his embrace for very long; I guess because it didn't feel the same way it did with Jason.

"This just the beginning baby," Steven whispered in my ear.

Wow, the beginning of us as a couple? Steven and Gina? I guess he really does like me a lot, I'm just not really sure why? I haven't done anything to this guy or for this guy. "Come on sexy," he said leading me back to the couch to continue watching the movie.

We laughed as we watched James Stewart and Donna Reed dance the "*Charleston*" with their backs to the indoor pool at the school dance, completely unaware of it being opened by some students playing a prank. I felt Steven's arm on my shoulder and eventually his grasp pulled me under his wing. I sat there cozy, leaning into his right-side chest and shoulder. I admit, I didn't have that same longing for Steven that I had for Jason; however, with Steven I didn't feel like the weaker species, the mockingbird. Instead I felt empowered with hope and life, like a butterfly—a beautiful butterfly. Naw, maybe a beautiful black butterfly! The black will continue to represent the darkness that exists in my life when Steven is not around.

"Damn...I guess the people just go let them fall in the pool" Steven said amused.

"Yeah!" I laughed myself. When everyone jumped in the pool behind them, including the original mischievous students who orchestrated the opening of the under-ground pool in the first place, Steven and I just continued to laugh.

"So...you like watching movies?"

"Yeah...I love movies...but I mostly read though," I replied. Steven was gently massaging my right shoulder.

"Oh, for real. What you be reading?"

"Novels... I finished reading *The Color Purple* a few months ago..."

"*The Color Purple...* I thought that was a movie?"

"It is a movie now, but it started out as a book...and I read it. Now I'm reading a book called *Black Boy* by Richard Wright."

"*Black Boy*! What the FUCK!?" Steven exclaimed, pulling away from me. "Who the fuck wrote a book called *Black Boy*? And why you reading it?"

"I...I guess cause my English teacher suggested it after I read a short story by Langston Hughes called, "*The Negro and the Racial Mountain.*"

"Negro!" Steven yelled jumping up off the couch. "You reading books about White folks calling Black people Negro and black boy?"

"Steven calm down, Langston Hughes is Black...or was Black. He died in 1967. Richard Wright is Black too; he wrote *Black Boy.*"

"Is he still alive?" Steven asked slowly sitting back down.

"No...I mean, I guess he is dead...if he not...he real real old! Both of them were writers during the Harlem Renaissance." I turned to look at him as I attempted to explain.

"The Harlem Renaissance? What's that? Ain't Harlem in New York? What they was doing...writing at a party?" I laughed, but Steven looked seriously confused.

"I still don't know a lot about it, but I do know it was during the 1920's and a lot of Black artists, writers and musicians had become known by a lot of people for the stuff they were doing...cause it was good stuff and everybody wanted to see it and hear it." I replied, doing my best to explain the specific time period.

"Oh...so what the book about?"

"Well, *Black Boy* is about Richard Wright when he was young living in Jim Crow South and...."

"Who the fuck is Jim Crow South?!" Steven's look of confusion returned.

"No, it's just Jim Crow...the laws that said Black people couldn't drink from the same water fountain or use the same bathroom as White people back in the days. The South is down here where we live, Texas, Alabama, Mississippi...you know where it was real prejudice."

"Oh yeah, I remember learning about that shit in school. I remember my grandma used to work for this white family, the Powers...they was cool though... they was real nice to her. She had to catch the bus downtown to Woolworth and transfer to the bus that took her to the River Oaks area. When she would try to go to the lunch counter to get food, they would refuse to serve her; she had to go around back cause she was Black!" Steven shook his head in disgust. "Man...I couldn't have lived back then...I would have been smoking fools and kicking asses!"

"Well, I'm reading the part of the book where he realizes he likes books...or I guess wanted to read...but Black people wasn't allowed to check out books from the library, so he had to convince a Jewish man he worked for to allow him to check out books in his name."

"Damn, that dude wanted to read bad! I wouldn't have asked him to do shit for me!" So, what's that Negro mountain story about?" Steven asked sitting back down and relaxing.

"That story is good. It's about a poet that said he wanted to be a poet—not a Negro poet. Which means he wanted to be a White Poet or just White period! I know a lot a Black people like that! Especially the people that live here on my street!"

"Them fools that live in those fantasy houses in Inwood Forest by the golf course be acting like that!" Steven exclaimed. "They Black asses be driving down Antoine in they Mercedes Benz and Volvos. Shopping at that high ass Randall's. I ain't never seen none of them riding around the neighborhood in those golf carts though...shiiittt...I guess they don't have it as good as they think!" We both laughed, agreeing with one another about the attitudes that the upper middle-class Black people in the area had, and how their noses turned up on us, the economically disadvantage. I continued to explain to him how I thought it was really sad that the poet who perceived himself as a true artist would want so desperately to fit in to these so called "societal norms," instead of being true to his self and his culture. According to Langston Hughes, "An artist must be free to choose what he does, certainly, but he must also never be afraid to do what he might choose." This single line in the story always stuck with me...how awful it must be to be afraid of your choices in life.

We continued to talk and watch the movie for the next hour and a half. When the movie ended, Steven asked where the bathroom was. I showed him, and in his absence, I went to open the front door to check out my immediate surroundings. The air was very chilly and no one was outside. I gazed down the street to the right; Jason was still not home.

"So...where your room at?" Steven asked as I came inside and closed the door.

"Why you wanna know where my room at?" I asked bashfully, knowing full well why he wanted to know.

"Why we can't chill in there?" He said shrugging his shoulders. I knew it was coming; he wanted to go to my room and have sex. Sigh, well I guess I could or should since he'd been so nice to me. All the outings with my sisters, the money and now the beautiful necklace. Well, I guess I could or I should do something nice for him if that's what he wants.

I lead him to my room and closed the door behind us. It felt kind of strange having a male in my bedroom who wasn't related to me. Besides the awkward encounter with my mom's friend some weeks ago, there has never been a guy outside my family in my semi private sleeping chambers. "Here it is." I said, while picking up a few pieces of clothing off the floor. It's really nothing special, just a bed, dresser and bookshelf." I had an old cherry oak bookshelf in the corner of my room that my grandmother found at a garage sale a few years ago to house all the books I have collected over the years.

"Damn you got a lot of books!" Steven exclaimed. "I guess you do like to read." He walked over to me and put his arms around my waist and pulled me close. "What else do you like to do?" Steven began to kiss me on the lips before I could say anything.

His kisses eventually lead to his hands traveling underneath my t-shirt and finally unfastening my bra. I didn't stop him, even though his touches felt weird, too unfamiliar. I took a deep breath and tried to imagine us making love so I could get in the mood. It didn't work. Was I nervous about getting caught? Naw, I knew my mom wasn't coming home anytime soon. I guess it just didn't feel the same way it did when Jason and I were about to have a sexual encounter. Awwww, Jason, I do miss his touch, his aggression, his...oh hell, why am I thinking about Jason while Steven is cupping my breasts with his hands and sucking my neck.

"Lay down," said Steven. As I move towards the bed, he took out a small square package out of his pocket, then began to take off his pants and underwear. I followed his lead pulling my sweat pants and panties off and kicking them on the floor. I lay down, still wearing my t-shirt awaiting his entry into my domain. Steven used his teeth to tear open the wrapper and pulled out a condom to protect his fully erected penis. He walked towards me as he rolled back the latex. He lay on top of me and raised up my shirt while using his lips to locate my breast. He began to suck one nipple with his mouth and caress the other with his hand. I moaned a little to signal to him I was ready for the insertion of his manhood inside my vagina.

I lay there trying my best to participate in the sexual act by returning his kisses as he repeatedly inserted his penis inside of me. I cradled my thick thighs around him as he attempted to force me to orgasm with his rhythmic thrusts; it didn't work. No matter how rapidly he pushed in and pull out, I found it harder and harder to stay focus. My mind continued to wonder. I had thoughts of Jason; his touch and our various sexual acts kept surfacing as I continued to engage in the less than great act of making love to a guy that I deemed as just this really cool dude. But I had to stay focused, focus Gina! I wondered what time my mom was coming home? I couldn't wait to show Diana my necklace after Christmas; mom would usually let me go to her house at least once during the break before the girls came home. Damnit Gina focus!!

"You alright baby?" Steven asked. I looked up at his face, noticing immediately the sweat beads forming on his forehead.

"Oh yeah," I lied. In order to keep my constant arousal and not have my vaginal walls dry up like the Mojave Desert in July, I continued my thoughts about Jason. Thoughts of him and our many sexcapades sent my body into immediate stimulation sensation! What has this man done to me? Why are my constant thoughts centered around a guy who could care less about me or my feelings?

An individual who had no problem with inflicting harm on me whenever it was convenient for him

After several final minutes of rapid power drives into my genital canal, Steven made a series of gropes and gasps that were followed by jerking contractions, indicating the sex had come to an end. Steven collapsed on top of me and continued to lay there until he caught his breathe. And as I lay there smothering under his moistened body, I couldn't help but wonder about my mom and all the empty relationships she's been involved in. Did she ever feel this empty and unfulfilled after sex? Sex with a person was meant to satisfy not annoy. But I'm nothing like my mother; she gives up the coochie for cash at the drop of a hand.

"How you feeling sexy, you good?" Steven asked slowly raising up off me. I breathed out a sigh of relief; he had finally gotten up!

"Yeah...I'm fine," I lied again. I tried to think of a way to get him up and going, even though my mom wasn't going to make it home anytime soon. I kind of wanted this to be over and Steven to be gone. It wasn't because I didn't like him, because I did, I think.

"I wanted to talk to you about something before I go," Steven sat up right in bed. I curiously sat up and rested my back on the bookshelf headboard.

"What's up?"

"Well...I wanted to know if you had a bank account in your name?"

"A bank account...why would I...what would I do with a bank account...I ain't got no money!" I said laughing.

"Well would you be willing to get one for me?" Steven looked down at the old patch work quilt on my bed and began to trace the outlines of the artistic details with his finger.

"Why you want me to get a bank account," I asked, curious about two things: his answer to my question and when he was planning to get up and get dressed. I was starting to feel a little paranoid, thinking about the possibility of my mom coming home and surprising us with an early arrival home from work.

"I just think you should have an account with your name on it; that way you can learn how to use checks and balance your money and shit!" Steven exclaimed, jumping up out of the bed. "Black folks need to learn how to manage they shit like the White folks do!

"Boy, I ain't got shit to manage!" I exclaimed with a chuckle. I got up to look out the window from my bedroom to see if anyone was outside. I saw no one; even Jason's house was out of range since there was a large shrub in front of my window that prevented me from viewing his home.

"You will, Ima give you money to put up." He walked over to the window and closed the single curtain I was holding in my hand, then turned to look at me. "Every time I give you somethin, you put it up...it's that simple."

"Like the money you been giving me after you drop me off?"

"Yeah...and once you open an account, I will give you more money." Steven reached down and grabbed both of my hands and placed them on his chest, kissing my knuckles. I will never understand how this man could be so gangster and so loving at the same time!

"Well....I got about $240 now." I pulled away gently to reach underneath my worn feather mattress to retrieve an old white sock I hid the cash in. I pulled out the neatly folded, wrinkly bills and showed Steven. He walked over to his black Adidas nylon pants, picked them up off the floor and reached in the pockets and pulled out some cash. It wasn't a large roll of money, just a few bills folded once.

"Here...add this to your stash." Steven handed me the money. I unfolded the loot and counted; it was $300!! My mouth dropped!

That brought my total to $540! Fuck putting money in the bank, I'm going shopping!

"I wanted to buy me something with this money..."

"You can buy stuff sexy...you just can't spend it all. Put the $400 in the bank and spend the $140; that way you have money put up." Steven leaned in and kissed my forehead before collecting his clothes so he could get dressed. "You gotta towel?"

"Oh yeah...my bad!" I grabbed my t-shirt, slipped it on and headed to the bathroom to wash off and wet a washcloth for him to clean himself with so he could go! It was after four o'clock, and my paranoia had reached an all-time high! He wanted to discuss my financial future, and the only future I had on my mind was my immediate future which consisted of my mom and her belt and hands if she were to catch him here in my room!

After a few kisses and plans to meet after Christmas day, Steven and I said our goodbyes and he left the same way he came, through the back door. I exhaled a final sigh of relief as I closed the door behind him and locked it! I made my way to the front of the house into the living room to see what was on the set, but before I changed the channel, I needed to sneak another peek out the window, hoping to find what I was search for. I found nothing. The parking spot like my heart was still empty.

Chapter 17

Reba and Rene played quietly with their Happy Meal toys that accompanied their meals from Mc Donald's in the backseat of Steven's sport's car as we sat in front of the Texas Commerce Bank on North Shepard Dr. It was the Wednesday before New Year's Eve, and Steven picked me and the girl's up early afternoon while my mother was at work. Since our conversation on Christmas Eve concerning my obtaining an account in my name from a nearby bank, he continued to press the issue and insisted that the account be opened before I went back to school from the holiday break. He told me Texas Commerce Bank was well established and his grandmother had been a customer for years. When he was younger, she took him and his cousin Eric to open up their very own individual accounts.

"You gotta know how to handle your money sexy!" All I could do was shrug my shoulders, I guess he was right; I mean money management is important when you have money to manage. But up until recently, I didn't have the pleasure of having money to manage, handle or secure. My mom didn't even use the banks to house her wages from work, well at least not anymore. After having a number of bounced checks at Weiners Department stores, B & W Meat Market, Kmart and Sac-N-Save, her picture taken and posted in their offices, and several criminal court hearings in the check fraud division downtown, my mother's money got buried in a sock and hidden under the mattress until it was time to be used.

"Nae stop it!" Reba yelled from the back seat of the vehicle. "Sister, tell Nae to give me back my toy!"

"I just wanted to see it for a minute," exclaimed an annoyed, yet sneaky Rene.

"Nuh un! You trying to take mine cause you broke yours!" I turned around and saw the detached Garfield figurine from its pink skateboard lying in between both girls on the seat and Rene holding the unbroken Garfield character attached to the pink skateboard in her hand. I didn't utter a word; instead, I quickly snatched the toy from Rene and handed it back to Reba. In response, Rene crossed her arms in front of her chest and began to pout in anger. And even though her thick red wool overcoat made it difficult to keep her arms folded, it didn't stop her from maintaining the pose. Such a mean spirited, stubborn kid! Reba just continued to play with Garfield.

"Damn girl! You be handling them girl...huh?" Steven said, not really looking for an answer. "Yall good back there?" He turned and looked back at the girls. Neither one responded. Reba continued to play and Rene continued sit in a silently throwing a fit. "You ready?" Steven turned back to me.

"Yeah...I guess so," I said again shrugging my shoulders. We pretty much discussed everything on the phone yesterday, how I needed a state issued identification card to open up the account. I was glad my grandmother took me to the Department of Motor Vehicle's office this past summer to get my ID. She knew I was very eager to start working a job that would pay me hourly wages, but, of course, my mom wouldn't allow her only babysitter to get a job! Funny, she wouldn't give me any money and she wouldn't allow me to go out and make money.

I was to walk into the financial institution, and before I got to the teller booths, sign the log sheet that sits on a small table in the lobby area next to the chairs.

"Ask for a light skinned chic named Mary Barron when you go in, since you not old enough to open no account by yourself. Don't worry...she cool... she always help my granny when she come up here," said Steven. But why would I be worried. I didn't care if I had a bank account or not, he was the one who kept insisting I get one in the first place. Who cared about taking care of my business and money management, I just wanted to go shopping and buy nice things for the first time ever. But I guess I would cooperate, especially since he was the reason I had accumulated all these funds in the first place.

"Yall behave until I get back," I turned looking back at my sisters.

"Okay sister," said Reba as she continued to play with Garfield. Rene continued to pout and remained silent.

I grabbed my small black leather Chanel purse with the gold link chain strap that I bought myself for Christmas, or at least the day after Christmas when I went to the mall with Diana and her mom. My sisters were still at their grandparent's house and my mom, like most years after Christmas, allowed me to go to my best friend's house and spend the day, as long as her mom or dad were in close proximity. The purse housed my Texas ID card and exactly $420, four hundred for the bank deposit and twenty to prevent my small designer bag from going broke. I got out of the car and made my way into the bank to open my very first account. Wow, now that I thought about it, it did sound exciting, a sort of--mature adult move.

I entered the bank solo, and the setting was exactly the way Steven described it. Just as I was about to sign the lined sheet attached to the clipboard, a fairly tall, light skinned black woman wearing a black fitted cashmere sweater, short royal blue suede skirt, whose borders rested just above her knees, black pantyhose and short black career heels, approached me.

"I can help you ma'am," the pretty young lady said greeting me with a smile. "You can follow me this way," as she led me down the short hallway to a small office. As we walked past the first three offices, I could hear conversations from consumers wishing to obtain loans and open new accounts. "Have a seat," she said motioning me to sit in one of the vacant arm chairs placed directly in front of the executive desk. As I sat, she proceeded to the opposite side and sat down in a large leather executive office chair, sitting in front of an IBM desktop computer. Ms. Mary Barron, was what the fancy gold-plated name plate read on her desk.

"Are you here to open a new account today?" Ms. Mary Barron asked.

"Uh...yeah," I responded. I unzipped my purse and took out the photo identification and handed it to her.

"Thank you," she murmured, reaching across the desk to take my card. She picked up a pair of reading glasses and placed them on her pretty face, then began to silently type my information into the desktop computer while I waited. I just sat there, also quiet, waiting for her to complete the setup. "Is this your correct address?"

"Yes ma'am," I politely responded. She continued to peck away at the keys. I didn't want to stare too hard at her, I was just admiring how pretty her long dark silky hair looked hanging down past her shoulders. She must be of mixed race, Black and Hispanic because my classmate Sandra Barron was Latina also and they both have the same last name.

"How much do you plan to deposit today," Mary asked looking up over her reading glasses from the computer screen.

"Ummm, $400," I said opening my purse and pulling out a wad of cash from the Chanel purse. I began to recount the money omitting the $20 I planned to keep while Mary watched to make sure the amount was correct... I handed her the cash.

"Thanks, I will be right back with your receipt," she said as she rose from her seat.

As I sat alone in the small box shaped room, I began to look around at the pictures on the credenza behind her desk. There was a picture of two small boys, who were clearly African American or one kid's skin tone was slightly darker than the other. They appeared to be between the ages of five and seven years old. There was another picture with Mary and the same two boys, only they all appeared to be younger in the photograph. There were no pictures of a man indicating she was married or involved.

When Ms. Barron returned, she handed me a slip of paper showing receipt of deposit, with an account number. "Do you want your checks delivered to your home address?"

"Uh? Checks? No...I don't need no checks..."

"Well checks automatically come with the account; plus, the bank is running a special, 8 books for only $12.95, that will automatically be deducted from your account balance...and you can choose the design." Mary reached inside a desk drawer and pulled out a booklet and handed it to me. I reluctantly opened the brochure and reviewed the different check features thinking about my mother and her past negative encounter with writing bad checks!

"But...don't check writing get people in trouble?" I asked as I slowly turned the pages, admiring the variety of designs to choose from.

"Only if they are misused and you don't have money in your account to cover the amount," Monique answered without looking up from the computer.

"I don't want them; I don't even know how to write checks. I sat the booklet on her desk. Ms. Barron stopped typing on the computer and looked at me in a semiserious manner.

"Ms. Jones, checks are a part of a checking account; you don't have to use them. As a matter of fact, just put them up in a safe secure place when you receive them and leave them there for safe keeping. Just because you receive them doesn't mean you use them; besides, you are a young lady now and writing checks will eventually be a part of your regular routine."

I picked the pamphlet up and finally settled on the character Betty Boop to grace the cover of each of my newly ordered checks.

Ten minutes later I headed outside to the car with a book of temporary checks and a folder that enclosed everything I needed to know about my brand-new checking account at Texas Commerce Bank. I wondered how Jason and his parents would feel about me now that I had money in the bank? I should at least be closer to being an acceptable mate for him. I was sure Lisa didn't have a checking account with hundreds of dollars available whenever she wanted it.

I stared out the window at the scenery during the ride home. The girls continued to play, as I listened to Steven blasting the song "Cinderfella" by Dana Dane. I guess he figured this was more appropriate since the girls were riding along in the back seat. He was pleased with how well everything went with Rachel at the bank.

"You taking care of yo business sexy!" Steven said, all giddy, almost excited about his giving me money to put up for my benefit. I guess he really did like me.

Since it was still early, we decided to go back to T.C. Jester park so the girls could play. My mom had been working lots of overtime at work lately and was not going to be home for at least another two to three hours, depending on how soon her ride from work gets her home. You would think that with all her laboring from her job and money collections from men, she would have a vehicle of her own by now! But instead, after bills were paid, her remaining funds were being contributed to the successful operating of the local bars and neighborhood cafes! Yet she always wanted me to listen to her rant and rave about how mannish and nasty boys were and they only wanted one thing, but in the same breath she continued to make her famous quote, "Don't fuck for free!" What a hypocrite, when all she did lately was give away all her "goods" to a young mannish guy who appeared to be one pay check away from the poverty line himself! Well, I knew I was nothing like her; Steven provided me with plenty cash, and we'd only had one sexual encounter! With Steven I didn't feel like the weaker species, the mockingbird. Instead I felt empowered with hope and life, like a black butterfly, with the black continuing to represent the darkness that exists in my life when Steven is not around.

We pulled up at the park and parked the red sports car in the first available slot and unloaded. The girls hurried out the back seat and made a mad dash to the monkey bars and swings to play. "Stay where I can see you!" I yelled, closing the car door. I walked to the back of the car to meet up with Steven and we both headed to the playground together.

"Have you ever wrote a check before?"

"No," I replied, shrugging my shoulders wondering why he and that Mary lady made such a big deal about checks. Damn, I probably end up throwing them away once they're in my possession. "Why you ask?" I asked with a slight attitude

"Just wondering, that's all...calm down sexy!"

"I mean...you and that Mary lady act like having checks is so important...I didn't even care about getting a bank account, let alone some checks! I told her I didn't know nothing about no checks! And now you keep asking me about checks!"

"Look Gina," said Steven saying my name for probably the first time ever. His tone wasn't stern; however, it was a little more serious than usual. "We just trying to look out for you...that's all. Hell, if I didn't give a fuck, I wouldn't have given you the money to open it in the first place! So why you trippin with a nigga?" Steven stared at me with his deep dark brown eyes, waiting for a response.

"I...I didn't mean nothing by it...yall just keep asking me...and I didn't want them because..." I began looking down at the ground and kicking around the dirt in my dingy, off-white canvas shoes, which were in desperate need of being replaced. "I just remember my mom's had a bunch of bounced checks when I was little. I remember sitting in the courtroom with her. I just always figured checks were bad!"

"Girl!" Steven said with a chuckle. "Your moms was just careless with no money! You got money sexy! Ima make sure of that!" He grabbed me and pulled me into a strong bear like hug. He then lifted my chin and gave me a kiss, "trust me...I got you!"

The familiar voice, yelling out profanity made me pull away and look at the incoming traffic. The black two door Toyota truck pulled into the parking spot next to Steven's car, with the passenger side door swinging open before the vehicle could come to a complete stop. Out jumped Ms. Deborah Rochelle Jones in a complete rage heading in our direction, yelling and cursing every obscenity under the sun. How did she know we were there? My feet froze in place; I couldn't move, even though I knew a woman of mass destruction was heading my way. The driver's side door opened and out jumped her young guy friend, running in her direction trying to stop her.

"Who the fuck is that? "Steven asked, completely unaware of what was about to happen.

"Its ...its my mama!"

"Oh SHIT!!!" Steven exclaimed.

My mom's friend did his best to try and slow down the raging bull, but all she saw was red and was ready to attack. He tried grabbing her hands she snatched away. He pulled her back by the arm; she jerked it back. Just as she approached me and was ready to swing, Steven stood directly in front of me and caught the blow. He continued to shield and protect me from her direct charges, keeping her from getting to me, but at the same time not retaliating back.

"Come on baby...calm down, they just at the park." My mom's friend softly yelled, hoping this would calm her down. It didn't! He was finally able to restrain her by placing his arms around her medium frame in a strong bear hug from behind. She tugged and pulled but was unable to break loose from his strong hold.

"Why you got my babies out here hugged up with this damn no good ass boy!" My mom yelled, panting hard after finally giving in to her friend's strong grasp. She was completely out of breath and still managed to utter loud, harsh obscenities to me that could be heard clear across the city park lines. The unfamiliar rage bulging from the debts of her eyes sent my heart into a nervous panic. I was afraid! I immediately turned and ran to get Reba and Rene, but I didn't have to go far; they were already heading our way, except their pace extremely slow, clearly illustrated their fear of the unknown. "Yeah bitch! You better go get my Goddamn babies!" She continued to yell, "and get yo ass in the truck! Ima beat yo ass when I get home!"

Just as I grabbed the girls' hands, I heard Steven speaking directly to my mother in my defense

"Please ma'am, don't get mad at them...please," pleaded Steven. I saw them walking to the park and gave them a ride."

"The hell you mean a ride? It's a park right down the street from my house! Gina bitch-ass ain't got no business getting into the car with you or any other man around here! She ain't have no business outside anyway...and she damn sho shouldn't be this far away from home! So...you just shut the fuck up and get yo sorry ass the fuck out my face!" She continued yelling as I passed her with the girls heading to the truck, they began to follow close behind; I was thanking God her friend still had her contained in the confines of his arms. However, all the cursing, yelling and physical threats still didn't stop Steven from continuing to offer an explanation for our being in his possession.

Several people with their children at the park stared at all the commotion that surrounded us as we finally made it to the truck. "Alright Deborah, calm down so I can unlock the door," exclaimed my mom's friend as he attempted to reach into his pocket to retrieve his keys. She took a deep breath and paused as he released one hand from her body to reach into his pocket and before we could blink an eye she had broken loose from his grasp and was heading my way with the quickness. She took two giant steps my way and landed her back hand and forearm to my face hard, knocking me to the ground. She pushed the girls to the side and jumped directly on top of me slapping each of my cheek bones at least twice before someone yanked her up off me.

"Oh...hell fuck no!" Steven yelled as he pulled me off the ground. "You ain't going no fucking where with her! I don't give a damn if she is yo moms!" He was holding me and pulling me towards his car as my mother's friend regained possession of her in his tightly gripped arms.

"What kinda fucking mama fights her child like a nigga in the streets! Hell naw! You ain't going with her," an angry Steven yelled as he opened his car door and pushed me into the passenger side seat.

"You better bring my motha fucking child back here you bastard!" My mother continued to yell while my sisters began to scream my name.

"Gina...Gina...Gina!!! Don't go! Don't leave us!" Reba began to run towards the car. I could see the tears pouring out from the depths of her eyes, slamming down hard onto her cheeks. Steven slamed his door shut, started the ignition and proceeded to put the car in reverse.

"Wait!" I yelled as Reba made it to my side of the vehicle pulling on the locked door latch.

"Watch out little lady, your sister got to go!" Steven yelled out the cracked window.

"No! I don't want her to go! Sister...stay!!! Mama not gonna hurt you." Reba continued to sob. I looked at Reba, then looked in the direction of my mom; she was still being restrained by her boyfriend. I opened the car door and gave Reba a long sincere hug and just as I was about to let go, I felt the small arms of another individual, Rene. I held them both and gave them a kiss goodbye.

"Sister will be back...I promise...and I'm gonna take you both to Showbiz...I promise!" I began to sob, hard, as I got out the car to walk them to the sidewalk out of harm's way. "I love yall, be good till I get home!" I ran back to the car, closed the door and Steven took off that early afternoon to his house. I wanted to look back, but I couldn't look back, as if one glance behind me would cast me into a pillar of salt. But let's face it, not only could I not stand the torture of seeing my sisters' weeping on my behalf, but I no longer wanted to be the weaker species. I no longer wanted my mother To Kill Regina Jones.

I cried all the way to his house, while he continued to yell in anger, still unable to take in the harsh, cruel behavior my mother displayed towards me at the public park. I paused from the constant weeping to enter into the small white shot gun house on brick piers because I didn't want to have to explain to the residents inside my tear shedding, but the house was empty and dark. We headed to his room. "Lay down for a while and get you some rest," insisted Steven as he helped me to remove my shoes and jacket. "I be right back." As he left the room. I lay down in the bed rolled up like a human ball with my knees almost to my chest. I felt the tears began to swell in my eyes once again. "Here you go baby." Steven handed me a cool wet towel to wipe my face.

"Can you turn off the lights please."

"Yeah...you okay...you want to eat something? Drink?" Steven asked as he shut off the lights.

"No...I just want to go to sleep." He briefly walked out the room and returned with a soft blue velvet blanket that I could tell from its fragrance it was freshly washed. He spread the blanket over me, kissed my forehead, and closed the door behind him, leaving me alone in the dark room... I cried all day. I cried all night. I eventually cried myself to sleep.

Chapter 18

"Girl where you at?" asked a surprised Diana on the other end of the phone line.

"How did you know I wasn't at home?"

"Cuss, when I called your house, your mom asked me did I know where you were...I told her I didn't know."

"What did she say?" I curiously asked.

"She said... She not here baby, have you seen her? Seriously Gina, she sounded really sad and worried." My mom, sad and worried about my whereabouts? Yeah right, she just needed me to baby sit so she could go to her New Year's Eve parties!

I proceeded to explain to Diana everything that happened at the park and how Steven took me with him and didn't care about what my mom had to say about it.

"Damn! She jumped on you outside? You okay? Why didn't you call me?" My dear friend continued to interrogate until all her questions were answered. "So, when you coming home?"

"I don't know Dee, it ain't like my moms wants me there!" I felt myself getting emotional all over again.

"Girl please! I know your moms be trippin sometimes...ok...most of the times...but trust me, she loves you and wants you home!"

"Dee please! Go home for what? So, she can beat me! No...I think I'll pass!"

"So... what you gonna do next week when we go back to school?"

"Uh...I don't know? I guess I hadn't thought about it."

"Well you better think fast cause Monday will be here before you know it!" Diana was right; Monday would be here in the blink of an eye, and I wasn't sure what to do! What if my mom was waiting there in the school's front office to finish what was started at the park yesterday! Mr. Rickson, the principal would have to call the cops in hopes that they would be able to contain her inside the building!

"When Steven comes back...Ima talk to him," I muttered into the phone's receiver. "He got up, left, brought me some breakfast from Mc Donald's, then left again. I hope he comes back soon, I don't feel right sitting in his house by myself! I thought I heard someone earlier, but he said no one was here. His grandmother was gone to the country to visit family and wouldn't be back until after New Year's Day. He said his cousin Eric left to go out of town yesterday to take care of some business, whatever that meant. My full bladder began to weigh down on my lower abdomen indicating the fluids were ready to be released from my body. "Dee, let me call you back...I have to use the bathroom."

"Okay, I have to go anyway; my mama wants me to go to the store with her. But make sure you call me back!"

"Okay...

"Promise? "Diane asked in her worried motherly tone.

"I promise!"

"Alright girl...talk to you later!"

"Bye!" I rested the black phone receiver on its cradle, jumped out of bed wearing the same clothes I had on the previous day. I opened the door and stood in the doorway, looking both left and right as if I was following all necessary safety precautions for adhering to oncoming traffic approaching my direction. The hall was clear to cross over to the bathroom, so I hurried in and secured the door tight behind me.

I couldn't believe I was still wearing the same clothes again today, were my first thoughts as I gazed at my reflection in the bathroom mirror. My eyes were puffy and swollen with dark rings outlining the outskirts because my mascara and eyeliner had run from all my constant crying. I annoyingly looked away from the mirror, unable to continue staring at the reflection of a girl who can't seem to escape predicaments that put her in situations that seem to take her away from home to unfamiliar territory.

After I relieved my bladder of the excess urine build-up and washed my hands and face, I exited the bathroom, but instead of heading back to Steven's room, I decided to explore. I was a bit curious about my current setting, and I felt this was the perfect time to do so, since there was no one else in the house but me. I slowly crept down the long corridor of the shot-gun shaped house and headed towards the kitchen, which was the direct opposite the living area and front door. The small kitchenette sat in the very back of the house, with a door that lead to the backyard. Just as I approached the kitchen, I noticed an old three shelf bookcase that I didn't recall seeing the last time I was here. The shelves at the end of the hallway, opposite the room Eric and Candace were in the first time I was here. The first thing I noticed was the gold and brown set of Encyclopedia Britannica on top. Wow! I had always wanted a set of encyclopedias at home! My grandmother had a set she bought years ago before I was born. She would always talk about the importance of having books of knowledge on hand whenever you needed to research a topic. She was right! Every time I needed to look something up that wasn't in the Webster Dictionary on my bookshelf at home, I had to wait and use the reference materials at the library at school. I randomly selected and picked up the letter C book, rubbing and admiring the silky gold-plated edges of each page my fingers came across. I opened the book and landed on information about "California" and then turn a chunk of pages to "cranium" then "cyst". I couldn't resist smelling each page. The satiny sheets of knowledge housed a vintage smell that was simply undeniable. I placed the book back on the shelf alphabetically in its correct spot.

The second level on the case had many random literary works: *Huckleberry Finn, Wuthering Heights, Pride and Prejudice, The Scarlett Letter.* I remember *The Scarlett Letter* I guess from school; the lady committed adultery and had a child with a minister she was in love with and had to wear the letter "A" on her clothing as punishment for her crimes. Hester, yeah Hester was her name and this had to be a very long time ago in a state far away from Houston, Texas! In my world, adultery was being committed all day every day, and the people in my world could care less about breaking the seventh commandment in the Bible. Hell, my mother alone would be covered with the letter A, all the time if the public made this a punishable crime.

The Invisible Man by Ralph Ellison; this must be a scary book. Even though I didn't like horror stories I picked the book up anyway, not realizing the old movie I refused to watch with my sisters about the transparent man wondering the land causing people to live in fear, was actually a book first. "I am invisible, understand, simply because people refuse to see me" was what the front cover read in italics. What an odd statement; of course, people can't see you, you're invisible! I noticed the wear on the book's paperback cover and realized it was the first book I noticed on the shelf that had actually been used. I didn't want to be judgmental, but it was hard to believe the people who resided in this house actually read! My curiosity lead me to read the back book cover, and its analysis was nothing like the few scenes I saw in the movie. As-a-matter-of-fact it wasn't the same story line at all! This book was actually about a Black man explaining how he came to live in an underground cell, spending his days smoking, drinking and listening to Jazz music because he felt defeated by the world he lived in. According to him the Black man was invisible in White society. I knew I needed to read this; hell I saw winos on the street corners all the time drinking, smoking and listening to Blues music, and I'm sure they hadn't written any books!

I picked up the "E" encyclopedia book to look up Ralph Ellison; he too was an author during the Harlem Renaissance era like Langston Hughes and Richard Wright. I decided to keep the book in my possession, to read while I was at Steven's house since I had an abundance of leisure time to spend.

"My paw paw used to read that book all the time before he died," Steven said walking towards me. I jumped scared from his unannounced arrival into his home.

"Damn Steven...you scared me!" I exclaimed with my right hand on my chest.

"My bad sexy!" He looked very casual in his denim Levi jeans, white t-shirt, white K-Swiss tennis shoes, solid white baseball cap and black leather jacket. His gold tooth was glaring through the seams of his lips. "I was just saying that book was my granddaddy's...who was always telling me about the Black man struggle. I was real little and I didn't understand all that shit! Hell, all I did was shrug my shoulders, listen to a little bit of what he had to say so I could get me a quarter to go buy an ice cream or some candy!" Steven looked down at the floor and smiled as he reminiscence about his past. "He used to always have the book on the table next to his chair in the living room. When he was at work, my grandma would beat our ass if we touched it! Grandma didn't play when it came to paw paw's shit!"

"I was going to take it in the room to read it...since you always gone," I murmured looking down at the book.

"Oh...my bad sexy, I was taking care of some business with the homies. I came on back so I can take you to the store...shiiitttt...I know you want to get out of those clothes."

"Yeah...and take a bath!"

"You talk to your moms?"

"No!" I snapped, wondering why he would even ask me that. "I don't need to talk to her!"

"Alright then...calm down. I know you mad and she was tripping yesterday...but she is your moms. Hell, I wish my moms was around! Hell, she can cuss and fuss all she wants...as long as she here...I don't give a damn!" Steven spirit suddenly becoming solemn.

"Why you never talk about your mama?"

"Nothing to talk about...shit...she just ain't here." Steven's solemn spirit becoming slightly annoyed.

"Oh...okay..." I murmured.

"Anyway...so what's up? You ready to go to the store?" I shook my head yes, went back to his room for my shoes and we were off.

Two days had past and it was New Year's Eve, almost a brand-new year. And, of course, I was subjected to having sex with Steven on multiple occasions. This morning I was awaken by his fingers carefully sliding in and around my clitoris, then eventually up the canal of my vagina. Like Celia from *The Color Purple*, all I could do was what was expected of me and that was open my legs and allow him to climb on top of me and do his business. And as usual, I forced my mind to think of happy thoughts of Jason and I making love, until his business was complete. I would sigh with relief at his completion, and Steven would simply roll over and go to sleep. I would stay awake reminiscing about the last time Jason and I were alone together in his car and I had lied and told him I would come to see him that night. I have to be the dumbest broad in the world. Why am I still thinking about a violent, lying, cheating guy like Jason? I have to learn to hate him, so I can learn to love Steven. Afterall, Jason, just like my mother only wanted To Kill Regina Jones!

Steven would leave me at night and come back really late. He always brought me food and drinks. After taking me to the store that very next day to buy me clothes, under wear and personal toiletries, I pretty much had everything I needed, so I simply spent most of my time in the house reading, *The Invisible Man* and watching television. "Am I destined to be here forever?" Was the question I often asked myself Probably so, I'm sure after everything that happened at the park, my mom could care less about my whereabouts. My sisters might miss me a little, well at least Reba might; the only thing Rene probably misses are the frequent outings to restaurants and entertainment with Steven! I'm sure my mom didn't care whether I was dead or alive, just as long as I no longer resided in her household!

"When do you think I should go home? School starts back up in a couple of days." I asked while we sat eating Whopper burgers from Burger King later on that same afternoon. "Your grandma will be home Sunday after New Year's...and...I don't want any surprises when I get to school Tuesday." I murmured eating on a handful of fries.

"When you wanna go? Shiiittt...I thought you liked it here," said Steven just before biting down on his double Whopper with cheese.

"I didn't say I didn't like it here," I lied, because regardless of what my mom did, I would much rather be at home with her than here. I didn't like my mom, mainly because she didn't like me, but I loved being at home in my domain. And as much as I hated to admit it, I missed my baby sisters, Reba and Rene! I even missed those rare times when my mother was in her rare jolly moods and she cooked us big dinners while singing along with the radio in the kitchen. A couple of times when she felt bad about wrongly accusing me of something, she would cook my favorite meal which was lasagna. I had decided last night while Steven was gone that I wanted to return to my life on Rolland street, live in my home and sleep in my bed. I didn't care anymore about the consequences I would face. Hell, I had grown immune to the beatings, what's one more?

"It's just that I feel bad for you...you have to keep coming home to check on me and stuff," I said, lying as I finished my food. I accidently spilled ketchup on my bright yellow, off the shoulder cashmere sweater. I needed him to know I appreciate his help, but this was not my life or the life I wanted to continue to live. I felt more like a prisoner, but this time I was in someone else's home. I would rather play the inmate in my own room.

"You ain't bothering me...shiiitt...tell you the truth, I like having yo sexy ass here laying next to me at night!" Steven smiled picking up a napkin to assist me with cleaning the freshly made stain on my sweater.

"You be coming in so late tho...I get scared...this not my house." I looked up at him.

"Yeah...I be taking care of business at night...shit just can't wait." I bet it couldn't wait--were my first thoughts. The life of a hustler never stopped! It was fast paced and dangerous, a life I wanted no part of! "But I wanted to talk to you about something before I take you home." We grabbed the uneaten food and soiled napkins and placed them back in the original bag to toss in the trash.

"What's up?" I asked still cleaning up the mess.

"Just wanted to tell you how proud I am of you for opening that account up the other day," Steven said sounding more like an afterschool special than a street hustler. "I brought yo papers in the house," he said pointing to the cream-colored manila folder with all that paperwork Ms. Barron gave me when I left the bank. It was sitting on the brown five drawer chest in Steven's room.

"No big deal...you gave me the money...I mean it was you that wanted me to do it...I honestly didn't care," I replied shrugging my shoulders. Hell if I cared; it was his money. And as long as he continued to finance the account, I would keep it open.

"Well I plan on putting money in it for you. Did the lady give you a pulse card so you can withdraw money out when you need it?"

"I think so, I guess it's in that folder," my uncertainty prompted me to get up and head to the dresser where the papers were. I picked up the folder and looked inside. With everything that happened that day, I never did go through all the information Monique told me to look over once I got home, but then again, I never made it home! I located a gray hard plastic card with the word "pulse" with a rainbow underline on the front. The name of the bank was on top and a long 16-digit number listed towards the bottom of the card. "Here it is," I handed the card to Steven and sat back down on the bed.

"Ima hold on to it...okay," Steven told me rather than asking for my consent.

"Oh...okay...I guess I won't need it anyway; you'll be the only one taking me to the bank if I needed to go.... I will just get it from you," I replied, not really feeling I had a say so anyway. It was technically his money, and he had the ultimate say in how it was used.

"I just wanna make sure you don't spend it...Ima give you money for yo pockets...so you don't need to mess with these dollars! Just leave that shit put up...that's how you save sexy!" Steven smiled softly placing his chocolatey hands on my knee. He leaned in and gave me a kiss on the cheek. I just simply smiled in agreeance.

"So, what you know about writing and depositing checks?" Steven asked, still insisting on staying on the topic of banking do's and don'ts!

"You mean...checks like the ones that are coming to me in the mail...?"

"Yeah baby...those," he chuckled slightly, not sure if he was amused at my ignorance towards the subject or lack of interest.

"I don't! Boy please, I told you that at first. But Ms. Monique said I need to learn and they will help show me at the bank if I needed help," I replied, still attempting to sound interested in the discussion.

"I can teach you how to write checks and deposit 'em in yo bank account so they can be cashed."

"Deposit...checks? Why I need to know that? What checks am I depositing?" I asked, confused, but interested in his response. Steven stood up and walked over to the five-drawer chest and opened up the top drawer. He pulled out a book of personal checks and handed them to me. They looked just like the example checks Monique showed me the other day. The check design was basic blue print with Bank of America logo in the top corner. The name of the checks read, Miss Barbara Thomas with Steven's address print underneath. "Isn't Barbara Thomas your grandma? Why you have her checks in your drawer?"

"Cuzz, most of my money go in my granny account, she don't have no money and she be needing me to pay bills with these checks...so I just put my money in her account. Plus, you know how I do, I hustle for mine! I don't ..need them good white folks in my business trying to figure out what I'm doing and how I'm doing it!" Steven murmured becoming a little agitated and defensive.

"My bad, I just asked," I responded looking down at my hands resting in my lap. I was puzzled and confused at his insisting that I open an account of my own, when he doesn't even have one.

"Look, my paw paw used to always tell us about putting money up, saving and all that shit...I just wanted to pass that on to you cause I cut for you big time!" Steven grabbed both of my hands and held them in his, "sometimes I will write you checks to deposit in your account so you can always have money. I might need to withdraw money out of it sometimes though...alright?"

"Alright..." I just simply shrugged my shoulders in agreement—again.

"Don't worry sexy...everything good."

I guess it was all good for me, a constant unexpected cash flow just for me! Trust me I wasn't worried at all!

"So... when you taking me home?" I asked changing the subject.

"You ready? Yo moms is ready for you to come back?" Steven said slyly.

"What? She ready? What do you mean...how you know that?" I asked, confused and panicked!

"Cuzz sexy...I went by there this morning and talked to her. She was trippin though, said she was going to call the cops cuzz I kidnapped her baby! She stopped trippin when I chunked her some cash!"

"Her baby? The cops? You gave her money?" I was really baffled at this point!

"Hell yeah I gave her money, I don't need them laws in my life! Plus, it made her hush so I could tell her you was okay and **wanted to** come home. Shiiiitttt...money talks! She ain't said a mumbling word until I finished!" Steven was amused.

"So...what else?"

"Long story short, she said bring you home and she gonna deal with you when you got there."

"Oh hell! I...I guess I have to just take the punishment!" I said becoming more perplexed and afraid of the possible near future events. But when we pulled up at my house on Rolland Street, my mom opened the front door and stood on the porch with a teal green, cotton fleece sweatshirt with the matching jogging pants. She wore thick white socks and house slippers to protect her feet, along with a silk scarf over her roller curled hair to protect her head from the cold New Year's Eve weather. I told Steven thanks and goodbye before exiting the car knowing full well, she was watching our every move.

"Come on in here!" Ms. Deborah Jones said, in a slightly raised voice as I made my way to the house from the car. "Alright, you can go now...we good!" My mom yelled to Steven as I walked past her, through the doorway and into the house with my head down purposely not wanting to make eye contact with her. And shockingly, we were good. "Yo sisters ain't here, they with they grandparents, so go take your ass a bath gal! You smell like you been fucking for days!" was the last thing I heard from her before closing my room door behind me as I entered my safe domain. Later on that night, after taking a long hot shower and straightening my room, I lay in my bed--thankful to be at home. I could hear my mom and friend in the living room watching Dick Clark's **"Rockin' Eve"** on television. They were laughing and having a good time. She never entered my room that night. Wasn't sure if that was a good thing or not...Happy New Year to me!

Chapter 19

It was approximately one month into the new year and my return home had been just like Steven assured me the day he dropped me off. It had been 30 plus days, and my mom had not reprimanded me at all for being away from home that short period of time during the holiday season. She would pass me in the hall and make indirect statements to me about the girls needing their bath, or she took meat out the freezer for me to cook for dinner while she was out or at work. When the girls made it home New Year's night, they were so happy to see me. They jumped on me hugging and kissing me, screaming, "Sister you home!" Even Rene hugged me tight not wanting to let go. "Don't leave us no more sister! We missed you sister!" They ended up sleeping with me in my bed that night. "We wanna make sure you don't leave us again sister," said my sweet Reba while yawning and falling fast to sleep, in the debts of my bosom. Rene had cozied up to my backside lying in the curbs of my spine. I was completely sandwiched in for the night!

Steven came back to my house a day later after my return and boldly stepped to my front door and knocked! My mother was at home in the living room watching television and popped up off the couch the minute she heard the blaring bass from the music being played from his red sports car.

"How you doin Ms. Jones," Steven asked while standing in the doorway. "We good?" Then he reached in his pocket for what looked to be cash and handed it to her.

"Call me Ms. Deborah baby. You can come on in," she said in a tone I was used to only hearing her take with my brother when she knew he was wrong but was ready to excuse his poor choices or inappropriate behaviors. "Gina, come on in here and see yo friend!" She stepped to the side and allowed Steven to enter. It was the first of his many visits to our home. "Yall go on in your room, I'm tryin to watch my stories!" This last statement left me completely speechless, a boy in my room? What was next, the door remaining closed, uninterrupted sex, overnight visits? So basically, as long as Steven kept her fed with cash, she was cool with us being together, regardless of the setting. I guess money can buy anything! And all this time I figured no dollar amount was large enough to compensate for releasing complete control over your teenage daughter and allowing the unforbidden to take place on a regular basis under her roof. I guess I was mistaken, I guess everyone has their price!

Later that evening after Steven left, she walked into my room unannounced. Aaaawww, the old Ms. Deborah Rochelle Jones, I was wondering when she would make her comeback. "What yall was up in here doing for over two hours? He seems like an alright boy, but you too god damn young to be having babies!" Ms. Deborah Jones exclaimed, briefly not caring about the hush money that was passed on to her.

"We was just talking...that's all," I responded in a bolder, more defensive tone than I would have normally taken with my mother. I mean I figured she was being paid to keep her hands to herself and off me. I was sure she knew better than to renege on a paid agreement. Let's face it, my mom sees, speaks and breathes green!

"Don't lie to me girl, you don't think I see how yo ass is changing around here. You don't think I see that gap between yo legs, the way you walking now? Yeah, yo ass is fucking! Maybe not today, but yo ass been fucking!"

I just stared at her in a courageous manner as if to dare her to make or say anything that would disrupt the verbal agreement between her and Steven. I was not at all surprised at what she said, I just didn't know how to respond! Yes, I've been having sex since this past summer! I mean really, does she actually need to hear me admit to her foolish logic out loud.

"How am I walking different?" I finally asked. "And what gap between my legs?"

"That gap is letting me know you done had your legs opened too many times for more than one boy! Am I lying?" She closed the door and began to walk towards me. She was accompanied by a layer of fear that attempted to overtake me but I wasn't afraid. I will no longer be the weaker species, my mother will no longer over power me, she will not Kill Regina Jones.

"I did have sex with Steven...while I was at his house, but don't worry, we used condoms." I lied. "So, nobody having no babies here." She stopped dead in her tracks, surprised at my boldness.

"Well, at least yo ass got sense enough to be fucking somebody with some damn money!" she exclaimed while deciding to turn around and head back to the door to exit. She reached the door and grabbed the door knob, "just don't be out here fucking these niggas for free! I see that necklace and those clothes and shit, so I know you ain't being stupid!" She opened the door and proceeded out. "You make sure you get what you can get out of 'em, for as long as you can, cause they damn sho ain't gonna be loyal to you and nobody else!" she left closing the door behind her.

Whatever Deborah Jones, because as usual I tuned her out! I wonder what Jason was up to? After talking to Steven for almost two hours about a check he needed me to deposit into my account tomorrow when I got out of school, well at least that's what I think he said, I can't remember, all I know is that I wanted to see Jason. While talking to Steven, I saw Jason's parents blue Caprice Classic pass by my house through the window and at that point my attention was lost. I looked at the clock radio sitting on the stand; it was 6:03p.m. I looked out the window and saw the dimly lit sky, the sun had laid itself to rest in the west completely hidden from sight to make way for the moon to make its appearance. I decided to get up and take a stroll down the street to Rachel's house before it got too late. I figured Ms. Deborah Rochel Jones wouldn't mind, after all she did receive monetary funds from Steven to keep her from committing any violent acts against me.

"Sistah...where you going?" Reba asked slurring her words to keep the saliva from escaping her mouth, while sucking her left index finger. She has been sucking that lazy, crooked finger since she was a baby! Most of the time it was when she slept or was watching television, right now she was doing neither. She was simply standing next to my room door waiting for me to exit.

"To my friend house to get something," I answered.

"Can I go?" Reba continued to suck her finger.

"No Bee, I need to hurry before it gets darker outside. I be back." I headed to the living room and as I approached the door my mom rose from the couch

"Where you think you going?" My mom asked. She first started off staring at me then slowly turned her head away from my direction and back to the television set, pretending to not care, yet awaiting a verbal response from me.

"I just need to get my notebook from Rachel to finish my homework," I lied.

"Don't be gone long, them girls got to get to bed."

"Yes ma'am." I headed out into the cold winter air toward Rachel's house, with my hands tucked away in the pockets of my coat. This Houston weather was so erratic; during the day the sun is shining with a constant chill in the air but when the sun disappears, the cold frosty temperatures set in as nighttime falls in the sky. My warm breath had turned into steam as it hit the frosty air as I hurried to my destination.

The first thing I had noticed was Jason's car parked at his house as I headed toward Rachel's cemented driveway. Oh how I wish he would come outside to play! I don't understand why I miss him so much, knowing I have Steven now, but I do! The moment I had sex with Steven for the first time at my house right before Christmas, I knew I still loved Jason.

It's almost as if all the hatred I forced myself to feel for Jason suddenly vanished with each unfulfilled stroke of Steven's penis. Steven is cool and all and I would probably love him more if Jason was never in the picture, but my love for Jason is and always will be captured in this portrait of my life as my first and my only true love.

I knocked on Rachel's door at least three times before there was an answer. "What's up girl?" Rachel asked standing in the entryway to their home. She was wearing the same cute black and white polka dot tights that showed off those killer curves that the guys go crazy over, with a black rayon top she wore to school today. The short black ankle boots she wore with the ensemble was replaced by white bobbie socks with a pink cotton ball attached to the back of each.

Rachel's less than pretty caramel colored face was covered in a green facial mask while her dark shoulder length hair was pulled up in a ponytail. Despite her imperfections, she did have great hair that Mrs. Robinson, a beautician that owned her own beauty shop, took care of. Gorgeous hair, nice clothes and a sexy body still couldn't help that acne prone face! Let's face it, there is only so much a correction mask can correct!

"Nothing," I said with my teeth chattering from the cold. "You got some notebook paper so I can do my homework.... I forgot mine at school."

"Girl yeah, come on!" I followed Rachel inside admiring the beautiful Victorian couch, loveseat and chair set in the formal living room as she closed the door. I truly adored the décor in their home. "You been good...not trying to run away anymore?" Rachel asked as she led the way down a long hallway, where the walls were covered in wallpaper that displayed trees, grass, birds flying and other wildlife.

"Run away? Who told you I ran away from home?" I asked as we entered into her pink and white princess bedroom. Rachel headed towards her white canopy bed, knelt down on her knees, and raised the pretty ruffle comforter up to reach under the bed.

"Your mama!" she replied while pulling a medium to large box filled with packs of loose-leaf paper from under the bed. "She saw me and Vanessa standing on the street talking and called us over to ask if I knew a guy that drove a red sports car last month? One time she asked if we had seen you at school that day, but that was months ago," she said handing me two packs of paper. I had to admit, Rachel was very generous when it came to her things, or at least the things she didn't care much about. School supplies were a perfect example, since her mom was a nurse at Heights Hospital and dad a high school football coach at some school in North Forest Independent School District, she just figured she would always have an endless supply of everything she needed. And why wouldn't she feel this way, she pretty much got everything she wanted.

"My mama a trip! What yall tell her?" I asked grabbing the paper. I made my way to the fury pink armchair in the far corner of her room next to the window draped in powder puff pink

lace and sheer curtains. There was an overstuffed white polar teddy bear with a pink bow tied around its neck resting in the seat of the chair. I simply pushed it to the side, thinking that if I sat the animal on the floor, its value would be lost forever.

"The truth! Hell...we didn't know where you was!" Rachel exclaimed pushing the large box back under the bed and standing up. "So, where you was at...cause you wasn't at school?"

"My friend house..."

"What friend?" Rachel nosily asked, resting her right hand on her hips. Her eyes staring at me through the now cracked mud mask on her face.

"Candace! Damn...I wasn't with no boy!"

"Candace...Candace that stay in Yorkdale?" Rachel asked puzzled.

"Yes, she took me to my granny house cause I got mad at my mama and went over there," I said partially lying. Her nosy ass did not need to know that Jason eventually came and got me and took me to my grandmother's house.

"So when you and Banky started talking?"

"Who the fuck is Banky?"

"Girl...you know...the one with the mustang that be doing all that crooked shit at the banks! Steve...yeah Steve, I know you talk to him cause I seen you with him. Wasn't he at your house today right after school?"

Damn, this nosey bitch! "We just friends...but I didn't know they called him Banky! And what crooked bank stuff you talking about?"

"Girl...I don't know exactly what he be doing out there...I just know he goes into these banks and get money....but he not robbing them with a gun or nothing like that," Rachel sat down at the white vanity looking at her face in the brightly lit mirror. She began poking various parts of her face to make sure the muddy green substance had hardened to a solid state.

"I think he have somebody in the banks that be helping him though...I don't know...I just be hearing stuff. Dammit, all these cracks!" Rachel exclaimed, continuing to rub her face in the mirror, annoyed by the crooked lines forming from the mask. "Let me go wash this shit off my face!" Rachel rushed out of the room leaving the door open. I turned to the side and pulled the curtains back to sneak a peek out of the window. I lifted the plastic white mini blind in search of some familiar scenery but complete darkness had already settled in. I guess it really didn't matter anyway, Rachel's room was in the back of her house and therefore, if I did have a view of a yard, it would be the back yard and Jason's house sits on the right side, not the backside.

Well, there was always the phone. I could call him and ask him to come out? But he's going to want to know why I'm calling. Really Gina, do you actually need a reason to give the man you love a call? I got up, closed the bedroom door and headed to Rachel's night stand where her pink oval plastic phone was located.

"Hello?" I instantly recognized the deep baritone voice, on the other side of the receiver. I instantly felt volts of excitement racing throughout my body leaving behind drops of hope and sprinkles of anticipation. I now know how Mister felt when he knew his love Suge Avery was coming home to him.

"Hey Jason."

"Who dis?" Jason asked, knowing full well it was me, Regina Denise Jones, the almost mother of your first born, the female you love to hate or the mockingbird you love to kill.

"Its me Gina." Silence. "Well...I...was just seeing what you was doin? I'm next door at Rachel house...but I'm bout to go home though" Still silence. Well...I was just seeing what you was doin...I'll talk to you later."

"Where yo crazy ass man at?" Jason asked just as I was about to lay the receiver down.

"Who?" I asked, knowing full well who he was referring too. Silence times three. "You mean Steven? He not my man...we just friends."

"That ain't what it look like to me," he responded with a dry smirk not believing a word I spoke. "Where Rachel at? She know you on the phone with me?"

"No!" Now I was annoyed. "She in the bathroom and I just wanted to call...that's all."

"I was doing something for my moms...I have to hit you back later."

"Alright," I said disappointed

"Alright then." There was a click and the dial tone soon followed. I laid the receiver down to rest on its cradle, sighing in disbelief. Not sure what I was expecting, but I definitely wasn't expecting that. Rachel walked in drying her face with a fluffy blue bath towel. Not sure what she had planned to accomplish with the mask, I just know looking at her results from the facial after the solid was removed from her face, wasn't much different from how she looked earlier!

"Girl I gotta go," I murmured as I grabbed the paper packs and headed past her out her bedroom door.

"Why you rushing off...who you was on the phone with...Banky?" Rachel asked with an inquiring mind. Nosey Bitch!

"No! I'm going home...I wasn't supposed to be gone this long. Thanks for the paper girl...your face looks good!" I lied.

"Giiirrrlll! I know Ms. Deborah be trippin! Let me let you out...oh...and thanks girl!" We headed down the hallway, in the opposite direction of her room to the front door. As we walked Rachel rambled on and on about how her big sister Stacy bought the mask at Dillard's in The Galleria. She claimed she's been using the product for a month and it cleared away her acne. "Well, see you at school tomorrow," she finally replied after six minutes of her unnecessary talking and my nodding in agreeance at the door.

The cold wintry air slapped my face as the door closed behind me. I zipped my pink hoody fleece jacket, stuffed my hands in my pockets with the paper safely tucked under my arms and proceeded down the cemented pathway that lead to the street. As I approached the end of the driveway, I felt the artic breeze seeping in through the crevices of my hoody, which made me increase my pace. It was cold!

"Hey!" The familiar baritone voice shouted from several yards away behind me just as my feet touched the street. I turned to my left and there he was standing at a distance on his well-manicured grass next to the large oak tree that was centered in the middle of his yard.

"Hey," I replied once I realized it was Jason. My teeth were chattering, I was cold!

"Come here," he asked, while standing in the shadows of the yard, adjacent from the lights mounted on the corner of the house just below the rooftop. I turned and headed his way walking through the grass to where he was standing. He looked really nice standing under the tree wearing a turquoise Charlotte Hornets windbreaker jacket, acid wash jeans and white sneakers. He was rubbing his hands together blowing the warmth of his breath into them for comfort, "So, what's up?"

"Nothing...just headed home," I replied, now standing directly in front of him with the pack of paper dangling under my arm. "How long you been standing out here? I thought you had to do something for your mama?" I asked staring down at the ground. I wanted so badly for him to reach for me and wrap me in his warm loving arms and shield me from the frosty air.

"I did it already," Jason replied watching me in a deep stare as if his life depended upon his watching my every move. "You got to go home right now? You want to sit in the car with me to warm up?" Jason asked noticing my frequent shaking.

"Okay...that's cool," I replied. What I wanted to say was HELL YEAH I WANT TO GET IN THE CAR WITH YOU! But I kept my composure. We headed to his parent's blue Caprice Classic, Jason jumped inside the backseat, I followed him inside.

"So, what's up...I saw your man down there earlier today. So, what's up, yall serious now? That fool ain't go be trippin cause you talking to me?"

"We just real cool...he like me...and I think he cool...but he not my man or nothing like that," I replied, not sure if that was a lie or not. I guess I wasn't really sure how to define the relationship Steven and I had. I know he has feelings for me, but I wasn't exactly sure of my emotional connection to him. I just knew right here right now is where I wanted to be, in the backseat of his parent's blue Caprice Classic.

"So...he won't mind if I did this?" Jason asked resting his right hand on my left knee. An electric volt sent waves throughout my body, instantly responding to his touch

"Why would he mind?" I asked taking a deep breath, trying to keep my composure. I didn't realize how much I missed his touch. Jason began to squeeze and rub my knee simultaneously--eventually working his way up my inner thigh. I wanted him, and I wanted him bad. I immediately jumped on top of him straddling my legs across his lap. I looked him square in the eyes and began to kiss him seductively. He didn't see it coming. I pressed my lips onto his, forcing him to release his tongue so they could connect, intertwine and dance within the compounds of our moisten crevices. He tasted good. Eventually, a high degree of warmth began to rise inside the vehicle causing a thin layer of fog to cover the windows. Wow, not even the cold air could stop the blazing heat sensation I was feeling at this point.

"So... you gonna give it to me like you use too?" Jason managed to utter in between kisses. He began to unzip my hoody and his hands began to aggressively travel inside my shirt, cruising over my belly, my back and now my bra that protected my breast. And before I could respond he yanked up my brasserie, exposing my breasts and stuffed the left one in his mouth and began to suck, hard. He moved to the right breast and sucked even harder. My body began to burn with intense passion, I wanted him inside of me now! He pushed me off of his lap onto the seat and immediately began to remove his pants and sneakers, so I followed his lead only undressing from the waist down. Before you know it, Jason was lying between my legs. I raised my left leg up over the back seat resting it on the head rest and my right leg on the back-shoulder rest of the driver seat for deeper insertion, I wanted to feel all of him deep into my stomach.

He then did something he's never done before, instead of his immediate insertion of his penis into my vagina, he paused and began to stare at me. Jason rubbed my cheeks with the back of his hand and kissed them sweetly, then began kissing me softly in the mouth with extreme passion while gently rubbing on my body. After about five minutes of intimacy, he slipped his fully erected manhood through the compounds of my womanhood, I cringed, he asked, "are you okay," and began to carefully stroke at a gentle pace. We made love, in the back seat of his parent's blue, four door Caprice Classic. His kisses were soft, his touch was gentle, I was in awe! My multiple explosions onto his genitals gave him life and left me lifeless. Jason's erection finally released an eruption that sent him to a shivery state of satisfaction that was accompanied with low cries and yelps. There was no collapsing onto my body, but instead Jason slowly raised up and sat in his original seat staring down at my nudity. After a long minute passed, he turned and stared out the front windshield. Another long minute passed. Then suddenly the trance was broken, he hurried and put on his clothes, bumping my hips and feet.

"Jason...what's wrong?" He said nothing. On went his jeans, his windbreaker jacket and eventually his sneakers. Still no words. And before I could sit up to gather my things to get dressed, he yanked the door latch, opened the door. He jumped out the car and slamming the car door behind him leaving me inside. I reached down on the floor for my pants and when I looked up, I saw the front door of his house close behind him. I quickly got dressed, grabbed my paper pack and ran home thinking, "somethings just won't ever change!" To Jason I will forever be the weaker species. I will forever be empowered by him; Jason's actions will always be To Kill Regina Jones.

Chapter 20

I opened the flimsily, black leather bond case that housed the Betty Boop checks that I ordered a few months ago at Texas Commerce Bank, as Steven and I headed downtown to the First City National Bank of Houston. I rubbed my fingertips over the gold calligraphy raised print that spelled out my name, Regina Jones, followed by my Rolland St. address in Acres Homes. Wow, the fine print made me look so important, my very own checks and check book! I didn't even have a job--well at least not one that required me to punch in on a time clock and work an hourly wage. The manual labor I was subjected to required my spending the bulk of my leisure time with Steven and his explaining the banking system and teaching me the art of check writing. The very next check in the book read #152, even though the count started at #101, I used the entire first book practicing how to fill them out. All I know is that Steven wanted the checks filled out perfectly, absent of any errors and he would not allow me to stop until the complete product was flawless in his eyes.

I closed the book and began to tap my perfectly manicured French tips with a single diamond in the center of each nail. They were gorgeous! I got the idea from Diana who had seen the design on a friend of her mom's one Sunday at church. So, I paid to have both of our nails done at a local popular nail salon called, Nails by Pros on Antione Dr. It felt good to always have money, I just got tired of these frequent trips to all these different banks and writing checks to cash because he needed cash out of my account. Now, the first time, which was over a week ago, I thought it was a little strange that he wanted me to write a check for $3000.00 at the Ameriway Bank on the 610 Loop Frwy, not too far from Northwest Memorial Hospital!

"But I only have a few hundred dollars in my account...that's not gonna cover that check!" I exclaimed. But he went on to explain that the lady, Mary Barron that opened my account lets him deposit money into my account without my being present.

"Don't worry sexy...I got you covered! My girl Mary be hooking me up. I just meet up with her in the morning before she get to work and tell her to put the money in yo account...shid...you got about $6000!" Steven murmured, flashing that gold tooth. "And every time you cash a check for my grandmother for me-- I will give you $500...$250 to keep and the other two fifthy to put back in your account."

"So...what about the amount for the check? And why can't we just go back to my bank where Mary work? And why do your granny have accounts at so many banks? And why we have to travel so far away...?"

"Damn baby! Yo sexy ass sho ask a lot of questions!" Steven chuckled. "I don't like that damn bank, mofo's always wanna be looking at you crazy when you come in there...like a nigga can't have no money or something, so I go far out to bank. I learned that from my granny and grandpa, they always traveled out the way to bank. And when my grandpa died, he left my granny some insurance money and she put the money away in all these places. Now, since she don't drive I have to go to the bank for her." Steven grabbed my hand and looked my way, "I really appreciate you helping me out...hell granny appreciates you! That's why I don't mind chunking money your way."

He seemed so sincere and a great guy for taking care of the people he cared for. I have hundreds of dollars at home, and would probably have more, but I shop all the time! And my spending is not limited to just the Weiner's Store on Antoine, I actually go to the mall and make several purchases from Express, Bakers and Foleys! I always buy toys and books for my sisters at Toys R Us, and Steven keeps my mother laced in cash regularly. He of course doesn't give her nearly as much as he gives me, but its more than she had before and clearly enough to keep her hands, comments and strict regulations to herself and out of my proximity.

Steven and I continued to make our way downtown on I-45 frwy in his red Mustang blasting "Boyz in the Hood" by NWA on the radio. The extreme bumping and thumping of the music sent pulsating rhythmic beats throughout my heart, pumping harmonious melodies instead of blood throughout my arteries. Instead of turning the volume controls down, he commenced to yelling over the lyrics stating he was going to get us tickets to see them in concert this summer at the Summit.

"Yeah them niggas go hard! Gotts to go see my boys!" Me, at a concert? Me at a concert to see NWA? Me at a concert with Steven to see Eazy E, Dr. Dre and my favorite Ice Cube? Oh wow! Life was good!

As we continued on to our destination, I couldn't help but reflect on the bizarre episode with Mrs. Ringold while I was at my locker yesterday, right after the bell dismissed us home. I did my best to avoid her at all costs lately in hopes to avoid the numerous questions and comments about my new clothes, new shoes, new jewelry and according to her, my new attitude. My only desire in life at that very moment was to put my books inside the small secured compartment and grab my jacket without my wise, influential role model noticing me. I grabbed the black suede jacket and tossed the Chemistry book and binder inside, then proceeded to close the door when I heard the voice of authority ask her series of questions.

"So what's this I hear about you being absent from school 11 days last month and already six days this month?" A concerned Mrs. Ringold, was hovered over me with her arms crossed expecting a response. She looked as lovely as ever in her carriage red, chenille sweater and black slacks. "So...I guess this new look is bringing about this new negative behavior...does your mom know you're not coming to school?"

"Ye—a-h," I hesitated in my response, never sure how to answer her very blunt and direct questions. "She knows...I be taking care of my sisters...they was sick," as usual I lied.

"So, your mama doesn't care that you are missing school?" She gave me that deep cut straight through my soul stare, waiting for an answer.

"I told you...my sisters were sick," I surprisingly snapped slamming the locker door.

"Well that's a lot of days...were they in the hospital or something?" Her sarcasm was annoying me. Why can't I just get to my personal belongings in peace without her third degree?

"No Mrs. Ringold, they had colds...chest colds with really bad coughs," I lied again, hoping this would be enough to get her off my back about not regularly attending school. Afterall, what did she want to hear, that I would rather hang out, shop and do the nasty with a guy I really didn't like, in exchange for monetary gifts during the day, when I should be attentive in class, constructing thesis statements, calculating algebraic expressions, or analyzing the composition and reaction of matter.

"Well, were your sisters full of cold and coughing when you were out shopping for all these fancy new clothes I've been seeing you in lately?"

"I have to go!" I began to walk off before I said or did something totally disrespectful and out of character towards someone I truly admired. She grabbed my right arm swinging me around to face her hard-concerned stare.

"Not sure what's going on with you Regina, the new clothes, bad attitude and irresponsible behavior...it's not you!" I gently pulled away from her hold, careful not to upset her but enough to let her know I didn't appreciate her assumed accusations against me. She didn't know my life and the constant hardships I faced daily. And how could she? She was a beautiful, privileged, upper middle class, middle aged white woman; she couldn't possibly understand the life of a poor urban girl with an abusive, psychotic mother whose soul purpose in life was to make mine miserable because hers had become such a letdown.

"I'm fine Mrs. Ringold ...dang! I'll talk to you later!" I walked off and headed to the bus ramp with the rest of the remaining students headed home.

"I'm here if you need me Regina!" I heard Mrs. Ringold yell as I turned the corner out of her sight. My eyes began to well with tears, I didn't mean to be disrespectful, I just needed her to get off my back trying to fish for answers to affairs that didn't concern her. The moisture in my eyes quickly dried as I jumped onto the school bus with the other students and headed home to wait for Steven to call and make arrangements for us to hang out today.

The musical notes continued to explode out of the speakers and dance around the inside of the car as Steven and I continued our ride down I-45 freeway heading south. I stared out the window watching the variety of cars in the different lanes travel alongside of us, some accelerated ahead while others fell back behind us. I continued to admire my nails as thoughts of this morning's events, after Steven picked me up from the school bus stop, started to pop up in my mind. He treated me to breakfast at Denny's, then afterwards, we went to his house to have intercourse and discuss our plans for the day before it was time to get my sisters off the school bus.

During our sexual encounter this morning, I realized that there was a clear distinction between having sex with Jason versus Steven inserting his fully erected penis into my pre-moistened vagina. Yes, the sex with Steven consisted of me making an excuse to go to the bathroom right before the act and inserting the KY jelly I purchased at Walgreens into my vaginal hole for instant lubrication. I actually got the idea from Freddy one morning during breakfast at school. I had told Diana about my dilemma and she didn't know what to do to alleviate the problem. So, we made up a story saying one of Diana's older cousins from Louisiana had vaginal dryness before sex with her husband.

"You better tell yo cousin to get some KY jelly at the store...I heard that shit works wonders on a dry pussy!" Freddy exclaimed laughing in his extremely flamboyant tone! So, bye bye desert and hello rain forest!

However, with Jason, the excess fluids just seem to flood the scenery upon contact, especially last month in the back seat of his car. It was the last time I saw him. It was the last time I was able to experience multiple orgasms for the first time in the history of our sex-capades. It was the last time I received intense simulations that aroused immediately after our genitals connected. It was the last time I heard from him.

Steven pulled up to a parking meter directly in front of the First City Towers on Fannin Street in downtown Houston after circling the block twice. The streets were flooded with cars heading in the same direction. Individuals of importance wearing power suits and carrying brief cases, had crowded the sidewalks and walk ways.

"Alright sexy...just go in and look for a black chic named Joanne...she told my grandma this morning when she called her that she gonna be working the last window...so make sure you go to her line...Ima wait out here," Steven murmured as he put the car in neutral and out of gear.

"Okay...be back!" I jumped out of the vehicle and headed into the black glass tower building. Brrrrr, I guess all the assumptions and sayings were right, it was much colder and windier downtown! I hurried through the crowd of white-collar workers, hustling and bustling to get to their desired destination. I stepped up to the revolving door and waited for an opening to slip in and out through. The inside of the building was beautiful! Gorgeous artificial plants paved the dark marble walk- way leading to the front entrance of the bank. The enormous financial institution was filled with table counters, velvet ropes and a long row of bank teller windows to service all their customers downstairs. Then there was the upper level loft area that housed all the executive desks and most of the bank employees wearing dark suits.

I quickly located the single black female teller window at the end of the row, which wasn't hard since she was only one of two African American females occupying one of the glass protected compartments. The other lady of color was located in the second booth on the opposite end. I headed towards the middle of the red velvet ropes and stood in the man-made line to wait my turn. The line moved swiftly and before you know it, I was next in line to be served.

"Next please!" yelled teller number four, a middle-aged Caucasian lady with frizzy, curly, brownish blonde hair. Well, since I had to wait for Joanne to assist me, I did my usually, "oh shoot... I'm not ready, ma'am or sir... you can go ahead of me," until the designated teller was available. If it were up to me, I would simply go to the next available, but Steven insisted that I go to the teller his grandmother specifically contacted prior to our visit. So, after the fourth person I allowed to pass, Ms. Joanne called me to her booth to complete my transaction.

"Hello," I spoke cheerfully as I slid her the pre-written personal check for $5000 under the window. I was immensely surprised at the large amount when I filled out the check, but Steven said his grandmother needed the cash to pay for her hip surgery. I didn't realize she had a bad hip, but he promised me $300 for taking care of his granny for him.

"Hello," said Joann. For whatever reason, she seemed nervous and would never make eye contact with me. "How would you like the cash...in large bills, small, or a combination of both?"

"I guess you can do both," I shrugged. No one ever asked me how I would like the funds distributed. I definitely didn't care, since hardly any of it was mine. The mocha colored, pleasantly plump young woman pulled out a book of cash and began to count me out $3000 in $100s, $50s, and $20 dollar bills.

"Is there anything else I can help you with?" Joanne asked.

"No," I replied as I stuffed the cash into my purse. "Have a good day!" I waved and headed towards the exit that lead back to the busy streets of downtown Houston.

Chapter 21

The black two door Toyota truck was sitting in the driveway in front of my house again. My mom's much younger, pedophile friend, was occupying space once again at our home. I hadn't seen him in awhile or at least since right before Valentine's Day. He just sort of disappeared from my mom's life and our home. I don't recall hearing the typical arguments, cursing out or threatening the other individual with a weapon. He just simply became a complete no show the latter part of January or early February. I was glad! I was tired of his constant inappropriate behaviors towards me when my mother's back was turned.

It was still a little early when Steven dropped me off with my $300. He said he needed to take his grandmother the cash and would try to come back later or if nothing else call me later on tonight like he usually does.

I entered into the house and there he was resting his medium build, high yellow body on the couch watching the show "Good Times" on the television set with his shoes off. My mother was apparently at the stove preparing a meal fit for a king because the aroma stemming from the kitchen was a combination of fried chicken, cheesy pasta and a chocolatey sweet. While the strong scent of a five-course meal filled one of my nostrils, the fresh smell of pine filled the other. A clean house, good food, and great sex was Ms. Deborah Rochelle Jones' three-way strategy for acquiring guaranteed funds from her victims. But I guess any unexpected fool would lack sound judgment if and when they are lying in bed comfy cozy, with a full belly and they are thinking with the wrong head! I'm sure no man is capable of being rational when all of the blood in their body has suddenly rushed to their groins.

"How you doin' Miz Lady? I haven't seen you in minute." My mom's friend looked up at me from the television set.

"I'm good." I continued to walk towards my room, not interested in entertaining any extra conversation he was trying to bring my way.

"Life must be treatin' you good...." Was the last thing I heard him say before I turned the corner into the hallway and headed straight to my bedroom. I immediately closed the door behind me without responding, thinking-- *why in the hell are you talking to me as if we were long loss comrades.*

I sat on the bed, sneaked a peak at the clock and let out a deep sigh, it was only

2:33 pm! I still had a whole hour left before the girls were released from the school bus. I was rather hoping I had the house to myself; my plans were to sit in the living room so I could keep watch out the window at Jason's house to see what time he made it home from school. Lately, because of my frequent absences at school, I never see him, unless I catch him when he first arrives at home.

I didn't bother turning on the lights in my bedroom, the luminating ultra violet rays from the sun shined through the sheer cream-colored window coverings. I kicked off my bright white leather Keds tennis shoes and took off my pale pink denim jacket I bought from The Gap to lay in my bed; leaving on my matching pink, denim skirt, socks and white t-shirt. Lately, for whatever reason I am always so tired and in desperate need of a nap when I get home.

I lay there in bed wrapped in my favorite patchwork blanket thinking about Jason, when suddenly a hard knock accompanied by an immediate intrusion into my bedroom broke me out of my pre-nap trance.

"Regina!" I heard my mother yell my name as my bedroom door swung open. "Regina!" she yelled walking inside flipping on the light switch. I couldn't help but notice how nice she looked this early Spring afternoon. Her hair was in short curls with chocolate highlights glowing as the light from the ceiling fixture hit each curly brown streak. She wore a nice black knee length cotton dress and black jelly sandals that I've seen her wear on several occasions. Her face was beautified with ebony liquid foundation to enhance her deep complexion, which had given her the image of perfect smooth skin. Her lips were distinctly traced with black liner and filled with matted dark plum lipstick. I also couldn't help but notice the glistening from her legs from the over use of baby oil. I guess she was making sure her man was happy, nothing like a glammed-up appearance to set the tone for a blissful evening of sex!

"Yes," I answered sluggishly and annoyed at being interrupted from my nap and possible dream sequence about Jason.

"Mama about to go to the store...I need you to get up in 'bout 20 minutes and check on my cake in the oven," she responded in such a delightful whimsical tone that if I wasn't looking directly at her I would have sworn she was someone else's mother!

"Okay," I responded dryly, not wanting the responsibility of making sure her baked goods were perfectly cooked.

"What's wrong with you?" Deborah Jones asked in a sassy tone placing her right hand on her hip.

"Nothin...just tired." I responded laying my head back down on the fluffy pillow. Go away! Was my every wish at that moment.

"Yo ass sho been tired an sleeping a lot lately! You sho you not pregnant?" She walked all the way inside my room and closed the door behind her so not to be heard by her male company.

Pregnant! Hell no! Why would she think I was pregnant?

"I like ole Steven...you need to be with a good man with some money...that don't mind handing it out!" my mom chuckled amused yet serious about her statement. "I always tell you to make sure you get a man with some money! Don't be fucking no man fo free!"

"I'm not pregnant mama...I just wanted to take a nap before I got the girls off the bus...that's all," I murmured. I just wanted her to leave me alone damn! If your plans were to go to the store, then please be about your way!

She walked over and sat on the corner foot of my bed placing her hand on my resting left foot, as if holding my hand was off limits or not an option. "Look baby, mama just don't want you to be out here getting caught up with some no-good ass nigga that ain't got shit!" Even though her tone seemed somewhat sincere, her dialogue was simply ridiculous! Why would a mother, a guardian, a protector, the keeper of the family, encourage her young to participate in sexual activity and adjust to the consequences of premature parenting, for financial gain?

"I know mama," I finally murmured. I just wanted her to go away! I guess she heard my thoughts because she suddenly popped up off the bed and headed towards the door.

"Well I can see you in one of yo moods...so Ima go...hell I got a man to tend to! So, if you know like I know...you better be tending to your man too...specially if you want to keep him and that cash flowing!" Ms. Deborah Rochelle Jones walked towards the door and grabbed the knob. She turned around before leaving out, "you hear what I say girl?" My mother paused before turning the knob, not sure if she was waiting for me to respond and of course I didn't. "Make sure you watch my cake!" she left and closed the door. Finely!

I lay my head back down on the pillow desperately in search of the level of comfort I was in before my interruption. No matter how I tossed and turned and shimmed down into the mattress I was still unable to relax thinking about my mother and her ridiculous accusations and statements. How dare she assume I was pregnant? I don't even have child bearing symptoms. I actually feel fine, I'm just a little sleepy, most days. Suddenly, I sprang up from the pillow with my eyes fixated on a large chip in the egg white paint in the wall that revealed small pieces of sheetrock chalk. I actually bumped it with my dresser a few years ago while changing my room around and since it was never repaired, it just seemed to chip away more and more, little by little as the years went by. As I stared, I realized I haven't had a period in a while! As silly as this sounds, I guess its easy to lose track of my cycle since it's so irregular. I do remember having a period a couple weeks after I returned home from that short stay with Steven back in January. Its already the end of March now and with all of the bank visits, check writing, ditching school, and shopping, I've been too busy to even think about a menstrual cycle. To be perfectly honest I didn't give my period much thought in the past, it dropped in for a visit out of nowhere once a month and stayed the week! Just like an annoying distant family member that comes into town unexpectedly and camps out at your home, you tolerate the inconvenience until it's time for their departure.

Just as I was about to get up and check the wall calendar for more clues to my mysteriously missing menstrual cycle, I heard light tapping on my bedroom door. I didn't answer, wasn't my mother and her friend gone to the store? There was another knock that followed the door actually opening and my mom's friend slowly peaks in.

"Hey," he murmured in a loud whisper as he entered into my bedroom without permission. He took one last look out the door before closing it behind him. "How you been feeling, lil miss lady?" he asked as he walked towards my bed.

"What the fuck! Why are you in my room? What' chu want? Weh my mama at? I thought yall left and went to the store?" I moved quickly to the opposite side of the bed hoping I could leap up and make a mad dash to the door. Why in the hell was this man in my room...again!

"Shhhhh...calm down," he said waving his hands in front of him gesturing for me to calm down. "I just wanted to talk to you...I sent your moms to the store to get some beer and bread...I just wanted to talk to you for a minute while she was gone," he added in an extremely soothing tone in hopes to keep me aloof. It didn't work, I wanted him out, NOW!

"You need to get the fuck out of my room! I'm good and don't need you checking up on me!"

"Well you do look good! Yo moms tells me you got a man now.... you like him? You love him?"

"That ain't yo damn business!" I exclaimed, wondering why he was so concerned with my relationship status. "Why do you keep coming to me like this? You know my mama be trippin! I don't have time to be getting into it with her...behind her man!" I was hysterically pissed at this point. It didn't matter that the relationship with my mom and me was secure due to her being financially compensated by Steven on a regular basis. The simple fact remains, he does not belong in my room attempting to seduce me behind my mother's back! What a sick twisted individual!

"Just relax lil lady! I'll leave you alone...I...I just like you and thought we was cool! Thought we had a connection or something," he said while grabbing the crouch of his pants, smirking and grinning simultaneously.

"Fool, I don't know you! I don't even like you! You belong to my mama! So, you need to take yo ass back in the other room and wait for her in there!"

"You mean...we can't be friends?" He starred slyly at me caressing the outer zipper area of his pants. As if his actions were going to change my mind about his being in my room.

"Fuck no! I don't need no more friends! Especially not an old pervert like you! Go be friends with my mama...she's the only friend you need at this house!" I darted out of the bed towards my shoes and jacket lying on the floor. "You one twisted motha fucka!" I yelled while lacing up my Keds. "I suggest you leave me the fuck alone...cause trust me...my boyfriend don't play!" I grabbed my jacket and rushed out of the room leaving him with a hard on! I headed out the door and decided to go to the bus stop early and wait for the girls' bus to come. I slammed the front door leaving behind a warm bed, a horny child molester and unnecessary frustration! Of course, this only happens in the world of Regina Denise Jones.

DAMN! Was all I could think as I stood in my front yard gazing at the dark cloud formation in the sky. Rain! Wow! The last thing I needed right now was a mid-day out door shower. I searched the time on my watch, I still had at least 20 minutes before the school bus pulled up for me to collect the girls, but I don't think God was going to give me 20 minutes of dry time. The sky had fallen into an emotional state of mind and was preparing itself to shed a few thousand tears. Hopefully the cry will happen more later than sooner.

It was too early to stand on the corner of the main street at the bus stop, but I was definitely not staying here for the pervert to reappear! I decided to go to Rachel's house and see if she was home. Since I didn't attend class today, I didn't know when, who or where my school mates were. I headed up the street with my eyes on Jason's house, he wasn't home of course, which was ideal because I was even too upset to see him! I just didn't understand what could possibly possess my mother's man to think there could ever be anything between us!

"Rachel not here right now," yelled Rachel's mom, Mrs. Peggy through the door without even bothering to open it at my arrival. She wasn't the most socially driven individual; plus, her solemn demeanor and total lack of common courtesy for me as a person was adding fuel to the fire that was ignited earlier in my bedroom. "She still at school baby...come back later."

"Yes ma'am." I turned around and stood there for a few minutes, I needed additional time to determine my next move since plan A was a no-go. Where can I go to wait for my sister's bus and steer clear of the rain that was soon to be falling. I looked to the left at Jason's parents cream colored brick house with dark midnight blue shutters attached to each window; the driveway was still absent of the blue Caprice Classic Jason drove. I looked ahead at the brick homes across the street and began to slowly head in that direction. I needed to buy some time; I had no intentions of going back to that house to be alone with that sexual maniac! As I moved down the road at a glacier pace, aggressively kicking loose gravel, I became more and more annoyed with time for deciding to stand still at a time like this! Then suddenly the black truck turn onto Rolland Street, with the driver purposely hitting a large pot hole on the corner. It speedily made its way down the street and stopped abruptly before turning into my driveway. Great, my mother was back from the store!

I quickly increased my pace in hopes to make it to my mom before she entered into the house. When she hopped out of the truck, she leaned back in and grabbed a brown paper bag with the plastic ruffles from the top of a loaf of bread sticking out. "Mama!" I yelled as she slammed the truck door. She didn't hear me. "Mama!" I yelled waving my hand as she turned in my direction. I ran the rest of the way to her.

"I thought you was laying down?" she asked heading towards the house.

"I was..." I began to say while bending over trying to catch my breath once I reached my destination. I stood up straight and took one final deep breath so I could begin my dialogue about her man and his tacky antics while she was gone. "I was laying down, but I hurried up and left out the house...." Suddenly, the front door opened and out walked her boytoy.

"Deborah...what took you so long? I need to go!" He exclaimed heading towards the truck before I could finish tattling on him.

"What you mean you leaving? Why you have to leave? I cooked!" Deborah had become instantly annoyed.

"I just got off the phone with my dad...he need me to ride to the country with him...my bad...I forgot." He held out his hands for the keys. A reluctant Deborah slowly handed over the jingling ring that connected the small metals instruments.

"Mama, this nigga ain't got to be nowhere...he just tryin to hurry up and leave before you go off on him!" The angry words flew out into the soring air.

"Go off fo what?" Deborah Jones was confused. "What the fuck is going on?"

"Ain't nothin going on...I just need to go!" He grabbed the keys heading towards the truck. "Yo daughter trippin...you need to get her fass ass in check! Every time I come over here, she checking me out! I ain't no damn sex offender!"

"You a damn lie! Nigga every time you come here...and I'm here...you come on to me!" I was pissed beyond the point of return!

How dare he lie on me before I could tell the truth about him! "Mama...I was in my bed trying to go to sleep and he came in my room trying to see what I would do!"

"What!" my mom yelled! "Why the hell you checking my man out? Ain't yo hot ass got a man!" she yelled while following her man to his truck. "Baby wait!" She dropped the bag of food grabbing his arm. "Wait...don't leave!" My mother jumped in front of the door preventing him from pulling open the latch.

"Don't leave!" I repeated her statement first in my head then out loud as if I mistakenly heard wrong. "What you mean...don't leave? Mama...this nigga is a liar and a damn pervert! He don't want you...he been after me since the first time he came over!"

"Fuck you mean he don't want me!" She took her main focus off him and gave me that stare of fury that I unfortunately had the displeasure of witnessing several times just in the past year!

"You think I'm stupid? I see how yo hot ass be prancing around here trying to get my man's attention! Introducing your body to him...letting him know that young pussy of yours is hot and ready!"

"Introducing my body to him? Hell does that mean? I don't wont yo old sorry man! While you sitting here taking up for him...he keep coming on to me!" I yelled, with no intentions of bowing down to her this time! Enough is enough!

"Don't you be cussing at me Goddamit! Who the fuck you think you talking too?" She turned to head my way fuming in anger.

"Wait a minute baby...just calm down," her friend grabbed her arm to hold her back.

"Ain't no wait a minute! She not fins to be disrespecting me and trying to take my man too! Hell naw!" she snatched away from him heading directly for me.

"You know what...FUCK you and that sorry ass man! Damn shame a woman got to be this damn hard up for some dick and act like this!" I yelled and turned to go in the house. I ran off towards the door with my head about to explode because it was so full of anger! She was yelling curse words while he held her in his tight grasp. When I turned the knob and pushed the door open a thin layer of black smoke slapped me in the face. The cake!! I rushed into the kitchen where the bulk of the smoke was floating around to the tops of the ceiling. I grabbed the only visible cloth in sight and pulled open the oven door, the thick black smoke forced its way out covering everything in sight. I reached in the hot compartment and pulled out the completely scorched baked good! I place the hot pan in the sink to cool off and made my way to the back door to open it and allow the kitchen to breath in some clean fresh air and blow out the filthy mixture of gasses and vapors it just recently collected.

"What the fuck!" I heard my mother exclaim as she made her way through the front entrance of the house. I took off to my room to get me some things including money, I wasn't staying here! I have cash, I don't have to take this shit! I will no longer be the weaker species, so Ms. Deborah Jones can empower me.

I flipped on the light switch and grabbed my blue duffle bag out of the closet. I could hear the faint sound of a large school bus pulling up, followed by the laughter of kids as I began to fill the bag with clothes, shoes and underwear. Damn, Reba and Rene were home. I didn't want them to have to witness my mother and I fighting and me leaving again! I quickly filled the bag and reached under my mattress for all the money I had stashed, which was several hundreds of dollars. I decided to run to the bathroom while my mom and her friend were still in the kitchen. I planned to escape out the bathroom window. I looked out into the still smoke-filled hallway coughing a little, it was all clear. I took off towards the bathroom and went inside and just as I was about to close the door behind me, there was a force pushing me back inside. Deborah Jones made her way into the bathroom locking the door behind her. I stepped back several steps until the back of my knee bumped the toilet and I fell back on the toilet-- seated upright.

"So yo ass grown now? Yo hot ass finally got caught in yo shit...now you wanna leave?" she headed towards me with her right hand in a fist swinging and throwing hard punches to my head once she was directly over me. "Yo ass ain't going no fuckin where! I run you!" I was silent and fear was attempting to take over, but I was bold and wouldn't allow it. There was a sudden banging on the door and I could hear the doorknob being switched back and forth because it was previously secured by Ms. Deborah Rochelle Jones. Protecting my head and face from her constant blows, I just simply starred down at the base of the dingy tub where the caulk glue connected it to the white linoleum floor. "Since yo ass wanna to be a woman and fuck with other people man...I'm gonna whoop yo ass like the woman you think you are!" she continued to yell and punch me while ignoring the forceful strikes to the door.

"Deb! Deborah!! Open the door! Open it now!" Her friend sounded as if he was going to break the door down to get inside.

"I run yo ass...you hear me girl! I run you!" my mom exclaimed as she paused from passing licks.

"No!" I screamed.

"The fuck you say? I said I run you!" She punched the right side of my temple near my ear. "I said I run you! You hear me!" she asked again clearly expecting a different response.

"No! I run me! Not you!" This time I yelled back looking her square in the eye. She looked back contemplating her next move since my response was unexpected. The door suddenly came open and her friend bust through. I pushed my mom back towards the tub hard, not realizing my own strength, and grabbed my bag. "I run me!" I yelled looking back at her trying to catch her balance to keep from falling in the tub. She didn't fall, thank God! She was able to evenly distribute her weight and remain upright and steady. I left before she could utter another word to me thinking to myself, she will no longer kill Regina Jones.

I could hear the girls barging in the front door, so I headed to the kitchen and out the back door. They didn't need to witness another episode of the mother daughter chronicles of violence. The rain was starting to come down, so I stuffed my purse and cash in my bag and draped the strap on my shoulder. I took off running outside through the heavy showers to our neighbor's house to call me a yellow cab and arrange to have them take me to the Baron Motel on West Montgomery Rd. Steven has taken me there several times--always stating they never bother him about a driver's license, he simply pays cash each time he visits. I will stay there the night and in the morning call Steven to let him know where I am. I would call tonight, but, well, I really just didn't want to be bothered with him especially since our every encounter has to involve sex or running errands for his grandmother! But I guess it's a small price to pay when a girl like me needs to get paid.

Chapter 22

Three days passed and I was still at the Baron Motel. I'm sure it didn't offer the same luxuries as the Hilton Hotel, or the comforts of the Holiday Inn, but it had to be sufficient for now because my funds were quickly running extremely low! The day I checked in I paid the taxi driver $28, the fare was actually $22, but I asked him to stop at a restaurant in the hood called Fish King so I could get a three-piece fish dinner with fries, I was hungry! When I arrived at the motel, the female Pakistani clerk at the counter charged me a deposit of $100 for incidentals--what the hell was an incidental? She claims I will get it back when I checked out. The room itself was $70 a night, which was hi-way robbery since the queen size bed had a dingy blanket and sheets, a broken antenna on the 19-inch box television set, which made the channel selection limited, and a flashing white vacancy light that shined through the window keeping me up all night!

I also spent at least $20 a day on food walking across the street to a small food store owned by an Asian family called Olano's. I was limited to buying summer sausage, crackers, cheese, chips, cookies and more sodas, since it was the only store in the area and I didn't have a stove to cook regular meals on.

Yesterday I rode the Metro bus downtown to Woolworth to purchase toothpaste, deodorant and other toiletries, that I didn't have an opportunity to pack before leaving home. As a matter of fact, I didn't pack underwear, socks or matching sets of anything. On the bus ride from downtown, I ended up stopping at Northline Mall and bought two outfits from Lerner's Department Store then I walked over to my favorite BBQ restaurant, Hunger Farmers and got a large chopped beef baked potato and large coke to take back to the room. That entire trip cost me $138.

I called Steven the second day of my arrival but got no answer until late that afternoon, his grandmother responded after the third ring saying Steven hadn't been there since

yesterday, but she will let him know I called. Therefore, no one knew of my whereabouts; not even Diana received a call from me since I've been gone. I know I will eventually contact my best friend; I just didn't want to talk to anyone. I guess I just needed some time to myself to think about everything, because I definitely didn't want to go back home--ever! At some point the unhealthy cycle of violence, distrust and accusations had to be broken. There was no amount of money or apologies that would tempt me to return to Ms. Deborah Jones' house on Rolland Street. I have money--I can make it on my own!

I decided to call Steven from the motel room phone again to see if he could come get me or bring me money—mullah--that all mighty dollar! I needed Steven's help to keep me free and independent of my mother, but I continued to get no response from the other end of the phone line. I was tempted to call Southwestern

Bell and ask the operator if the lines were down in the area or any interrupted services, I needed to be aware of, but I simply just had to face the fact he wasn't home and unreachable.

Feeling defeated, I decided to pick up a novel I checked out of the large public library downtown the other day off the nightstand to read. The title read, *Their Eyes were Watching God*, by Zora Neale Hurston. Ordinarily I would stray away from reading spiritual books but two things caught my attention about the paperback read. First off, I recognized the author's name, Hurston, she was a writer during the Harlem Renaissance era with a very interesting, very unique first name, Zora, how exotic. But it was the illustrations on the cover of the book that piqued my interest the most. It was a young girl lying in a field of grass looking up into the heavens as if she was waiting on God. Waiting to be rescued from the world of never-ending heart breaks, let downs and turmoil, and I could definitely relate to that. My 16-year life span has been one let down after the next.

I continued to read throughout the evening, deciphering through the intense dialect the author uses when the characters were dialoguing. And how ironic, the story was about a young girl Janie, her time spent under the pear tree which was really symbolic for her longing to be loved, but instead she was forced into an arranged marriage at a very young age to an elderly man named Logan Killicks. All because her grandmother wanted to make sure she was taken care of after she passes away, since Janie's parents abandoned her at an early age. I can't say that I blame Janie for wanting to be loved, even if it was with a young grungy poor field worker like Johnny Taylor.

Night began to fall as I continued to read about Janie's second marriage, the town of Eatonville and wondering when this Teacake fellow would eventually surface. While reading, I decided to turn on the ten o'clock news after the television drama "Dynasty" went off.

I usually don't watch the news at night, but since I've been away from home for several days, I figured the logical thing would be for me to stay informed. Dave Ward, the head newscaster began the segment with breaking news out of Southwest Houston. Apparently four-armed and dangerous Black men were apprehended for attempting to rob the Washington Mutual Bank in Bellaire, Texas. I released my book ignoring the dull thud noise it made as it hit the floor. I raised upright in the less than comfortable bed and had to blink several times--rubbing my eyes to make sure they were correctly focused and I was not imagining seeing on the nightly news segment, the images of the four suspects displayed side by side on the television screen. Suspect number two

was definitely my Steven and number three was his cousin Eric! The other two guys were unfamiliar to me, and although the picture of Eric seemed a little foreign because I hadn't seen him in a while, the mug shot of Steven was definitely a match. Dave went on to report that the men were charged with aggravated robbery and aggravated assault with a deadly weapon after beating up the security guard in the building during the robbery attempt. I ran to the phone to dial his number, there was still no answer! I dropped my head back down on the pillow and my body went lifeless, what was I going to do about money now!

After tossing and turning most of the night worried about Steven and the criminal charges that were brought up against him, I got up the next morning in a very drowsy state of being. I didn't know what to do. I sort of felt terrible after realizing my initial thoughts about his incarceration was--*how am I going to survive without him supplying me with daily funds.* However, I needed money and decided to go cash a check for at least $500, I figured that should hold me for at least a week. I had a mere $52 left in my purse and since Steven wasn't here to provide, I needed to take action into my own hands. I know he told me I should never cash a check without him because I was under age and needed one of his friends working in the financial institution to complete my transaction, but I needed money now! Plus, I saw a young teenage girl writing a check at the store and she said as long as you have an identification, you can write a check anywhere that accepts them. And since I had plenty of cash in the bank, thanks to Steven, I will just write and cash one there.

I got dressed and headed out to the bus stop, bypassing a dirty male crack head staggering out of the motel parking lot to cross the street in pursuit of more street drugs! After waiting several minutes for the Metro bus to pull up, I entered, paid the fare and patiently waited for the bus to reach my destination as it took off down the street. Luckily the route wasn't too long because I sat behind a woman and her two children, one child was a preschooler sitting quietly in her seat scribbling in a coloring book with crayons. The other was an infant the lady held in her arms who reeked of puke and poop! I now see why it was the last empty seat on the only means of public transportation in Houston.

After about six stops, I hopped off the Metro bus at my designated stop, which was directly across the street from Texas Commerce Bank on N. Shepard Dr. I made my way across the busy intersection after the bus pulled off and the traffic subsided and hurried to the building's entrance. And just like a few months ago when I initially opened the account, I headed to the line and waited patiently for a teller to assist me with my transaction. I neared the front of the line looking for the familiar face but didn't see Ms. Barron anywhere, I guess she had the day off.

"Next please!" yelled the young blonde teller behind her assigned counter space. "How may I help you today?" the young lady asked as I approached the counter. Her name badge pinned to her purple rayon blouse read Pilar, and I thought what an interesting name.

"Yeah...I need to cash a check," I replied opening my purse and pulling out the prewritten personal check and my identification and placing the two on the wooden surface. "How do you pronounce your name I asked as she grabbed the items and began to tap the keys on the IBM computer keyboard.

"Oh...its Pee-l-are," she responded, more focused on the transaction than the conversation. "But don't feel bad, sometimes people call me pillow!" she chuckled still tapping the key board. I quietly laughed as I waited for her to release the cash to me. But she continued to type, and type, and type some more. I looked at the clock on the wall, the bus was coming in less than ten minutes, she needs to hurry up because I need to go!

"Wait here a minute ma'am," said Pilar as she stood up and walked over to an older male employee wearing a grey suit holding my check and ID. They began talking amongst one another for several minutes then walked off in the opposite direction through a door and closed it behind them. I looked at the clock on the wall again, my bus was scheduled to be there in five minutes and the teller girl disappeared behind a closed door with my check! I began to lean on the counter with my face in hand annoyed!

"Excuse me ma'am," said a male voice from behind. I jumped, I stood up straight and turned around to face the unfamiliar Black man who was accompanied by a security guard. Not only did their sudden appearance directly behind me without warning slightly startle me, but it also brought me into an instant state of confusion. "Can you follow me to the back offices to discuss an issue we are having with your account"

"What problem...I got to go catch my bus," I replied looking again at the clock on the wall. I only had one or two minutes before the Metro bus arrives!

"It will only take a few minutes ma'am. Please follow me." I reluctantly followed the short, stubby bald African American man wearing a red polo shirt with the bank's logo, khaki pants and penny loafers.

"Where did the white lady go...she got my check...did she say I'm too young to cash a check? Cause a girl at the store told me I could," I said following the bank employee to the private offices in back while the security guard walked directly behind me in close range. We passed Ms. Barron's office on the way but there was another individual occupying the room. "Where is Ms. Barron?" I asked, but no matter what I said or asked, neither gentlemen responded to my questions or statements. They just continued to lead me to an unoccupied room at the end of the hall. The room was very plain with an empty metal desk in the corner, an office chair and two simple iron guest chairs with beige vinyl cushions on the back of the seat.

"Have a seat here," said the bald guy instructing me to sit in one of the vinyl chairs. I sat. "I'll be right back," he said while walking out the room and closing the door behind him.

"Why do I have to sit in here?" I asked as the door closed. No answer. Wow I thought, all of this because I wanted to cash a check? I guess everything Steven said was true, they be tripping at this bank!

Swiftly and abruptly the door swung open and in rushed two HPD officers. "Regina Jones, you are under arrest for bank fraud and illegal check fraud. You have the right to remain silent..." recited one of the officers, as he grabbed me out of the chair, swung me around, then inappropriately frisked my entire body.

"Arrest...for what? I just came in to cash a check!" I yelled as I attempted to jerk away and resist arrest. It was no use; they had a tight grip on me and weren't letting go! The next thing I knew I was on my way downtown to be booked.

Then began a series of events that started with a guard taking all my possessions and placing them in multiple large yellow envelopes. Then I was pushed to the next section where I received a thorough body check from a female guard. She used rubber gloves to search the very insides of my butte, vagina and underneath my breast, I cried the entire time not understanding why I was there and the reason for my arrest.

"I didn't do anything...why are you doing this to me?" I sobbed. After I was instructed to put back on my street clothes, another guard took me to a room to have my blood drawn and a urine sample collected. Finally, just before I made it to a jail cell or shall I say pushed into solitary confinement, one of the officers attached several wristbands on the lower part of my arm, a yellow, an orange and a white. I reluctantly entered the small room with the steel doors slamming shut behind me and continued to cry an intense sob begging for one of the female jailers to let me call home, because for the first time ever--I wanted my mama.

"Bitch...go sit you ass down and shut up! You ain't goin nowhere...no time soon!" was the last words the overweight female guard yelled to me before turning to go back and sit at her desk. "That crazy ass girl thankin she go use da phone, she betta sit ass down on one of those bunkies! Ass shouldna been out there breakin the damn law!" I overheard her tell her co-workers as she was writing on the clipboard. I sat on the hard lumpy, bottom bunkbed and continued to sob. Even though the cell was equipped to house two or more inmates, I was the only one there. I slowly lay down on the extra firm pillow and put my entire body upon the bed. Even though the dark grey blanket I lay on was rough and filled my nostrils with questionable foul odors, my every thought was still on my unknown reasons for being incarcerated, I began to cry even harder eventually dozing off.

I dreamt that Jason and I were walking on Galveston Beach holding hands, laughing playing, and engaging in intimate talks about our lives together in love. The sun was beginning to set and we found a quiet spot away from the general public and sat down in the warm sand to watch the sun disappear into the horizon. He looked at me and leaned over to kiss me gently on the lips. He put his muscular arm around me and pulled me in close and looked me in the eyes saying my name repeatedly, "Regina Jones...Regina Jones...Regina Jones!"

I jumped out of my dream and back into the nightmare of being in jail. "Regina Jones!" yelled the guard at the high security steel bar cell door.

"Yes!" I responded rising up off the bunk. There was a very petite Caucasian female sprawled out on the cell block floor asleep. She lay there directly in front of the half toilet, half water fountain attached to the far wall of the cell. She had on a very short dirty red dress that was slightly lifted above her waist, unknowingly revealing to me and anyone that passed by that she had on no underwear.

"Let's go, they are ready to transport you to the county." The jailer unlocked the steel bar door and opened it to allow me to exit, then quickly handcuffed me from behind.

"Where am I going?" I asked as I crossed the threshold to the other side of the cell.

"Because of the severity of your charges, you're going to the county jail, that's why you have on a white band," the middle age officer spoke with authority.

"Can I call home?" I asked afraid of the unknown.

"Your parents will be notified once you get to Harris County Precinct two. All juvenile's parents have to be notified, which is why you have on the orange band," she replied as we walked down the long hallway towards an iron door.

"So why do I have on the yellow band too?"

"Because of your pregnancy you have to be labeled for medical safety and treatments."

"Pregnant! I'm not pregnant!" I yelled.

"That's not according to your lab work," the officer replied with a sigh as we continued to walk the long stretch. *Me pregnant? Again? Me in jail?* Were among my many thoughts running loose in my head.

Once outside the door I was handed off to a sheriff wearing a cowboy hat. He escorted me outside to a white Precinct two police car and placed me in the backseat; then we were off. I tried asking him questions only to be ignored and was eventually told to be quiet. The ride was very short, less than 15 minutes and I cried the entire time. When we reached the Harris County Jail, I was placed in a holding tank and stayed there for several hours.

"Regina Jones!" once again my name was called.

"Yes...that's me," jumping up off the floor rushing to the guard.

"Your mother and grandmother are here to get you." The doors were once again opened and once again I was led down a hall. This time instead being released to another officer, my mother and grandmother stood up as they watched the guard buzz the door so I could exit. Not only did my grandmother grab me, but my mother also embraced me in her arms with tears of relief that her oldest daughter was finally safe in her presence--in one peace.

Chapter 23

Returning home from my days of living independently in the hotel seemed a little odd at first. Consequently, my mother and grandmother reported my disappearance to the Houston Police Department, the very next day of my departure. Apparently, Steven came over that afternoon looking for me because I hadn't called him or answered any of his phone calls. My mom just assumed I was with him and when she realized I wasn't and none of my friends could give her or the police any leads to my whereabouts, a missing person's report was filed. Therefore, all the neighbors on the street knew I was gone!

Two days after my return I put on a light jacket, stuffed a $5 bill in my pocket and started walking, not sure where I was going, I just knew I needed to get some air and get my thoughts together. As I strolled down Rolland Street, I could feel the neighbors stares' and faint chattering about me and their assumptions about where I could have been all this time. They were like the porch sitters in the book, *Their Eyes were Watching God*, when Janie returned home from her rendezvous with Teacake. She was all disheveled and exhausted, just trying to make it to her home so she could rest, continue to mourn and begin to celebrate the life of a man who brought the bloom back to her pear tree and singing bees! I really need to finish reading that book, luckily my belongings were still at the hotel when my granny and mother took me there after leaving downtown.

Even my so-called friends whispered their opinions about Steven and me, especially since the news about my being held in jail seem to spread like wild fires. Rachel, Vanessa, and even Trent were in on the gossip, spilling the beans about Steven and how he had to stop hanging out with him because he was getting into too much trouble! Liar, he was made to stop only because his supplier, Steven was imprisoned. And why not talk, I was a criminal, I was a pregnant criminal, I was a broke pregnant criminal, who managed to hold on to $52! And that will soon diminish into the cash registers of retailers. But they were nosey like the porch-sitters of Eatonville, except this was Rolland Street! But just like Janie had her best friend Phoebe there to defend her, I had my very loyal comrade Diana, who was always in my corner ready to defend me.

I finally made it out of harm's way walking through the back trail that lead to Carver Rd. I was still not sure where I was going, but I was definitely headed in the direction of the Tois's Food Store, which was at the end of Carver Rd. As I walked, I thought about my appearance in court the day after I was released from jail—totally unprepared to go before the judge to attempt to plead my case. The public defender, or shall I say public offender, encouraged me to plead guilty to the charges since I was a minor with no prior record or criminal convictions. I should get two years of probation and hundreds of hours of community service! However, he did assure my mother that as long as I didn't break the law in any way, this incident should drop off my record once I turned 18.

"You are lucky," said the young, cute, Caucasian lawyer who looked to be in his late twenties. "The checks you wrote were for sizable amounts and typically federal charges are brought up against persons who commit this crime. But you and three other female minors were linked to a same man who is currently in the custody of Harris County Criminal jail."

"Three other minors? Females?" I asked, shocked at the new details surrounding my case.

"Yes...a Steven Washington," he responded as he read from a manila folder. "He and several others were charged with bank fraud, a Mary Barron, Joanne Ruud, Carrie Phillips and Molly Franks were all charged and being held in the county jail for their part in a check writing scheme at various banks in the Houston area," he continued to read.

"But I met these ladies...Steven said they were nice and would cash the checks for me because I was a minor...they worked at the banks Steven took me too!" I exclaimed extremely disturbed at the new information the attorney was presenting.

"These ladies along with Mr. Washington worked to lure young minors into their illegal check writing scheme, you...the minor, wrote the check, the tellers cashed the checks and kept a sizeable amount of the money. It was Mr. Washington's job to find the minors and Ms. Barron opened the accounts. The rest was on the tellers to cash the checks in order to keep the money flowing. We are still investigating and we're confident more individuals will surface in the very near future," he stopped reading from the documents in the folder and looked in my direction. "As for you young lady... and the other minors, since you did in fact write the checks and spent money that did not belong to you...it made you liable for your actions and criminal charges were brought against you. But you are lucky, you are still considered a minor and the state cannot try you as an adult until you are at least 17 years old. But you can and will be punished...since the crime is considered punishable in the court of law."

The lawyer continued to discuss with my mother and grandmother the severity of the crime and what the judge's plans for disciplining me and the other minors involved with this case. This really upset my mom who felt like I should have been let go with a warning since I had no knowledge of what was going on. But the lawyer insist that the judge wanted to send a message to me and the other juveniles about making better choices in life. So, I was served probation and community service with a side of stupidity and humiliation. It was clear, Steven did not have my best interest at heart! I can't believe I was carrying this man's baby!

I continued down the road, still deep in thought, when I spotted the familiar blue vehicle headed my way on the other side of the road. Jason! Because of everything going on, I hadn't been thinking much about him. However, I did often wonder if he was disappointed in me for getting caught up with a criminal like Steven. The car passed me up and turned in an empty lot nearby, then backed up and headed back my way, pulling up on the side of me.

"Get in!" Jason commanded in a low tone. I ran to the passenger side and jumped in the blue Caprice Classic without thinking twice, I guess somethings will never change! We drove off down Carver Rd.

"Where you headed...the store?" he asked solemnly.

"Yeah..." I replied. Nothing else was said, not a single word was uttered. He pulled up at the store, parked and waited inside the car for me to go in and get what I needed, which was really nothing. Once inside the store I decided to purchase a pint of Blue Bell cookies and cream ice cream for a $1.59. The Asian store clerk handed me my $3.41 in change, which I stuffed in my pocket. I grabbed my bag and left the store.

"Where you been all this time? Folks was worried...that nigga got you out here doing illegal shit?" Jason finally broke the silence as we headed back down Carver Rd.

"My mom...she made me mad and I left. You know how she is!"

"So how you get caught up with Steven? Shid...you know how that nigga is and what he all about!" Jason said matter-of-factly while raising his voice.

"It's a long story! Trust me...Steven and me is no more! That's a promise!" I murmured as I turned to look in his direction. He looked pale for some reason. "Are you okay?"

"I've been sick, throwing up every morning! The doctor don't know what's wrong with me though...said it's probably an ongoing virus or something. Said I need to stop eating so much fried food. But hell, I only be getting sick in the morning! I can't stand his sarcastic ass either! Told me it's just morning sickness, when the baby come it will stop...then he started laughing! Stupid mofo!" Jason said with a small chuckle.

Baby, I didn't want to think about the baby growing inside of me, but I had to do something soon. There was no way I was having Steven's child!

Jason pulled up to the trail that lead to our street to drop me back off. "I'll talk to you later...stay yo ass out of trouble!" He smiled as he drove off.

"Yes sir," I replied sarcastically while watching him drive off into the mid-day sun set. Just reflecting back on all the unnecessary turmoil Jason put me through doesn't even come close to the illegal dealings I had with Steven.

I made my way through the trail and up my street, thankful that the porch sitters decided to find another victim to verbally slander.

As I continued to head home, I continued my thoughts--this time about the unexpected conversation I had with my grandmother. She ended up staying overnight after she and my mother rescued me from the big house. She came to my room to talk to me that night--saying things like my mom was wrong for putting a man before her child, especially a man she barely knew herself! She also went on to say my mother had always made poor choices in life when it came to men and the one or two men who came into her life that were actually decent, she always managed to run them off!

"I tried to always make sure my late husband did right by her...and he did...as far as I could see." Nana sighed deep as she sat at the foot of my bed. I sat up in bed watching her watch her hands; which were wrinkle, worn and cracked, from years of being over worked and neglected. I could hear the rough, scratchy skin create friction as she moved them repeatedly back and forth.

"Huh? Do right by her? Who...her daddy?"

"But I do remember once...only one time when my Debbie was bout six-years-old," my grandmother continued ignoring my questions. "I come home after a long day of cleaning after White folks...I remember being so tired! Yo Uncle Lonnie was out back feeding Queenie and Duke, our dogs...said Debbie got in trouble and daddy made her go to bed." Nana looked at me shaking her head. "It was only seven in the evening...too late to be napping...too early for bedtime. I went to her room and found her fast asleep in da bed." Nana continued to look down at her fidgeting hands, trying to hide the single tear that began to roll down her face. "The white sheet that covered her body had several red streaks. When I pulled the sheet back...my baby's legs were bloody red with whelps from being beaten by a switch my husband cut from a tree!"

"I lost it! I ran to the kitchen and got the butcher knife...and headed straight to the living room where he was sitting his behind on the couch...NOBODY HARMS MY BABIES!" Another tear dropped. "Yo Uncle Lonnie saved him...came stood between us...kept me from stabbing him!"

"But...why? Why would grandpa beat mama?"

"Claim she got in trouble at school!"

"So he beat her?" I asked, wanting to cry myself.

"Baby...yo grandpa..." Nana paused. "Ain't yo grandpa...cause he ain't yo mama daddy."

"What? Not my grandpa?"

"When he was in Korea...one of the soldiers he fought with, wrote me a letter saying he got shot. My husband, Mr. Jeremiah Jones...we had only been married a little while when he got drafted...I thought he was dead! Yo Uncle Lonnie was a baby and I was so depressed! I made a mistake and started taking up time with a young fellow name Harry Stone...he lived in Anderson, Texas—not too far from Dobbin. The way I figured...if I can't have the one I loved...I might as well try to love the one that was willing to love and take care of me and my baby!"

"What! Nana...you was wit another man besides grandpa?" I was in a state of shock!

"Yeah...but Harry was no good...stayed in the juke joints partying! I ended up getting pregnant...and when I told him...he didn't see fit to wanna stop all the partying...so I left him alone...went back home to my parent's house...didn't care if I saw him again."

"I was two months pregnant when Jeremiah came knocking on my parents door looking fo me with that wound to his leg. I was so happy...so surprised to see the man I loved! I wasn't showin then...and I couldn't tell him knowin' he was goin back...so I didn't. I just waited for my husband to return to me. By that time Debbie was born. Fo couple years I said nothin...but the guilt was tearing me down! But I knew I had to make things right before we moved into this house...so I told him." Nana raised up from the bed and walked to my bookshelf.

"What he say?" I asked anxiously.

"You mean...what did he do? He left me. The rage...never seen a man so mad...he was beyond angry! Said he ain't raising no other man's child."

"But...he...you guys..."

"I know baby...he came back...said only a fool would leave a woman like me." Nana headed back towards my bed. "Said he would always treat her like his own...but when I saw my baby's legs all bloody up from being beat...I shoulda left him...I should have left his sorry ass then!"

"Why didn't you?" I asked, still shocked.

"Cause he a man...a man I loved...and he promised he would neva do it again. Went and worked long long hours to buy her that necklace and me another ring."

"Did he ever renege on his promise?"

"No...far as I know...he was good to her. And...she seem to love him too."

"Do mama know he not her daddy?"

"Yes! Told her the next day...and made sure she knew to come tell me anything he did to her that wasn't right...but she neva did...so I always figured everything was alright." Nana sighed deep again and sat back down at the foot of my bed; she had a look of defeat in her eyes.

"I tried to always make sure my late husband did right by her...and he did...as far as I could see. But...it jus seem like something happened...something happened to her growing up...and it jus seem to get worse right before my husband died," said Nana. "Yo uncle Lonnie strayed away a bit...he took his daddy passing hard! But he eventually got it together...but yo mama...just couldn't get right. She neva has...and I guess...she neva will..."

We continued to talk a little while longer, then finally Nana kissed my forehead goodnight before leaving my room to go sleep on the couch in the family room.

Chapter 24

When I finally made it home from my walk to the store, I headed to my bedroom to eat my ice cream in peace with the complimentary free wooden spoon I took from the store's freezer.

"Come here Gina," my mom yelled from the hallway. "Somebody wants to talk to you."

What now? I just wanted to sit in my room in peace. I usually get like this after Nana leaves. Thoughts of our conversation that night, me being pregnant, seeing Jason for the first time in weeks—oh, and let's not forget my brand-new criminal conviction, were all running through my mind. I just wanted to get in bed and bury my face in my pillow, in hopes that my problems would find themselves six feet under—dead and gone forever. I wish Nana would have stayed; I needed some grand-motherly love!

I paused then turned in the opposite direction of my room and headed towards the kitchen where my mom and sisters were.

"Here...somebody wanna talk to ya," said my mom as I entered the kitchen. She handed me the yellow wall kitchen phone.

"Sister its..."

"Shhhhhhh! Yall hush and let your sister find out for herself!" my mom exclaimed, cutting Reba off before she could finish.

"Hello?" I asked holding the phone receiver to my ear.

"What's up lil sis?" I immediately recognized the deep baritone voice on the other side of the receiver.

"Ray? Hey...how you doin? Wow?" I replied, shocked and excited to talk to a man that I hadn't seen in almost two years!

"Yeah baby girl...its me Ray! I'm cool with one of the guards and he let me use the phone to call home."

"Oh man...its so good to hear from you!" My eyes began to well with tears, they were tears of joy of course! It was my big brother Raymond, the one who always had my back! If Ray were here to protect me like he did when we were kids, I wouldn't be in this mess!

"Look Gina, yo brotha ain't got a lot of time to talk. Mama wrote me a letter saying you was missing. I was worried...so I called. I was jus talkin with mama and she telling me some dude done got you caught up and in trouble with the law! What's up with that?" Raymond asked concerned, trying to control his anger.

"I guess I trusted the wrong guy...got caught up...he was giving me money to help out around here and for school...you know clothes and stuff." I responded, attempting to defend my actions.

Raymond sighed, "Look I know it's rough around there...mama always working and goin out...and I know I should have set a better example for you and the girls...but lil sis...this life ain't for you! You hear me baby girl? It ain't for you!"

"I know...well I know better now..."

"Naw sis, you don't know! I've been locked up down here in Beeville, Texas for almost two years! If I could turn back time and just listened to at least one person that was tryin to school me on the right direction to take in life...hell I woulda listened! I'ma fucking caged animal here! I have to eat, shit and sleep when they tell me too! I work in the kitchen to stay out of trouble. I see mo fos die on a regular! Baby girl...believe me, this life ain't for you!"

"I know Ray...I know," the tears began to pour out.

"And I know moms be trippin sometimes...trust me, I know...she was my mama first! But one thang is for sho...mama love her kids! Never doubt her love for you, even when and if she never shows it! You hear me sis?"

"Yeah...I hear you."

"Now stop all that crying...you got me all emotional and I cain't be having all these emotions up in here! I gotta go now...you behave...go read a fuckin book or somethin, do you. Love you sis!"

"I love you too Ray!"

"Tell mama and those lil ladies I love them too."

"I will!" The phone clicked following the dial tone. I didn't realize just how much I missed and needed my big brother.

"Where Raymond? He hung up?" My mom asked as she walked back in the kitchen wearing her favorite purple house dress and dingy white cotton slippers and sat down.

"Yeah...he had to go. Told me to tell you and the girls he loved yall." I picked up a folded napkin off the kitchen table where my mom was seated. I needed to absorb some of the moisture from my face which had formed during my dialogue with Raymond. I could feel my mother's stares as I patted my skin dry even though the tears continued to form in my eyes. I wanted to confide in her, question her, scream at her! Why didn't she do more to encourage my older brother to make better choices in his young adult life, instead of making him feel obligated to take care of her family by any means necessary, like she has made me feel all these years?

When he goes before the public officials to face judiciary review, the appointed judge has no way of knowing the kid within the hard exterior. They don't know that the same guy that stole cars off the street--also read bedtime **stories to his little sisters. This same young man, made spaghetti with super large meatballs every Thursday for the ladies in his life because** it was his favorite and he loved to see us devour his specialty dish! They didn't understand that money and finances were so scarce in our world that you were almost forced to live a life of crime to make sure mouths were fed and the family's needs were met. Necessities like food and clothing became his responsibility, since my mother alone, although a struggle, seem to only be capable of maintaining **the shelter in our** lives. Raymond lied, he cheated, he sto*le, all in* the name of love for his family. But was it love or was he made to feel obligated to take care of us like I was made to feel this same obligation when it came to taking care of Reba and Rene?

"I didn't always do right by yall..." my mother murmured as she lit a Kool Filter King. She sat at the table slowly inhaling the cigarette smoke into her lungs, then parted her lips to push out the circles of shapely white gas into the atmosphere. "I didn't always do right by yall..." she repeated while tapping away the fresh ashes formed from the cigarette into the small black circle ashtray. "Yall my babies and I didn't always do right by yall...and I'm sorry." A single tear began to roll down her face as she inhaled the cigarette smoke. The visible white blankety silhouette **of vapor and gases seeped** slowly through her slightly parted lips as she wiped the single tear from her face with the same hand she held the cigarette with.

"I lost trust in men a long time ago..." I sat down in the chair next to her—wanting to let her know that I knew about grandpa not being her dad. But I was also awaiting the answers to questions I've had all of my life regarding her--her lifestyle--her relationships.

"Your granny got really sick and had to have emergency surgery at Jefferson Davis Hospital, when I was bout 13 years old. I was left with my best friend's parents and your uncle was left with his friend's parents while mama was at the hospital." She sighed continuing to inhale, puff and talk about her past experiences. She went on to tell me about her first night there, her best friend Gwedolyn had one small twin bed that could not hold them both, so she made a pallet of blankets next to her friend's bed and slept on the floor. Then, after midnight when everyone was asleep, her friend's dad Malcolm, crept into the room to wake her up--claiming she needed to go home. His claim was that her mom was released from the hospital and wanted to see her children. "I left with him cause I wanted to see my mama to make sure she was alright. I should have known somethin wasn't right...that nigga was quiet as a church mouse...nobody even heard him leave out of the house with me!" Ms. Deborah Rochelle Jones exclaimed. Her face was in a blank state, harden by the retelling of this story. "He put me in the car.... an old ass, turd brown, Pinto. I still remember the cool breeze blowing through the long cotton night gown I had on," she sighed deep, contemplating on whether or not she could or wanted to continue the story.

"I kept asking that bastard where we was going...he would never answer...just kept driving down some dark ass dirt road...I thought we was lost...but that nigga was tryin to find somewhere dark to take and have his way with me!" The tears rapidly poured from her eyes as she reflected on the highlights of the negative encounter.

"He tried to rape me...sorry bastard...I was 13!" the violent eruption of words came pouring out of her mouth. "He pulled into some damn woods and parked the car...till this day I don't know how I got loose. All I know is that I kept fighting and biting...and kicking...then finally I got loose! But he grabbed me again and slapped my face...then held me down! I kicked his ass one mo good time and I guess I musta kicked him in the right place...cause I left his ass bawled up howling like a hurt dog!" she sighed and took a deep breath. "I got out of that damn car and ran barefoot through these fields to the main road...and I walked and walked until I made it home to my own house. By this time it was daylight. The sun was up and peoples was going to work!"

"When I got there my daddy's car was in the driveway...I ran in ready to tell off on that fool Mr. Malcolm!" My mother paused briefly, staring straight ahead as if a picture of the story she was telling was illustrated on the wall. "He was havin sex with some woman." My mother's tone became solemn, sad and filled with disappointment. "Jeremiah Jones...while my mama laid in a hospital sick...was fuckin another woman in our house! When I saw that shit...I just took off running again...cryin...hard!" She **contined** to stare at the wall then took a deep breath. "I ran and ran and ran...till I got to the other side of the bayou! I just fell out on the ground crying! I couldn't believe it!! I sat there at that bayou for over an hour...I was pissed! When I finally decided to go back home...he was waiting for me on the porch with a fucking belt!"

She crushed the final blaze of fire on the butte of the cigarette out in the ashtray and jumped up out of her seat and rushed to the kitchen sink. She twisted the hot water knob on, then stopped and began gripping the edges of the black and white checkered countertop with both hands, trying to fight back her tears of anger.

"He beat me--saying Brotha Malcolm told him I had snuck out the house and left with some boy!" The cries suddenly stopped abruptly. "And no matter what I said, no matter how I tried to explain...he wouldn't listen...and why should he...I wasn't his child! I started off as my mama's baby and daddy's maybe!" she murmured while releasing the counter to turn off the water. I walked over to put my hands around her but she rejected my sympathetic touch of affection. "My step-daddy...made me get in the tub to take a bath...then began scrubbing me his self! I can still hear him yelling..."

"Ima scrub that no good ass nigga you was wit offa ya!" My mom yelled, trying to imitate her mother's husband.

My mother released the counter and let out a deep sigh, as if she was relieved that the storytelling was over. "I ain't neva trusted no man! I ain't neva had a reason to...he wasn't my daddy...and he had ways...he had ways about him that showed me he neva got ova my mama gettin pregnant while he was at war! He always took time with yo Uncle Lonnie...making sho he always had what he needed. He only did right by me when my mother was watching or simply willing to turn a blind eye to his resentment towards me! But many times...as soon as her back was turned...he was just plain mean! He only bought that necklace out of guilt...cause he wanted to put on a show for my mama...makin her thank that he loved me like his own...and that was a damn lie! He loved Lonnie and was in love with mama...always makin sure they were happy...he just tolerated my black ass...letting me know every chance he got that I was the only one that was not apart of him in this house."

She turned and faced me with an unfamiliar look of hatred and disgust. "I was glad when he died! Made me sick to my damn stomach every time I saw that damn "pity" necklace he bought me...I wore it to the funeral cause mama made me...but the first chance I could...I hocked that shit at the pawn shop!"

"Did Nana know?" I asked, not totally shocked about what she just told to me. I never met my grandfather; he had already passed away before I was born but I had never heard of a single bad thing uttered about him or his character. He was often described as hard working, loving, a family man. This new found information about him these last few days were definitely a surprise that helped me to better understand why she was the way she was. My mother, Ms.

Deborah Rochelle Jones, 36-years-young, with four kids, two baby daddies, and a mouth so bad she could put pirates to shame. She wanted a partner in life and love, but would definitely trade it all for a man with some money. I learned today that my mother too was a mockingbird, she was weak and lacked power and everyone she came in contact with, Mr. Malcolm, her step-father, her kids' fathers, saw this lack of strength in her personality and felt the need to overpower her. My mother never did tell my grandmother about the incident, she didn't want her mother To Kill Deborah Rochelle Jones too.

Chapter 25

"I can't have no baby Dee!" I exclaimed. "Not for a guy that's in jail and ain't getting out no time soon!"

"Look, I didn't want to tell you this at first...but...I know a lady that can get you some pills to make you have a miscarriage," Diane murmured looking down at the ground as if admitting to knowing this information would condemn her for life.

"Some pills? What kinda pills? What lady?" I asked eagerly searching for answers.

"This lady in the ghettos...she gave my homegirl Sonya some pills last year, and she ended up losing her baby the next day."

"Where...Lincoln City Apartments? Can you ask Sonya to get me some and how much they cost?" Diana didn't respond right away. "Dee please...I need help!"

"Alright...alright, I know where her apartment is, I will take you to her in the morning...but I think she charge $20? Plus, I heard that shit is dangerous!"

"I cain't have no baby Dee! I'll take my chances!"

When we arrived at apartment number 26 in Lincoln City Apartments that Saturday morning, a petite dark-skinned woman in her late forties answered the door. She wore a long silky dashiki house dress with a matching silk scarf tied around her head.

"Is Ms. Noemi here?" I asked.

"Who wants to know?" the lady responded in a Caribbean accent. She was clearly not a Native Houstonian or citizen of the U.S.

"I...I do. I need help with my pregnancy..."

"Come in!" she quickly responded and moved out of the doorway so Diana and I could enter and immediately closed the door behind us. Her apartment was very dimly lit with blackout curtains hanging to prevent sunlight from coming through. The only light shining in the room was the low reddish beam coming from a lava lamp on the coffee table. "Wait right here," she exclaimed rushing out of the room through some beads hanging from the doorway. And before the beads could settle, she reappeared holding a small paper bag. "$25 please."

I reached into my pocket and pulled out a twenty and some ones. "All I have is $23..." I murmured hoping and praying she would take it. She snatched the cash and handed me the bag.

"Take all four pills at once...best if done at night before you go to bed cause yo stomach gonna hurt afterwards."

"Yes ma'am."

"You take at yo own risk...no refunds! You go now." She opened the door and let us out.

"I hope you're happy," said Diana as we drove off. I was happy and relieved that I didn't have to go through another abortion or pregnancy for a guy I didn't even love or expected to see ever in life! Who wants to have dealings with a man that had me unknowingly committing federal crimes!

That night after everyone was in bed, I went into the bathroom with a glass of fruit punch juice. I figure since it had a lock on the doorknob the bathroom gave me the most privacy than any other room in the house, so I didn't have to worry about my sisters or mom barging in on me while I inhaled the large pills.

I turned away from the bathroom mirror unable to gaze upon my reflection. I was still in disbelief that another fetus was growing inside me. I stared down hard at the bag, following one wrinkle line after another. I needed to pick the bag up and release the pills so I could go to bed, yet I did not move. I looked up at the mirror once again forcing myself to take a good look at the person on the other side. She looked scared and confused. Her brown eyes seem distant, sorrowful, screaming to be rescued from this thing called life. Isn't that something, Regina Jones wanted to be saved, but willing to harm her still developing baby. "Stop Regina!" I looked away from my reflection rapidly shaking my head in hopes that the ideas of protecting an unborn, under developed fetus would exit my mind. I took a deep breath, opened my eyes and gazed back down on the brown bag, "Do it Gina, do it now!" This simple task grew increasingly complicated the longer I stalled. Finally, I picked the bag up and proceeded to open it and release the pills into my hand. It's now or never.

"NO, that's a man child!" spoke a loud deep voice out of nowhere! I threw the bag on the floor on the far end of the bathroom and fell down in fear, searching my surrounding for the person I just heard spoke. There was no one there, absolutely no one in sight! I unlocked and opened the door and ran to my bedroom without looking back. I jumped in bed and wrapped in the covers in fear that the person or voice would come back. It didn't work, I got up and ran up the hallway to my mother's room. She was asleep. I quickly walked in but slowly got in the bed with her.

"Gina?" she called out groggily out of her sleep.

"I'm scared mama...can I please sleep in here with you?" I sighed in fear of what her answer might be. However, yes or no, I wasn't leaving. She immediately responded by putting her arm over me and pulling me close. I eventually fell asleep feeling safe and secure in her arms. The next morning, I got up early to use the bathroom while everyone was still asleep and the bag, the pills were gone.

Epilogue

"Damn, I have to fuck this old bastard again!" A pregnant, exhausted Regina Jones plopped down on the worn metal dinette chair and threw the single cash bills on the dinette table. Her tips from work weren't nearly enough to cover her rent. Even though it was Sunday and she covered a double shift at Denny's today. She couldn't understand how the restaurant stayed packed with customers yet the tips given today were lower than what she was anticipating.

Regina looked down on the living room floor where her sleeping babies lay together on old thick blankets and sheets she found at Goodwill. She knew she was invading their sleeping quarters since the only bedroom in the apartment belonged to her. When she first came to live there, the single bedroom belong to them and she slept on the old, lumpy, grayish-blue couch that she found in the for-sale section of the *Greensheet* circular. But it became harder and harder to entertain company, including Stanley Bates, without the use of her bed. Stanley is a 56-year-old retired army veteran that liked Regina a lot. She found herself entertaining often, since he didn't mind leaving a little cash to help assist with bills before he left. And she desperately needed this money, especially since the kids' daddies hardly ever contributed to her household—they barely even came around!

Mathew, Regina's eldest who is five has it the worst! His dad Jason, makes a series of false promises to his son, but never follows through with any of his commitments. She knew getting pregnant for him was a shock at first, especially since she was involved with another guy at the time of conception. But the blood tests his parents, Lester and Monique Wallace, insisted that they take one year after Mathew's arrival into the world, confirmed that he was 99.9% his biological child. However, Jason and his parents were still reluctant to acknowledge the new edition to the Wallace's family. An entire year had passed and Jason was away at college-committed to a longtime relationship with his girlfriend Lisa, so of course they hesitated to embrace Mathew. But once Jason's mom, Monique Wallace, saw her first grandson looking the splitting image of her very own son, she willingly accepted him into the family and was ready to shower him with any and everything he could ever want and need. The problem is, she wanted Regina out of the picture. She wanted Mathew at home with them. Full custody. They paid a high-priced lawyer to help prove in the family court that Regina was unfit to care for a baby. Of course, the judge ruled in favor of the mother and allowed Regina to remain the custodial parent.

At the time, she did provide a stable home and a safe environment for her son—she was living at home with her mother. But when Regina got pregnant with her two-year-old twin toddlers, Elizabeth and Victoria, her mother, Ms. Deborah Rochelle Jones, told her she had to go. But it didn't matter to Regina, if it wasn't for her baby sisters and their help, she would have left a long time ago!

And now that she is unstable, living in a small one-bedroom apartment, with three kids and one on the way, her fear is that the courts will take her sweet babies away! Which is why she can't file for child-support or get assistance from the government.

Regina just needed to see their sweet faces before calling Stanley over. She wanted to love on them, embrace them so she can be constantly reminded of the responsibility she has to care for them by any means necessary. Afterall, they are her babies, her hearts—she is responsible for providing for them and ensuring that they always have a safe secure place to live. And if any means-- meant her having sex with an old geezer like Stanley Bates to ensure the rent payment is made, then--a girl just has to do what a girl has to do.

~The Heart of a Black Butterfly~